The Other Son

J.M. Hewitt is the author of eight crime fiction novels. Her work has also been published in three short story anthologies. Her books usually incorporate twentieth and twenty-first century events and far-flung locations, and her novels explore the darker side of human behaviour. In contrast to the sometimes dark content of her books, she lives a very nice life in a seaside town in Suffolk with her dog, Marley.

Also by J.M. Hewitt

The Life She Wants
The Eight-Year Lie
The Other Son

THE
OTHER
SON

J.M. HEWITT

🔟 CANELO

First published in the United Kingdom in 2022 by

Canelo
Unit 9, 5th Floor
Cargo Works, 1-2 Hatfields
London, SE1 9PG
United Kingdom

Copyright © J.M. Hewitt 2022

A CIP catalogue record for this book is available from the British Library.

Print ISBN 978 1 80032 460 2
Ebook ISBN 978 1 80032 459 6

Look for more great books at www.canelo.co

Printed and bound in Great Britain by Clays Ltd, Elcograf S.p.A.

1

For my brother, Darren Hewitt

With love

Prologue

Before

It only happened in movies, but the dread of real life was so much more intense than anything Sara had ever experienced.

The call came not from the school itself, but from one of the other mothers. Dianne was her name, and Sara didn't know her all that well, but she was the closest thing she had to a friend-among-mums, and their boys were in the same class.

Dianne was shrieking, screaming, and Sara, in the quiet of the local florist, held the phone away from her ear. The woman behind the till, clutching the white roses Sara was in the process of purchasing, stared at the phone, wide-eyed, before lifting her gaze to Sara.

Sara put the phone back to her ear. 'Dianne,' she said, and then, when there were only cries as a reply, long and thin like the noise of a kitten, she raised her voice. 'DIANNE!'

A shuffling sound down the line, and another voice came on. 'This is Dianne's sister,' announced the newcomer.

'Do you have the right number?' Sara asked. 'This is Sara, our children go to the—'

'Yes, Sara, I'm so sorry. Can you get to the school?'

The florist was only a few minutes away from the school where her sons, Scott and Ryan, went. She turned towards the window, aware now of the single police car that had sped past a moment ago. This was London, however, and sirens were a part of everyday life. But now Sara saw that something was going on out there, great crowds of people rushing past the florist's shop. And not a single one of them was walking.

The caller on the line – Dianne's sister – was quiet now, but in the background, Sara could hear the sirens. She knew then that it was something terrible. Life-changing. Life-*ending*?

'Wait,' she said into her mobile. 'I'm coming now.'

Dianne's sister started to say something, but Sara hung up. A defensive, unconscious move, because something deep inside her didn't want bad news relayed to her by a stranger. She turned to the woman on the till, about to apologise, to say that she had to go but she would come back and pick up her purchases later.

The assistant was looking at her own phone, though, and her face was as white as Sara's roses, which now lay on the side, forgotten.

The woman behind the till raised her eyes to meet Sara's.

'There's been a shooting,' she said, breathlessly, 'at the school.'

1

Sara
Now

Sara moved slowly up the path, pausing as she always did at the white rose bush. It was in full bloom, and she reminded herself as she had every day since she had moved here that she must dig it up and discard it. She pulled a rose off; let it drift to the path. Stared at it for one moment before she ground it underneath her heel.

She scrutinised the bush for a long time, carrier bags hanging loosely from her hands, until the hairs on the back of her neck prickled. Turning her head sharply, she angled her gaze upwards. Her elder son stood in the bedroom window, staring down at her, his expression as blank as she knew hers was.

He didn't come downstairs when she slammed her way into the little wooden chalet cabin that was now their home. A year on, and Scott still missed the hustle and bustle of London life. Their new home, set deep in Kielder Forest, north of the Pennines, was surrounded by 250 square miles of nothing but trees. For Sara, it was required; for Scott, even though he never said, she was sure it was hell.

But this was their home. It was peaceful, nobody bothered them here. It was quiet, and most importantly, it was *safe*.

And so was her family.

–

The joy had gone out of cooking, Sara realised, as she dumped the salad in the wooden bowl and half-heartedly stirred it around. The joy had gone out of most things, she thought now, putting the bowl down and staring out of the window.

The move here was supposed to be the start of something new. Something positive, hopeful, living here among all this nature.

But it was quiet. Too quiet. She dipped her head as she thought about her previous home, always noisy with the two boys. Although that was unfair. Scott was always quiet. Ryan, however, could never seem to just *talk*; everything was a yell or a shout – even normal conversation. It had got on her nerves back then, but she'd give anything to live in a house like that again.

Can't go back.

She snapped to attention, brought out of her reverie. Yes, there was no going back. What had happened had impacted all of them, changed them beyond recognition. All they could do was get on with it.

She pulled herself away from the window and set out three plates on the dining table.

Overcome with a sudden fatigue that felt like smacking into a brick wall, she slumped into a chair.

Footsteps on the wooden stairs, as slow as her tread had been earlier. They didn't pause, and she didn't look up as

Scott slipped out of the house and closed the door behind him.

In the oven, the chips began to burn. Sara put her head in her hands, unable to bring herself to care.

–

'Scott!' yelled Sara up the stairs. 'Dinner!'

It wasn't unusual for there to be no reply, but normally she heard the telltale sound of footsteps, or the squeak of a bedroom door as it opened. Now, though, the house was filled with even more silence than usual.

In the kitchen, she looked at the three meals she had served up.

'Where is he?' she asked the shadowy figure of her younger son.

There was no reply.

Nobody answers me any more, she thought.

Suddenly angry, she darted out into the hall and took the stairs two at a time. She paused outside Scott's closed door, remembered a couple of hours ago, his face at the window, looking down on her as she pulled the rose bloom off the bush and stamped on it.

Taking a deep, jerky breath that betrayed the fury she tried so hard to hide, she turned the handle and shoved the door open.

The room was silent, neat and tidy; the bed made and the cover smoothed. Not the normal room of a teenage boy. On the nightstand was his backpack. Sara shuddered, screwed her eyes closed before forcing them back open.

It wasn't the original backpack, not the one she had found last year, she knew that, but it was similar, same brand, same style; they all looked the same. But it was not that one. Not the one she had picked up, intending to throw away, the one that had been on his back at the school, covered in blood.

Falling back against the door frame, she raised her hands to her mouth as the memory crashed into her.

Almost a whole year ago now, in a different room but with much the same items in it. As much as she hadn't wanted to touch it, it was more important that he didn't come home and see it, covered in all that blood.

Protecting him. The way a mother should.

With a small hiss at the sudden reappearance of a horror she'd tried to forget, Sara swivelled on the balls of her feet, stepped into the hall and pulled Scott's door closed behind her.

The flashback diminished with the door shut, and she looked around the empty hallway. He wasn't here. Scott had gone out. *Now* she remembered. The light tread of footsteps on the stairs, the opening and closing of the door while she'd been slumped at the table, chips blackened and burned.

As she stomped down the stairs, she knew she should be worried. Even though they'd been here ages, Scott didn't know the area. What if he'd gone up on those moors? What if he got lost, stranded there after dark? All those hazards out there: the rocks and the water and the deep caves that lined the riverbed and forest floor she'd heard about when she was in line at the Co-op, half-listening to other people's conversations because it was preferable to listening to what was going on in her own head.

She knew anyway, without the well-meaning chit-chat of strangers. She had been there, walking miles alone, or with just Ryan by her side for company. Scoping out the

6

area, she'd spotted all the danger spots, because that was what her mind did these days. It searched for potential risk and threat. It remembered them, filed them away in a dark corner for future reference. Because she never wanted to be unprepared again.

But Scott didn't know them, he didn't go out enough to, even though she'd encouraged him at the beginning to go with her to the Centre, because surely sitting alone all day in his room wasn't healthy. She was supposed to be home-schooling him. That was the official line, anyway, but so far nothing even remotely resembling a lesson had happened.

It wouldn't heal him or repair him. Which had been the whole point in coming here.

Back in the kitchen, she dished up the burned chips and the tiny, shrivelled pork chops onto three plates.

Then she sat down at the table, head bowed, waiting, though for what, she didn't know.

2

Travis
Now

Travis Samuel followed Sara all the way from the Kielder Art Centre, down the small road that was laughingly called the high street, out the other end into the forest.

Travis knew everyone in the little village, but during the time he'd been away, Sara Doyle had slipped into the community under his radar. Back now where he belonged, after the silly misunderstanding, and who was the first person he'd seen after his six-month hiatus?

Sara Doyle. A newcomer, who seemed to keep herself to herself. Travis liked that; to him it seemed ladylike and nice. On the other hand, it was frustrating not being in the know.

He'd been back two weeks, and he'd made it his business to find out everything he could about the new girl he was preparing to welcome into his life. After all, didn't they say that a stranger was just a friend you hadn't met yet?

The obstructions he'd faced since starting his new project had been disheartening. Nobody knew anything about her. A voice had niggled at him that maybe they did, but after the furore and fracas of Travis's most recent 'incident' they didn't want to tell him. He brushed away that concern. Everyone in Kielder loved Travis. He knew that he was well liked and well respected among his peers. They all knew it was a lot of fuss over nothing. Even the head teacher, Mr Bridge, had practically said as much.

Travis had been aghast when Mr Bridge had suggested counselling. Travis didn't go to therapy; people came to him for that!

The Head had waffled on about procedure. 'We have to be seen to be following protocol,' he had said. His tone had been uneasy, as though he didn't like what he was clearly being forced to say.

Because Travis respected Gordon Bridge, he had gone along with it. In fact, he had read up on it, and it turned out it was normal for therapists to have their own treatments. Supervision, they called it. Counselling for counsellors. That had made him feel a bit better.

He had taken a sabbatical. His once-weekly sessions were not far away. For the first few months he had used the novelty of free days to head to the city. There, he had watched, mused, blended into the background and wondered how he could get his normal life back. After a while, the city had bored him, and apart from his supervision, he had remained in Kielder. He came out at night and moved around his forest, just like a bat or a fox. Sometimes he walked to the Centre and peered into empty classrooms through the closed, darkened windows. A few times, as he watched from the shadows of the trees, he saw *her*, the silly woman who had caused the mess with her overreaction to a bit of attention that really should have had her flattered.

Eventually, finally, the sessions had come to an end. *She'd* thankfully departed for pastures new; Travis had gone back to work.

9

And Sara had come to his attention.

From her application paperwork, which he'd sneaked out of the filing cabinet and looked at one day after hours, he discovered she'd been here almost a year. At first she'd worked in a packing warehouse in the city, before finding the job at the Centre. Dismayed, he'd turned her file upside down, desperate for more detail. There had been none. A letter applying for the job in neat, careful writing, and what looked like a hastily constructed CV that said just enough without actually telling him anything at all.

It was difficult to 'accidentally' bump into Sara Doyle. She was like a ghost or a whisper; like his nocturnal forest animals – there one minute, gone the next. She didn't court attention, and he liked that, even though it was frustrating for him.

After a few days of watching, he had her movements committed to memory. Today, he had timed it perfectly.

He smiled to himself as he followed her at a respectable distance down the track, imagining how it could be – would be – with her in the future. They would walk together. Both to and from the Centre. They would make their life here together, because Travis didn't intend to be forced out of either his job or his forest home again.

He was glad to be back.

Kielder Art Centre was not a place of formal education but rather a venue that was open all year round. It offered learning classes for adults and children alike, in all the arts. Knitting and crochet, pottery, yoga, Pilates and general well-being. There were evening groups held for book clubs, creative writing, and a few times a year guest teachers came to offer intensive language courses, at all levels.

Travis was employed at the Centre as an art tutor, teaching the kids the basics of landscapes, portraits, using different mediums and materials. Occasionally he stretched his classes into drama. He found that when the kids improvised, they presented a lot of tells about the environment they lived in.

As well as being a qualified art teacher, he was also a therapist. Unlike some of the other teachers at the Centre, he liked to think he went that extra mile. He was a mentor and occasional counsellor. Shrewdly, he had come to realise that nearly all the kids who came here had some sort of issue. Children from broken homes, children who were bullied, or different, hiding their sexuality, *confused* about their sexuality, on some sort of spectrum; some of them were depressed, struggling under a black cloud as they tried to navigate their way through the most difficult times of their lives.

Over the four years he had been working here, he imagined that he had built a kind of reputation and those in need gravitated towards him. Well, almost all of them.

He focused again on the woman in front of him, narrowing his eyes as he watched Sara's slow progress walking home after her shift.

Her progress shouldn't be slow, he noted. This path they were on ran slightly downhill, and yet every few minutes Travis had to do a little shuffle to slow his gait.

Finally, she reached her cabin. Travis ducked behind a tree to observe her. Halfway up the path to her home, she stopped, her head angled slightly. He lowered his face, partially hidden by the low-hanging branches.

Did she know he was there, watching, waiting?

But it turned out she hadn't sensed his presence as he'd thought. Instead she reached out a hand, pulled a single bloom from the rose bush.

He held his breath, taken by the lovely scene. His romantic side tingled; he expected her to lift the rose to her delicate snub nose and breathe in the heavenly scent. Instead, she opened her slender fingers and let it fall to the path, where she very deliberately stepped on it, crushing it into white pulp underneath her shoe. After a moment, she carried on to her door and let herself into the cabin.

With sweat prickling at his forehead, and unease nestling next to excitement that settled like a breeze on the back of his neck, Travis emerged from his hiding place and, with a last, lingering look at Sara's home, carried on walking.

–

When he reached the waterside, his skin prickled; he wasn't alone out here.

He slowed his step, unafraid of what or who was following him. This was his forest, his home. With his knowledge and his confidence, *he* was the one to be feared.

Plus, Kielder was the safest place he had ever lived, and Travis had lived in a lot of places. There was no crime here, no gang violence or robberies. The police presence was nil, because there was simply no need for any sort of authority here.

He stopped, surveyed the grass and fields that surrounded him. Brown and burned yellow from the scorching summer sun. It had been a good year, he acknowledged, weather-wise, and as he stared up at the glaring sun, he smiled. Summer was far from over. The break he'd had to take hadn't sullied it too much. Life was still good. His smile widened. It was about to get even better.

And soon, when the schools began breaking up, more people would come. More harassed parents and stressed-out, lost children. He would help them all, or at least as many as he could, at the same time reserving a special place in his heart and mind for Sara Doyle.

As he made his way over to the shade of a tree, a shape on the other side of the water caught his eye.

Travis blinked.

It was a boy, a teenage lad, he thought as he squinted across the water. He glanced at his watch. He worried that the boy was lost. Not such a big deal now, but when the sun went down and these moors turned as black as night, lost wasn't a good place to be. This wilderness, so welcome in the summer sun, claimed lives when the moon came, and even a professional hiker with a good sense of direction could be caught out. When that happened – as it did sadly once or twice or a handful of times a year – that was when Kielder *did* have a police presence.

It was going to be a hot night, absolutely no chance of freezing fog or soaking, chilling rain. But still, Travis had a duty of care.

He raised his arms. 'Hey, kid!' he called. 'Wait there, I'm coming round to you.'

The boy never moved a muscle as Travis made the ten-minute walk around the water. It was a little disconcerting, he thought as he got closer, deliberately slowing his step, aiming to get a better look at the lad, who stood statue-like at the edge of the water. Recognition – this was Sara Doyle's son – and a thrill of something shivered through Travis.

'Hello,' he said, aiming for casual as he stopped a few metres from the boy. From his secret reading of Sara's confidential files, he reached into his memory for the lad's name. 'You're Scott, right?'

Scott turned his head slowly, mechanically, and looked Travis up and down. 'Yeah,' he replied, and his voice was hoarse, almost a whisper.

Travis knew that Sara worked every day at the Centre, cleaning and tidying up. The great thing about Kielder Art Centre was that in the holidays, employees could bring their kids in for sessions in art, music, drama, or the various sports that were on the agenda each day. It was free for the staff, no charge, and they all took advantage of it given the exorbitant prices that breakfast clubs charged.

But Scott had never attended any of the classes. Travis checked himself. The lad was older than some of the other kids, thirteen or fourteen, certainly old enough to be left at home while his mother went to work. Which meant that he didn't *want* to take part in the activities that the other children seemed to enjoy so much.

Social anxiety? Travis mused. Or perhaps he was simply an introvert, a loner.

'I wanted to check you were okay. This isn't a good place to get lost in.' Travis swept his arm out, gesturing to the moors and the meadows and the dense dark forest beyond.

Scott looked across to where he was indicating. 'Why?' he asked.

'The moors can be dangerous; didn't you see the sign-post where you came in, warning just how many people get lost here each year?' Travis swallowed, hoped he wasn't coming across as condescending. 'I've been a bit lost myself at times, and it can get scary.'

Scott looked back at the water. 'Do they die?' he asked. His voice had dropped to a whisper.

Travis glanced at the river before looking back at the boy. 'Who?' he asked, momentarily confused.

'The people who get lost,' replied Scott.

It wasn't often Travis was lost for words, but it was an odd question, and he wasn't sure how he should answer.

'Very rarely. They usually turn up, dazed and frightened but whole and healthy.' He swallowed. 'Will you walk back with me? Make sure *I* don't get lost.' He laughed, aiming for hearty, but it sounded forced.

Scott wrinkled his nose and scowled. 'What're you, a paedo?'

Travis smiled; the question didn't offend him. He'd been called worse things, usually by angry youngsters who didn't know where or how to deflect the way they were feeling so settled instead for projecting.

'No. My name's Travis. I work at the Centre with your mum. She and I are friends.' It wasn't really a lie, he thought. After all, one day soon they would be. More than friends, he hoped. He lowered himself down onto one of the large, flat rocks that bordered the river. 'I don't see you at the Centre much, do you ever go there?'

Scott shook his head. 'No.'

Picking up a handful of stones, Travis flicked them in the air, watching as they skimmed the surface of the water. 'You should, we have a lot of fun things over there.'

Scott didn't reply. He didn't shrug or even acknowledge that Travis had spoken.

Hard work. Travis nodded to himself as he chucked a few more pebbles in the river. Potentially interesting work. A new case. If he could get to know Scott, then surely it would lead to getting to know Sara. He sneaked a look at the lad, still standing in exactly the same position he had been when Travis had spotted him. Legs a shoulder's width apart, arms hanging loosely at his sides, chin angled downwards.

Travis pushed himself up. 'So, do you want to walk back with me?' he asked. 'Your mother will be worried.'

At that, Scott barked a laugh.

Troubled and intrigued in equal measure, Travis raised a hand as he began to walk away. Moments later, to his relief, Scott Doyle began to follow him.

–

'So, will you think about coming along to the Centre?' asked Travis as they walked the final few yards to Sara's cabin.

Scott lifted his head, looking slowly around, as though he couldn't fathom where he was or how he'd got there.

Travis waited awkwardly at the bottom of the path, eyeing the rose bush and the flattened bloom on the ground. Scott waited too, and Travis frowned before moving past him and up to the door.

He hesitated before knocking, then leaned close to the door. No sound from inside, no radio, no television. He turned to Scott, was about to ask him if his mother might have gone out looking for him, when the door creaked open.

She looked tired, was his first thought. Still beautiful, though, even though her hair was pulled back in a simple ponytail and her face was scrubbed clean.

She didn't speak, didn't look behind him at her son still standing at the end of the path. There was no greeting, no smile.

Travis cleared his throat. 'Hi, I'm Travis. I work at the Centre.' He reddened, realising belatedly that he'd told Scott that he and his mother were friends. He chanced a look behind him, and noticed that Scott was paying no attention to the interaction going on at the door.

He turned back to face Sara, waited to allow her to respond, or for some sign of recognition. He tensed, worrying for a second about what she might have heard, before remembering that she didn't socialise with the other women there. Gossip clearly wasn't a part of her life. The knowledge that this woman might finally be different gave him the confidence to try again. 'Found this one on the moors, thought I'd walk back with him.'

Finally, she looked past him, but neither her eyes nor her expression changed at the sight of Scott. Travis, thrown by the total lack of reaction from both mother and son, decided to take the bull by the horns. He lowered his voice. 'Scott hasn't yet been to the Centre; we've got a lot of good stuff going on there.' He smiled gently. 'Things that might help him.'

Now she looked him in the eye. 'Help him?' Her tone was as quiet as Travis's was.

He nodded – over-eagerly, he thought later, when he went over their conversation from start to finish, so pleased was he to get *something* out of her. 'There are social activities, though of course you know that. You work there. Exercises and lessons that promote integration, team activities.' He drew in a breath, kept his eyes on her. 'Or if you think Scott might benefit from something on a one-to-one level, I could help you. I specialise in therapies, you see. Art, play, off-the-record chats.' He waited with bated breath.

Was she considering it? Behind those eyes, still and empty almost, he couldn't tell. Then she nudged the door open wider, and for one hopeful, splendid second, he thought she might invite him in.

Instead, she addressed her son for the first time. 'Your dinner's getting cold,' she said, tonelessly.

As Scott ambled up the path to the house, Travis stepped aside. He raised his hand in a goodbye gesture that Scott didn't see, before turning to Sara. She didn't look at him again, though, and instead the door closed softly in his face.

3

Sara
Before

It grew quieter the closer Sara got to the school. Even the sirens, squawking non-stop as they sped down the street, had faded to silence.

It was eerie. More than anything, the absence of noise seemed to highlight that something terrible, unthinkable, was happening.

She was holding the flowers, she realised now, belatedly. She didn't even remember picking them up from the counter. The stems wept through the tissue paper, cracked and cut in her grip. She didn't remember paying for them, and for a silly second that worry of an accidental theft eclipsed the looming sense of doom.

She slowed and looked down at them. Funeral flowers, she thought. And with a gasp that was almost a shriek, she flung them forcefully towards the brick wall that bordered someone's garden.

People were overtaking her now, parents, carers, grandparents. They didn't speak, they didn't look at each other or anyone else. Mouths set in a grim line, eyes forward, they marched determinedly onward.

Sara joined the throng, falling into step beside Dianne, the woman who had called her earlier. Just minutes before, the other woman had screamed down the phone. Now, her eyes and face were blank. On the other side of her, a woman, presumably the sister who had taken over the phone call, clamped an arm around her shoulder.

Keeping her upright, rather than comfort or support, thought Sara.

And since she had nobody to offer any such gesture to her, Sara straightened her spine and sped up.

The gates of Farenden came into view. Or rather, they didn't. They were obscured fully by the people ahead of Sara on the strange, quiet walk to the school. Here they stopped. The gates were apparently locked, the parents pressed up against them, faces no longer blank, but stretched in terrible expressions of fear, anger, pain, worry.

Sara swallowed and glanced back at the approaching crowd. It was like a march, or a demonstration, she thought with something like wonder.

Thoughts caught up with her, almost like now she had stopped walking, her brain had clicked into gear.

Where were the police?

As if in answer to her unspoken question, a siren blared, just once, drawing her attention to the half-dozen police cars that lined the verge.

She blinked, and when she opened her eyes, she saw the officers spread out like a fan around the bodies at the gate. Someone caught her arm. She looked down at the slender white hand that encircled her wrist.

'Do you have a child here?'

She stared into the eyes of the female police officer. In the other woman's gaze she saw an urgency that frightened her.

'Yes,' Sara stuttered.

'Do you know the community centre, at the end of the road?' the officer asked. Without waiting for a reply she went on, 'All parents are to go there, please. We need to keep this entrance clear.'

'Why?' Sara heard her own voice, a bleat, high-pitched, betraying the fear that she saw in everyone's eyes, now bubbling up inside her.

'Please,' said the officer.

Don't waste her time. The voice came from nowhere, a deeply instilled politeness in which the British had high stakes. Sara nodded and obediently shuffled a couple of steps backwards.

The police carried on, herding, a clever mix of soothing but strict, a gentle nudge on a paralysed bystander, a firmer grip that didn't quite amount to manhandling if it was called for.

In front of her, the school looked like it did when she walked past it on a weekend. Calm, still, empty.

Where were the kids? How many men were in there? Were they armed? Of course they were armed. The woman in the florist had said there had been a shooting. Knives, although deadly, were easier to dodge. A swiping blade wasn't quite as threatening as a flying bullet.

'Sara, Sara!'

The voice was breathless and low. Sara turned. The eyes that pierced into hers were green, familiar, desirable. The last time she had looked into them, they had glittered, colours changing as she stared. She'd avoided these eyes, and this gaze, for years and years.

'Sara.' He spoke again. She drew in a breath and began to talk, just to stop her name coming from his lips.

'Jojo. Jesus, what's going on?' Her teeth were chattering, she realised, as though she were freezing. And she was, but it was summer, and she shouldn't be.

'Are your boys in there?' he asked.

She nodded, saw his arms, oncoming, incoming, and unconsciously wrapped hers around herself, a protective gesture.

Stay away.

He ignored the slight and shoved his hands in his pockets. 'Police say we're supposed to go to the community centre. We're to wait.' He nodded towards her bag. 'Did you try to call them?'

'The police?'

He shook his head impatiently. 'The boys, your boys.'

Damn. She hadn't thought to do that. Stupid, stupid. What sort of mother wouldn't think to do that? She wrestled with the zip. It always got caught on the inside lining, always, and she would reverse the motion, pull the zipper carefully away and try again. This time, she kept on yanking, hearing the silk inside splitting, not caring, just trying to still her shaking fingers.

Finally, her phone was in her grasp. Jojo stood uncomfortably close, watching over her shoulder. She scrolled to the recent calls, Ryan's name, and jabbed at the call button.

'Straight to voicemail,' she whispered.

She went to put the phone back in her bag. This time, his hand caught hers. 'Try Scott,' he said.

She swallowed. 'Yes,' she said.

Scott's phone rang, and with each ring she gripped the phone a little tighter. No voicemail. No answer. Eventually a recorded voice told her the person she was trying to call wasn't available.

She thought of her boys. Scott would likely be alone. Ryan, the younger, would be surrounded by friends. She thought of how afraid Scott would be on his own, and she swallowed down the tears that threatened.

'I spoke to Jaden, but he got cut off – the phone went dead,' said Jojo.

Sara stared at the ground. She hadn't thought to ask after his son. What was wrong with her?

'I'm sorry,' she said. 'I should have asked. My thoughts...' She raised her hands in the air, scrambled them around her head. 'I'm sorry,' she said.

He nodded; his face, which she remembered as always laughing, grinning, boisterous, ready with a smile or a quip, was now grim and stony.

'What do we do?' She hated to ask the question. It was unlike her. She didn't ask others what to do. She was a single mother with a minimal support network. *She* was the decision-maker.

'Go to the community centre, I suppose,' he said.

They fell into step beside each other. Sara could see the centre up ahead, not far, a few hundred yards. It felt like a mile.

'I'm sorry,' she whispered again. This time, she wasn't apologising for forgetting to ask about his kid, or her inability to think and speak and act rationally.

She didn't elaborate. She didn't need to.

'Forget it. All in the past,' he said.

But his words were as stony and cold as his expression.

4

Sara
Now

Scott was standing in the hallway. Sara felt him watching her, a wary look on his face.

She closed the door on the weird teacher man, an action that admittedly was quite rude. She'd never have done that a year ago, but times changed.

Scott switched his glance to behind her, looking at the three meals on the table, all of them untouched, the room empty.

'What did you say to him?' Sara asked as she walked into the kitchen, past the table, to stand by the kitchen window.

She stared out with glassy eyes. That window was her post now, her lookout to a world she was no longer a part of. As though she were keeping watch, protecting her family from someone who would come into their new home and rip their lives apart again.

She felt Scott move to stand a few feet behind her, and watched as Travis walked away from the chalet, his head bobbing up from behind the hedge as if he were hoping to catch a glimpse of them.

'I didn't say anything to him,' said Scott.

She turned around, watching him now as he sat down at the table and picked up a cold chop.

A year ago, she would have reprimanded him, told him to use his knife and fork. But table manners didn't matter any more. He gnawed around the bone. The meat, overcooked and stodgy, refused to be chewed, and he forced it down with a mouthful of water.

'He said he wanted to help you,' said Sara, turning to look out of the window once more. 'What did he mean by that? What does he *do*?' She turned to face him again.

Scott abandoned the chop and picked at the blackened chips. 'I don't know. *You* work there, don't you know what he does?'

She thought about not answering him. She chewed on her lip, deep in thought, before taking a breath. 'Therapy,' she said. 'Counselling.' She spun around, her eyes fixed on something outside that only she could see. 'No,' she said, even though he hadn't said anything. Even though her heart told her that her refusal was wrong.

Nothing more was said. Scott slid out from behind the table and went upstairs. Sara waited a beat before following him soundlessly.

His door was ajar. She positioned herself to peer through the crack. He was lying on his bed.

'Leave me alone for a little bit, Ryan,' she thought she heard him say. His lips curved upwards as he softened his words with a smile.

Ryan, obedient as always, left the room, slipping past his mother like a ghost.

5

Scott

Before

The English class was late in getting under way. Mrs Fleecy cast long, lingering glances towards the empty desk.

Scott followed her stare. He couldn't recall who normally sat there. He wondered if the latecomer would face any consequences. He sighed and turned back to face front. Probably not. For some people, the rules didn't seem to apply.

People like Scott's own brother, Ryan.

Scott felt a flare of irritation inside him.

While Mrs Fleecy seemed to hold an internal debate on whether to start the class or not, Scott's mind wandered away to his home life, and to that day a little over a year ago.

'My best boy,' their mother, Sara, had said, grabbing Ryan in a hug and squeezing him until he squirmed.

Scott watched from the breakfast bar. The words rang in his head, a painful echo. *My best boy*. He clenched his fists in his lap. Ryan looked at him and rolled his eyes.

Scott looked away. *Don't roll your eyes. You love it, you love being the one who is loved best.*

He'd jumped off the high stool, walked past without glancing at them. Neither of them noticed him, still lost in their little embrace.

As he'd stood in front of the mirror and cleaned his teeth, his thoughts had gone to his father, dead for a while now. He wondered whether, if he were still around, they would have a special bond, like Ryan and Sara did.

Probably not. Mack, his dad, had been a sportsman. A semi-pro ice hockey player, he had excelled at everything physical, just like Ryan did. Even though Ryan was only eleven years old, his trophies jostled for space in the special glass-fronted cabinet in the hallway. Cups, medals and certificates for karate, football, swimming, even *diving*, for God's sake. Scott wasn't confident in the water, or on the football pitch, and when he was dragged along to Ryan's karate matches, the sounds of the kicks and the thump of bodies hitting the floor made him flinch.

No, his dad would have been just as enamoured of the younger son as his mother was.

'Scott!' Sara had called his name, clipped and sharp.

He remained silent, carried on brushing his teeth until she had no choice but to call again.

'SCOTT!'

He smiled, rinsed, put his toothbrush back. Made her wait before slowly opening the door. It was a small victory in a household where he never won, but it was a victory all the same. Even when he was out of the bathroom, he didn't call a reply. He simply stood at the top of the stairs, waiting.

'Scott!' she'd called a third time.

'I'm here,' he replied.

'Come on, come down here,' she said without looking at him, her attention still on Ryan, unable to drag her gaze away from him.

Scott traipsed down the stairs.

'Right, your brother will be at your high school today, as you know, for preparation for him moving up there in September. You are to walk him there, walk him home too. I'd like you to look for him at break times, just to make sure he's okay.' At last Sara dragged her eyes away from Ryan and appraised Scott. 'Do *not* let anyone be mean to him. I'm holding you responsible for him.'

Scott stared dispassionately at his mother. Ryan was a sporting hero, he was bright and intelligent, the most popular kid on their street, much more so than Scott. If anything, it was Ryan who should be looking out for *him*.

'Ready?' he asked him.

'Yep, let's go!'

One more hug, one more squeeze from Sara. Scott flattened himself against the wall and edged past them out of the door.

In the street, he waited for his brother to be released from Sara's grip.

Farenden High School was the best London state school in the league table. It hadn't been the plan; apparently a school that charged thousands would have been on the cards, but when Mack died and purse strings had to be tightened, the blueprint of Scott and Ryan's life had to change. Neither of the boys cared. Ryan just wanted to compete in all his many skill sets, and Scott just wanted school to be over with.

Three more years. Sometimes it seemed like a lifetime.

'You don't have to look out for me today,' said Ryan. 'I'll be fine.'

Scott smiled thinly.

'Do they bully you at school?' Ryan asked as they began the half-mile walk.

'Get lost,' Scott scoffed. 'Who the hell would bully me?'

Ryan shrugged.

They walked on in silence.

It was almost worse than being bullied, admitted Scott to himself only. He was lower than the kids who got beaten up or had their lunch money stolen. Scott was invisible; nobody even looked at him.

Sometimes he told himself he didn't understand why. He wasn't butt-ugly, he wasn't fat or stupid or lazy. He just preferred his own company to that of others. He couldn't really see the point in arguing or fighting or joining in with a group of kids who screamed and flaunted themselves and did the most obscure things just to be noticed.

Instead, during his lunch hour he sat in the library, sketching in his art book, or just sinking into himself and thinking about whether life was supposed to be more than this nothingness, pondering the fact that when he finally got to leave school, everything might change for the better. That something else might open up for him, and in doing so it might smother and close the black hole that his entire being seemed to be swamped in.

Ryan pulled him out of his morose thoughts by putting two fingers in his mouth and letting out a piercing whistle. Scott jumped, stumbling into the gutter, swearing quietly as the rainwater gathered there flooded over the top of his shoe.

Ryan jabbed him in his side. Scott staggered again.
'There's my mates,' he said. 'See you tonight!'

He jogged off, not casting a look back at his brother.

Scott stared at his wet shoe, the water seeping into his sock. Inside him, the black nothing swirled and grew, glowing with a red heat.

He pushed the feeling away and carried on walking.

Now, in the classroom, remembering that day, he rolled his collection of pencils together and held them in his fist, sharp ends enclosed in his grip.

He heaved another sigh, audible this time, and slumped in his chair.

Slowly it dawned on him that the chatter had subsided. It had been a free-for-all, a bonus, a chance for all the kids to swing around in their chairs and resume playground conversation.

He blinked and sat up straight. Had the lesson started while he had been miles away in his own head?

The thud of the door, rubber soles squeaking. A scream, loud and fear-filled and high-pitched.

Scott jumped, banging his knees painfully against the underside of the desk, and clapped a hand to his right ear before glaring at the girl who had screamed. Emily, a pretty blonde who wouldn't even know his name, stared past him. Scott turned his head, expecting to see a mouse or a spider. Halfway through the swivelling manoeuvre, he paused at the sight of Mrs Fleecy's face.

Paler than pale, eyes huge, mouth slack.

What the…

He swung around to face the rear of the classroom.

The gun sprouted, a dull silver, from the kid's hand.

It's a toy, it's pretend. It's not real. Guns are black, not silver.

30

There was no fear yet, not for Scott. A mild fascination, slight excitement at an anomaly in a day that had promised to be like all the others that had come before it. Today was going to be different.

Noah Miller, the kid who was late to class. The kid who'd moved here at the start of term from Germany or Denmark or somewhere. The only other boy in school who seemed to be as invisible as Scott. He'd never shown any comedic qualities before. He wasn't the class clown, he wasn't popular or a show-off, which was why, Emily aside, the classroom full of kids seemed to be looking at him with bemused faces right now rather than fear.

Scott leaned back in his chair and waited to see where this was going.

Mrs Fleecy was moving now, striding down the classroom between the rows of desks. Gone were the huge eyes and the stupid hanging mouth. Gone was the pale skin, replaced by two red cheeks, like she'd been outside in the snow or was mortally embarrassed.

'Noah!' she hissed as she walked. 'What are you doing? What is that? You can't bring something like that in here, frightening people like this.'

Scott remained staring, transfixed, at Noah.

In slow motion he saw the boy's thumb come up and over to pull back a little black catch on the top of the gun, just like they did in the movies. His forefinger tightened on the trigger.

The sudden, subtle sound of the bullet was more deafening than Emily's scream had been.

6

Sara
Now

Scott had been as good as dead since the shooting at the school, thought Sara. They all had, really.

Oh sure, he still functioned, got up in the morning, ate his dinner mechanically. Though not tonight, she realised, looking at his practically untouched plate.

And was he really so different to how he had been before?

No, was the answer, if she were brutally honest.

Sitting at the kitchen table, she looked towards the window. It was pitch-black out there now. No street lights down the little lane where her cabin was. Anyone could be out there, but Sara didn't feel the fear. The threat had happened already, it had passed, and now was the time for recovery.

She wondered how the man, Travis, could help her son. Oh sure, she knew bits and pieces about therapy; she'd been offered it herself. They all had, all the kids who remained, all the parents regardless of whether their children had lived or not, the teachers, the staff, the cleaners and the classroom assistants.

She had declined it. Her reaction had been to flounder. Later, as she learned more about what had happened, her instinct had been to run. To get away from London and Farenden High and the press and the total and utter devastation that hung like a rain cloud over the community. She hadn't told anyone where they were going; she had just planned it all very quietly, and when she had secured a new job and a new home, she had simply left. She had taken the batteries and SIM cards out of the mobile phones, used her mother's maiden name and stayed clear of social media and well-meaning people who offered their friendship.

Now, a year on, that day was never mentioned. But was that a mistake? Did Scott need to talk about it? Did *she* need to hear about it? Sara thought of Ryan, and closed her eyes, a bittersweet smile on her face. No need to worry about him. Scott was the one who needed her now. And she didn't know how to handle that. She couldn't talk to him. Never had been able to. He was so closed off, quiet and still in his own little world.

She came to a decision. Tomorrow she would track down Travis at work. She would thank him for bringing Scott home tonight, thank him for looking out for her boy, and maybe offer to buy him a coffee in the little café at the Centre.

There, she could figure him out, get him to tell her a little more about himself and his expertise, and then conclude whether or not to trust him with her son.

If it could help, it might be worth it.

The ache in her chest, always there these days, eased a little, and she leaned against the hard back of the chair, closed her eyes and thought of the therapy man.

He was all-right-looking, trim and smiley, friendly and kind. What more could a woman want? At that thought, a face flashed through her mind, but it was not that of her dead husband.

Jojo.

She trembled, blinked fiercely to chase the ghost away.

It was a face she never wanted to think about ever again. But it was hard not to picture him, especially when she was feeling tender and her nerves were frayed.

The tremble turned into a shudder. She forced herself to backtrack her thoughts to Travis.

There was an attraction there, she realised. On his side mostly. Attraction led to companionship, which led to sharing, which led to trouble when you were trying to stay hidden.

The teachers at the Centre were mostly temps. They came, they stayed for a year or a season and they moved on. Maybe that was what Travis would do. He must be discreet and quiet, as she'd been there six months and had never clapped eyes on him before; it was only in the last couple of weeks that she'd noticed him. Perhaps he was one of those who came, conquered and left in the space of a term or two. And if that were the case, she could make use of him, make use of his arms and his hands and his body and his mind and then wave him on his way at the end of the year. And if this 'friendship' helped her son, all the better.

She pulled Ryan's untouched dinner towards her and popped a couple of chips in her mouth. For the first time in a year, she could actually taste the food. It wasn't very good, the chips were burned and too crispy, but suddenly she was starving.

With more energy than she'd felt in a long time, she carried the plates to the bin and tipped the contents away. Pulling out two slices of thick-cut bread, she slathered them with butter and ate them standing up at the sink, watching out of the window.

Watching this time not for an attack, but for Travis, the therapy man.

It was late now. But tomorrow she would find him. Tomorrow she would try and fix Scott. And maybe, just maybe, if this Travis was as good as he claimed to be, he could fix her too.

–

The following morning, Sara waited until Scott was in the bathroom before slipping into his room. She was quiet, though he wouldn't hear her over the sound of the shower. Ryan never heard her either; the kid slept like a log, always had done, ever since he was a baby.

She paused in the doorway, thinking of her baby. He had been an utter joy from the moment of conception. He had contradicted Scott in every way. The pregnancy had been a breeze; no morning sickness, no bloating or swelling like she'd had first time round. Scott's labour had been a twenty-eight-hour nightmare culminating in an emergency Caesarean. Ryan had slipped out with ease exactly two hours after her contractions began. He had slept through almost immediately; Scott had had her up so frequently that she had almost had a breakdown and Mack had had to take over the night feeds.

It was partially where the discord came from now, she knew, and it made her sad. It made her feel like a bad mother.

And it had made Scott feel like he was a bad son, which was why he was the way he was.

She cringed, her entire body tightening, almost spasming. She clutched onto the door frame and edged her way into his room.

It wasn't a teenage boy's room, she thought sadly as she stared at the neatly made bed, the lack of possessions.

He'd been something of an artist at one time. It prickled her consciousness that she'd only recently remembered this. It worried her that she couldn't remember when he'd stopped drawing.

He had been good. His teachers had said that at a parents' evening one time. Was it primary school? It must have been. In high school, there was no time for such whimsy. That was the impression she'd got, anyway. Maybe it was around the time that Mack had died. Everything had stopped then. Time, her heart, her enjoyment of anything and everything. From then on, for a little while at least, it was all mechanical. Getting up in the morning like a robot. Dressing the kids, feeding the kids, getting the kids to school.

Time had healed, like they all said it would, but she didn't know when she had felt better. Maybe she hadn't. Maybe she had just adapted.

Like she was doing again now.

Travis the therapy man specialised in art, he had said. If he could get Scott interested in drawing again, that would be nice. It would be good for Scott to rediscover a passion. It would be excellent just to see him do something that didn't involve the television or video games or staring into space.

She had come up here because she had wondered if he might be secretly drawing again. She went down on her knees and lifted up the side of the duvet to peer underneath the bed, avoiding looking at the rucksack.

Apart from the bag, it was clean and empty.

The wardrobe and chest of drawers told the same story.

There was nowhere else to look for hidden sketch books or notepads.

Apart from… She side-eyed the rucksack, but couldn't bring herself to touch it, let alone unzip it and look inside.

In the room behind her, the rush of water slowed, then stopped.

Sara backed out of Scott's room and hurried down the stairs.

37

7

Travis
Now

The summer seemed to be racing past, mused Travis with something like alarm, as he left his house and began the half-mile walk to work. But it wasn't, really. It was the change in his schedule that had thrown him. All because of her, that whiny, witchy woman who had caused his life to go off kilter and lose almost a whole season in the process.

He paused at the gateway to his little cottage and tried to up his positivity. No, there was still plenty of green, always would be, with the firs that lined the path to the forest; they never lost their colour. Even the oaks and the katsura trees nestled among them were still glorious at the height of their summer hue.

In contrast, the day was warm, as it had been yesterday, and all the days before it. Travis shrugged off his jacket and stuffed it into his backpack. He walked on, glancing back once, offering a smile to the cottage that he had made his home and could now never imagine leaving.

He had always been a mover – circumstances and misunderstandings meant never being able to stop in one place for longer than a year or two – but Kielder had its claws into him good and proper. The cottage was a bonus. Previously, his houses or apartments had been a base, a place to put his stuff while he went on with his daily work, and a warm, dry shelter to sleep in. But this place had changed that, and he had begun to realise that the cottage had become a home.

All that was missing now was someone to share it with.

The woman, Sara, flashed through his mind as she so often did these days, and even after his first proper encounter with her the night before, he was unable to dash the hope away. It had been a disappointment, he acknowledged now as he stepped up his pace. He had thought she might be shy, or just one of those rare women who kept themselves to themselves in the workplace. But that wasn't what she was, or certainly wasn't what she had been yesterday.

She had been *cold*. She hadn't even been furious at her son's disappearing act, or embarrassed that Travis had found him. She had been… *nothing*.

Oh well, thought Travis as he tipped his face upwards and let the sun bathe it in its warmth. It could be a challenge, her and the boy both. Travis enjoyed a challenge.

–

The walk to work inspired Travis for his first Saturday session, which consisted of half a dozen teenagers in varying states of tiredness.

He surveyed them as they sat in front of him, their eyes heavy, then glanced at his watch. It was nine a.m., hardly early, yet these kids were slumped in their chairs as though the sun wasn't even up yet. What time did they go to bed? he wondered, grateful for his own strict rules on the amount of sleep he got in a night. With a pinprick of annoyance he realised that had he not been absent for the majority of the previous term, the children wouldn't be in this state now.

'Right,' he said, emphasising the need for a bit of energy with a clap of his hands. 'Today I'd like to see some creativity involving summer. I want to see the colours that emerge in our landscape at this time of year.' On a whim, he picked up his jacket and slipped it on. 'Come on, outside. We'll get some visual stimulation.'

They traipsed outside, and Travis led them to the field at the back of the Centre that bordered Kielder Forest.

He watched as they walked around, happy when he heard a shout or an exclamation of delight. They were waking up, he realised, and he pledged to do more outdoor sessions in the autumn term.

He let them be, sitting himself down on the stump of a tree, lost in his own pleasure at simply watching them. As he sat, he felt a cold draught on the back of his neck, out of keeping with the warmth of the day. He shivered, turned back towards the building, and there, like an apparition in the window of his classroom, stood Sara Doyle.

She was watching the children as they rummaged around the lower branches of the trees, but as though she felt his stare on her, she turned towards him. Slowly she raised her hand in a half-wave. His heart gave a little skip and he waved in return.

Abruptly she disappeared from the window.

He turned back to the kids, a frown knitting his brow, but within a few moments he heard the heavy clang of the fire door. He spun around again, startled to see her making her way towards him.

He appraised her upon her approach, comfortable enough at this distance to allow his eyes to roam over her tight-fitting jeans, the T-shirt that clung to her upper body. Her hair was tied back, as it always was, her face scrubbed and clean. She should look blooming, rosy even, but as usual, to Travis she seemed oh-so-tired.

Quickly he glanced at the kids, seeing the change in them simply by bringing them outside. Was that what Sara needed, fresh air and gentle exercise?

'Hello,' she said, as she neared him. 'I wondered if I could speak to you?'

He scrubbed his hands on his jeans and stood up, an absurd urge to pull her into a hug overcoming him. He resisted and put his hands in his pockets.

'Hello, Sara. How are you?'

He watched carefully as her eyes darted from him to the kids and back again. 'You're in a lesson, I'm sorry,' she said, ignoring his question. 'I wondered if perhaps you might join me in the cafeteria later for a coffee. There's something I'd like to talk to you about.' She waited a beat and moved a step closer, causing his pulse to accelerate. 'Something you said last night. When you mentioned art therapy.' Her voice lowered on the last word, as though it were dirty, or something to be ashamed of.

He didn't take offence. He was used to it. Mental health was still tinged with stigma.

'I've an hour between this class and my next,' he said. 'Are you free then?'

She nodded, and her lips turned up in what he supposed she hoped might pass as a smile. Then without another word, she turned around and headed back to the main building.

–

On occasion, there were deer in the forest. There were no borders, no fencing keeping them in or out, and they wandered close to the cottage where Travis lived. He had seen them numerous times. Once, he had been outside, on the porch, enjoying a cup of green tea when some of them meandered over. He had watched them with joy filling him; he had sunk into the atmosphere, a smile on his face so wide his gums had dried out.

He had reached for his tea. It was all it took. They bolted, fading back into the trees.

Just one slight movement was enough to spook them.

He had this thought now as he stood in the doorway to the cafeteria, watching Sara as she sat, ramrod straight, at an empty table.

Mustn't spook her.

The cafeteria was practically empty, it not being break or lunchtime. Any sudden movement, any loud noise and she would withdraw again. Sometimes he could be ham-fisted, overeager, and it led to misunderstandings, especially with women. He must pull his natural self back with this one. Because Sara was destined to become someone very special, of that he was sure.

He moved back into the corridor, walked the length of it, turned so he was once again facing the cafeteria. He strode towards it, his footsteps hopefully clear, a warning signalling his arrival.

It worked, he noticed, as he entered through the doorway again and saw that she had twisted in her chair. Her slender, pale hands clutched the back of it, her eyes narrowed and thin as he approached her.

Out of the corner of his eye, he saw Dora on the till, a bored look in her eye as she moved a cloth in circles on the counter.

'Coffee?' he mouthed to Sara.

Her knuckles whitened a little as she gripped the chair. Her jaw tightened, then she exhaled, raised her chin slightly and nodded stiffly at him.

'Dora, hi, two coffees, please,' he said as he stood at the serving counter.

He thought of the exchange that had just taken place. It could hardly be called that, really. Sara was so tightly wound, what should have been a normal, easy transaction had been almost painful to watch.

He glanced over his shoulder as Dora fiddled around at the hot water urn. Sara had turned, her back to him again. Her spine was a straight line, as though she were wearing uncomfortable armour.

What's her story? Travis wondered.

Dora averted her eyes as she passed him the coffees. He paid her, set them on a tray and collected milk and sugar. Finally, with no procrastination time left, he squared his shoulders and made his way over to Sara.

'Wasn't sure how you take it.' He set a coffee in front of her and frowned. 'I can get cream from Dora, if you'd prefer.'

She shook her head, said a soft thank you and drew the cup towards her.

Travis deposited the tray on the table behind him and sat down.

'What are your confidentiality policies?' She startled him by speaking first, and the question itself took him by surprise. It took him a few beats – more time than it should – to realise she was speaking about the therapy.

He was staggered, thrown off balance for a moment. Was now the time to tell her that he wasn't qualified per se; rather that he had collected experience through many years of being a good listener? He thought of the therapy that he himself had recently – grudgingly – undertaken. He had had a similar thought to Sara, though he hadn't voiced the question. He'd been smarter than that. He had known what the man wanted to hear, and had given him what he needed in order to get past the ridiculous bureaucracy and back to his life.

He felt the side of his mouth twitch. It always did when he was caught off guard. He couldn't tell her that he wasn't actually qualified. It made him sound like a fraud. And he wasn't. He was just someone who tried to help the kids. He'd had success because he never told them what to do.

He simply listened.

And that was exactly what therapy was.

Blindly, a reply came to mind. Almost word for word, he repeated a statement he had heard on a TV show, *Breaking Bad*. He'd loved the psychology of the characters on that show, had watched it time and time again.

'Anything you say to me is in the strictest confidence. I can't repeat anything you say, unless you make a direct threat of harm to someone else or yourself.'

He sat back, pleased with how smoothly the answer had come out.

She picked up her coffee and sipped at it, ignoring the sugar and milk. Travis watched her mouth, half aware that he was staring. He pulled his eyes away and fumbled on the table for a spoon.

'Are you close with people here in Kielder?'

Her voice was deliberately casual, but he recognised the undertone. What she meant was: are you a gossip?

'I get along with most people,' he lied, 'but I like to spend time alone. I live alone,' he added as an afterthought, and then worried that it sounded like he was coming on to her.

Time ticked on. Behind Sara's head, Travis watched the large clock on the wall. The second hand swung around once, twice… Five whole minutes passed before she spoke again.

'You've heard of Farenden.'

It wasn't a question and she didn't phrase it that way. Everyone had heard of Farenden. It sat uncomfortably between 9/11 and Princess Diana's death. It jostled for position alongside Dunblane and the Hungerford massacre.

Travis heard a sharp inhalation. His own, he realised. Not quite a gasp, but it denoted the shock he felt.

He swallowed.

'Yes, I remember it,' he said as mildly as he could manage.

Nothing else was forthcoming. But although she hadn't moved an inch, Sara's body language had changed. The two sentences – her statement and his subsequent reply – had been their first session, he realised. It was over now, for today at least. She would say nothing more, and that was okay. For now, he knew all he needed to.

She or Scott had been at Farenden.

In his mind, he was already at home, huddled in front of his old PC, one side of his mouth twitching as he waited for the patchy Wi-Fi to get some legs.

In his body, he was still here, sipping coffee in what he hoped was a companionable silence.

Behind Sara, the second hand of the clock moved around and around.

8

Sara
Now

Sara allowed the excruciating silence to go on and on. Soon, the cafeteria melted away. She was no longer at work, seated at a table, with a coffee rapidly going cold. She'd travelled back in time, fourteen years back, and was lying in bed in a hotel room that rented by the afternoon, gazing at the patchy, yellowed ceiling.

She looked at her feet, at the worn bedspread, at the awful panelled walls and the bare light bulb that hung disturbingly off-centre in the little room.

She looked anywhere but at the man in the bed beside her who wasn't her husband.

An age-old tale. Such a cliché. Her husband, Mack, sitting night after night in his chair, withdrawn and silent, his movements mechanical, the days now routines that left her depressed and stifled.

This one, this man in the bed, had been all over her in the bar on the corner of the street where she worked. Not in a slimy, groping way. It had been much more subtle: the eye contact, the smile when she served him as opposed to the polite-but-removed behaviour when one of her colleagues pulled his pints.

Bit by bit, day by day, they began to learn more about each other. The attraction was clearly mutual. Her heart leaped when he came into the bar. She started to take more care of herself when she went to work. A bit of lip gloss, eyeliner, hair straightened instead of pulled back in a band.

She blamed Mack, inside her head. They were young, for goodness' sake, they were childless at that point and not long married. They were both in work, and unlike a lot of their friends, they could actually afford to do stuff.

So why were they sitting in a darkened room every night, not talking, pretending to watch television, before Mack would invariably fall asleep in his chair, leaving her sneaking off to bed alone to lie awake and wonder. Wonder what she had done wrong. Wonder why he was no longer interested in her. Hurt and rejection had become her go-to emotions.

'Your hubby expecting you back any time soon?' asked the naked man beside her, casually.

Sara clutched the sheet to her breast and turned her face to the window. She feigned sleep, just like Mack did when she reached for him.

The man beside her fell silent.

This can't happen again, thought Sara as she closed her eyes.

But it would.

Now, there was a different man. In front of her, rather than beside her, in a cafeteria and not a bed. There were differences, but she was pretty sure the intention was the same.

He was interested in her, and his interest could well be genuine. Maybe he *did* care, about her and her kids and her life and her well-being. It was all nudged out, though, by the endgame.

He wanted to sleep with her.

Sara wasn't sure why. She wasn't the barmaid she'd once been. Back then, pre-kids, even afterwards, for a while, her body had been slamming, her hair shone and her face was line-free and filled with fun. Now, her figure was out of shape. A lean, thin, wiry form of forgetting-to-eat stress, with lumpy parts from binges when the pain got too much and the only way to calm it was to fill her gut with anything she could find in the woefully scarce kitchen cupboards.

These days, the time between hair washes stretched out longer and longer. She didn't even own a pair of straighteners any more, nor eyeliner nor lip gloss. Her clothes were baggy and shapeless, just like her personality. Today, though, she had rummaged in the back of the wardrobe and found a pair of very old skinny jeans. They fitted, barely, and though they smelled a little musty, they accentuated what remained of the figure she used to have.

But this wasn't about her. She was a mother, and as unnatural as it seemed — even now, when her elder boy was almost as tall as her — that had to be the thing that came before everything else.

The children's well-being. Their mental health. She couldn't talk about it with them, couldn't stand to. But as a mother, it was her responsibility to put them first.

Ryan was fine. Ryan was happy and secure and safe. But Scott… he was another story.

She stood up abruptly.

'I need to get back to work,' she said.

Travis nodded, his eyes fixed on her face. He pushed his chair back, a gentlemanly, old-fashioned move to stand because she had.

Sara averted her gaze. 'I'll try and get Scott to come in one day. Just for the art stuff, just... drawing and that.'

She turned before he could respond, but she could feel his smile on her back before the feeling faded and she heard his footsteps clicking away out of the cafeteria.

She stared at the cold coffee, then, checking her watch, decided she had enough time to get a caffeine boost and made her way back towards the serving counter.

'Another coffee, please,' she said.

Dora, the ever-present server, poured the drink in silence. When Sara held her hand out with the coins, Dora shook her head.

'Thanks,' said Sara softly as she collected the mug and turned away.

'Lass.' Dora spoke, the single word hushed and quiet.

Sara half turned, gaze down. From the corner of her eye, she saw Dora leaning in towards her.

'Careful with that one, darlin'. Just... watch yourself.' Straightening up, she busied herself with a cloth. 'Have a good day, love.'

—

Sara got back to work, hiding herself away in the cleaning closet and pondering on Dora's strange words. Probably the older woman felt nurturing towards the single, middle-aged teacher. Probably didn't want Sara spoiling him, the way she'd desecrated Mack and ruined Jojo.

Sara shook her head. Dora didn't know any of that.

She leaned against the wall, one hand on her chest, forcing herself to breathe. She turned to the shelves and counted the bottles of bleach stacked there. When she felt her spine begin to relax, she replenished the products in her cart and pushed it out of the closet, locking the door behind her.

The rest of her shift passed, slow and drama-free. She mopped and scrubbed and vacuumed mechanically. She had thought it before, and now it occurred to her again: she had become Mack, her late husband. All those days and nights when he withdrew, when even the television didn't get switched on any more and the only sound in the house was the ticking of the clock on the mantel.

Those black days. If anybody had told her that those days would not be the worst she ever faced, she'd have ended it all then.

But it went on. Life was a wheel. And she couldn't get off it now any more than she could back then.

–

On her afternoon break, she had borrowed the computer in the office and looked up recipes. A chicken dish that promised to be 'better than Nando's' sounded good. She had scribbled the ingredients needed on a piece of paper and quickly logged off.

There was a Co-op on her walk back to the cabin, and she blinked in the bright lights and shivered at the air conditioning blasting her bare arms as she walked the aisles.

The woman on the till was cheery and chatty, and not for the first time Sara wished she had moved elsewhere. A big city, Glasgow or Manchester or Liverpool. To get lost in the crowds rather than trying to hide in the middle of nowhere.

She forced a smile onto her face, accepted the woman's pleasantries with a nod and counted the items as they were scanned through.

The searing heat of outdoors was as much of a shock as the cool air of the Co-op had been. She looked back through the doors; the checkout lady had moved on and was deep in conversation with another shopper. Behind her, the closed doors of the cabinet that contained the cigarettes caught her eye.

What she would give for a cigarette right now. They had become so expensive she'd had to quit, but she recalled those dark days after Mack's death, and then a year ago after Farenden, when she had sat in the darkened kitchen and smoked one after another.

Mentally she calculated her bank balance, and how many days until payday. She could get a pack, or even some rolling tobacco, and she had decided and was just turning back to go inside the shop when movement at the top of the hill caught her eye.

A hundred yards away, and she had to squint in the sunlight, but she was sure it was Travis. And he was heading her way.

She stopped, caught in indecision as to whether to hide inside the Co-op or walk smartly and quickly back home. The shop was the obvious choice, but what if he came in, saw her skulking around the aisles? For a moment she entertained the idea of what might happen. There had been something when she sat opposite him earlier. A spark that signalled an attraction. Or a need. Didn't matter; were they not one and the same thing?

She licked her lips, suddenly dry. He was getting closer. Not close enough to spot her, she didn't think, but if she loitered here any longer, the decision would be taken out of her hands.

She put her head down, turned to her right, and walked down the track towards home as quickly as she could.

—

She'd made it home, unpacked the chicken and the spices and the potatoes and salad and stared at it heaped on the draining board. Tired, like the anomaly of a shopping trip with real purpose had wiped her out.

Outside, movement caught her eye. Travis, his head bobbing past the hedge, just like it had the previous evening. Behind the half net curtain, she was sure he couldn't see her. She watched him, convinced he was walking deliberately slowly, certain that his head was angled to catch sight of a member of the freakish family who lived in the cabin and interacted with nobody.

As he vanished from view, she looked away from the window. He had been kind today. He hadn't pushed her, had bought her coffee, and though she hadn't said very much at all, he had listened.

She'd said hardly anything, really. And it was just that one word which was now fixed in his mind: Farenden. It was enough. It was more than she could usually manage, and it was sufficient to give him a little bit of information about who she was, and why she was the way she was.

She pulled the chicken from the wrapping, sliced it, spiced it, shoved it under the grill. Her motions were mechanical, automatic, and as she waited for the meat to cook, she rehearsed her lines, silently, inside her head, until she was sure she had them down right.

'I want you to come into the Centre,' Sara announced as she dished up the dinner. 'That Travis has some good classes and I want you to join in.'

Scott seemed more interested in the contents of the table than in her words. She appraised it herself. She'd laid it out buffet style, three plates on the side, kitchen roll folded for napkins.

Scott reached for a piece of chicken and held it over the tabletop. He chewed it and looked at her cautiously.

'Okay,' he muttered.

Sara hadn't realised her heart was beating wildly until he gave his consent. She put a hand to her breast, felt her breathing slow at her touch.

'Good,' she said. She slipped into a chair and watched Scott as he picked another piece of chicken off the plate. 'Save some for your brother,' she said absently.

A scowl replaced the amiable look on Scott's face. He put the chicken back. Sara, smiling as Ryan rounded the corner, didn't notice.

9

Travis
Now

Travis was sure he saw movement behind the thin curtain of the Doyles' cabin. He didn't loiter, though. That deer came to mind again, how easily spooked it was. Sara had extended something to him today. A tiny snippet of trust. He had to handle her carefully.

And besides, he had things to do tonight.

He sped up as he walked the short distance to his own cottage. Usually, when he got home after his last class, he would kick off his shoes, walk barefoot out onto the deck and spend at least an hour watching and listening to the wildlife. Normally with a coffee or a beer, occasionally with a wine. Some afternoons he would sit there until the sun went down. Sometimes the night view was even better than the day.

Today, however, he had work to do.

He dropped his bag to the floor by the door and headed straight to his PC. As it fired up, he said a prayer out loud for a good Wi-Fi connection, and hissed a little 'yes' as the green lights blinked at him from the modem.

Pulling up a chair, he hunched over the keyboard. Where to start?

A general search, he decided, would bring up key information. He typed 'Sara Doyle' into the search engine and pressed enter.

Nothing. Well, something, plenty, actually, but none of them were her. Half aware of his mouth twitching, he added 'Farenden' and pressed enter again.

Lots of partial results, lots of Saras, lots about Farenden, but nothing that matched up to her. Finally, he deleted her name and let the hundreds of articles about the Farenden tragedy come up.

It was horrific, reading the stories, the witness accounts, the pieces about the funerals, and scanning the numerous images taken on the day and in the immediate aftermath.

Nineteen students and one adult dead. Six other kids wounded, some of them with life-altering injuries.

It was a massacre with a final victim count that surpassed Dunblane, Columbine and Parkland.

Travis remembered it vividly. He had been here then, in Kielder, and had heard the news when he got into work. He'd been early, because he was always prompt, and had been taking a leisurely coffee in the staff room when the headmaster, Gordon Bridge, had run in, phone in hand, and switched on the television.

They had watched in horror as the events unfolded on Sky TV news. The yellow ticker tape that ran across the screen had numbers on it. They changed with each new reported death. When the numbers reached double figures, Travis had left and gone to his first class.

They were waiting for him, eight kids aged between nine and fourteen, all blissfully unaware of what was happening in another classroom 300 miles away.

It was the rule at Kielder that phones had to be turned in or stowed away in lockers before classes began. And as Travis stood ashen-faced in front of the kids, he thought of one of the snippets he'd seen on the news. Text messages and voice notes coming in streams from the kids: to parents, grandparents, friends at different schools. They were all relayed to the police, and as a result the authorities garnered some sort of idea of what they were dealing with.

The next day, Gordon Bridge had put in a motion for the kids at Kielder to be able to keep their phones on them while they were at the Centre.

Nobody opposed it, though Travis always kept a careful eye that they were packed away in pockets or bags, and not left out on the desks.

Outside his cottage, dusk fell. The only light in the room was the glow of Travis's computer screen. He was scrolling through the images now, scanning the faces for one he recognised. Nothing; nobody was her.

With a deep sigh of frustration, he looked at the list of the victims' names, tasting them out loud. 'Quinn, Matty, Iozif, Amir, Sam, Chase, Chloe, Jessie…' He raised his hands above his head and stretched, before clicking off the screen.

The faces of the dead faded away.

As he moved into the kitchen area, he pulled his phone out and went onto Facebook, half-heartedly entering her name. He expected and got nothing. She was so private, he wasn't surprised. He tried Scott. Plenty of Scott Doyles, but none of them was the troubled young man who intrigued Travis so.

He put the phone face down on the counter and stared out into the now-black night. He felt sick, all those hours staring at all that grief. Nothing in here would help him. Only his beloved forest could soothe him tonight.

Taking off his shoes and placing them neatly by the door, he rolled up his shirtsleeves and walked barefoot out into the darkness.

—

Travis believed in nourishment from nature. His habits were quirky, sure, but the nice thing about living in a place where the population was just a couple of hundred, in an area that spanned 2,000 acres, was that barely anybody ever witnessed his habits. Even if they did, they wouldn't be perceived as overtly strange. This place was all about the unusual.

It was a haven.

And the forest floor did its job right now as he walked toe to toe with nature. He never carried a torch on his night-time walks, preferring to let his eyes adjust as fully as possible to the darkness and allow his other senses to be heightened.

He had run some classes last year that involved taking students night-walking. Two female staff had accompanied him, because to have one male guiding a bunch of school kids through the woods at midnight wouldn't be appropriate.

It might be something that Scott would be interested in, and perhaps even Sara would come along. Travis let his mind wander: Scott ahead of them, concentrating on his footing, Travis and Sara behind. She wouldn't be used to it, and he, knowing the forest as well as he knew his own home, would take hold of her hand, guiding her on until she too let go of all her hurts and anxieties and let her body do the feeling and the thinking and the sensing. All that tension that she held in her spine like a metal rod would vanish. She would be grateful to him for showing her how wonderful it was in his world. She would be soft and yielding and smiling—

A crack in the undergrowth up ahead startled him out of his dreaming state. He frowned, stopped, and scratched at his head, annoyed at himself for letting his feelings for a woman he barely knew disrupt his journey.

But that was Travis. When he fell, he fell hard and deep.

He closed his eyes and breathed in the night. The air around him had changed. He could smell something other than the natural forest scents now, and he knew he had walked further than he had intended.

The pit caves.

When the forest had been created by man a hundred years ago, it had been just 3 square miles. Over the years, technology had caught up, a reservoir had been constructed, and the machinery used had inadvertently created dozens of cave-like structures in the forest floor. Nature had played a part, the roofs falling in over time, though it was rumoured that some tunnels still ran underground, undisturbed except for the wildlife that inhabited them.

The locals called them the pit caves, and for a visitor, they could be as deadly as the surrounding moors.

The caves carried a scent on the slight breeze, of chalk and concrete and metal. This aroma reached Travis now and he shivered.

He considered himself an expert, well versed in the ways of the wild, but even his ego wasn't big enough to think he could walk safely among the pit caves at night. As if in answer to his concerns, he felt the sole of his right foot shift into dangerous nothingness. He yanked it back, turned smartly, and picked his way carefully in what he hoped were his own footprints back to his home.

The odd cracking sound came from behind him, always at a distance. Something heavy enough to snap a twig underfoot.

The deer, he told himself. Nothing else, just the deer.

In spite of his internal pep talk, he moved faster than he would usually walk, not lessening his pace until the outline of his isolated cottage came into view.

10

Scott
Before

The smile slipped from Scott's face as Mrs Fleecy's shirt bloomed red. Then he laughed. It was a nervous reaction, and it only lasted a second before he swallowed it back and looked at Noah.

Noah was staring right back at him.

'Yes, bro,' he said, and with the gun dangling from his forefinger, he gave Scott a thumbs-up.

Scott looked down at his lap. His heart beat faster, pounding in his chest.

The gun was real.

A hand landed on the back of his chair, and he jumped and spun around to see Emily, her usually flawless face stained red.

Mrs Fleecy's blood, flecks of it on Emily's cheeks. Scott felt bile rise in his throat as he edged away from Emily's outstretched hands, staring at her mouth, wide open, her eyes, filling and over-spilling with tears that ran rivers down her face.

It felt wrong, seeing someone so perfect looking so... dishevelled.

He looked away, and saw that everyone else's expressions looked like Emily's, so he lowered his eyes to the floor.

His rucksack was by his feet. It was also flecked with claret. Off to the side, Mrs Fleecy lay motionless, face down. Beneath her, blood began to pool and spread.

A flurry of movement in the corner of his eye. Scott chanced a look up. Noah was on the move, his own rucksack on his back, the gun held in its proper grip now, waving from left to right as he walked around the back of the classroom.

Emily's scream faded to silence, while around him, the rest of the class let out a previously held breath in unison.

'Stay where you are,' Noah said. 'I'll be right back.' He sidled along with his back to the wall. At the door, he paused. 'Now you see me,' he said.

He turned, and with a flash of his long, black coat left the room.

Scott didn't know what he had expected: kids springing into action, screams, shouts, released by the sudden absence of their perpetrator. But he didn't anticipate what was happening now.

Nothing.

Nobody moved. It seemed to Scott that after that first exhalation, no one was even breathing any more.

Now you see me.

Noah's parting words reverberated in his head, and he looked towards the windows that lined the left-hand side of the classroom. They were high up, but if they pushed the desks over and stood on them, they could get them open. Whether they were big enough to actually get out of was another question.

'Is anyone going to help us?' A voice, high-pitched, rang out, finally breaking the awful quiet.

Beth Cage was the speaker, and Scott watched as she half stood and observed her classmates.

'The gun had a silencer on it.' Scott hadn't meant to speak up, and he wished he hadn't when everyone's head swivelled to look at him.

'So?' said Beth. The squeal of moments before had gone; now she was rough, disparaging, the way they all were on the rare occasions they spoke to him.

He was sure he was right. Although everyone had jumped when Noah had pulled the trigger, it hadn't been that loud. So even though their eyes were boring into him, he pushed on. 'If it had a silencer, people might not have heard what happened in here.' Beth looked blank now. Scott expanded a little more. 'Help might not be coming.'

A gasp, theatrical almost as it broke the dead air in the room. It came from Emily, and she shuffled her chair a little closer to him. 'We should run,' she said.

She couldn't be talking to him. Surely she wasn't looking to him? Scott glanced around the classroom again, and then he saw it.

He'd thought they were numb and paralysed by events, slouched over their desks, heads down, staring into their laps.

They weren't. They were all on their phones, texting frantically, eyes flicking up every couple of seconds to look to the door.

Scott sank into his chair and reached into his back pocket for his own phone. He stared at the blank screen. It wasn't switched on. He rarely turned his mobile on. Why would he? Nobody ever called or texted him, apart from his grandmother. He turned to put the mobile away in his bag, pausing mid-reach as he realised that his rucksack was nestling next to the inert bloodstained form of Mrs Fleecy.

As if sensing his thoughts, or his line of sight, Emily slipped out of her chair, scuttled behind him and crouched beside their teacher.

'I don't know what to do,' she said.

As if they had needed just one person's motion, the classroom stirred. Phones, beeping now, ringtones hastily silenced, were answered as the fifteen other pupils surrounded Emily and Mrs Fleecy.

'…shot…'

'…Mrs Fleecy…'

'…chest… blood…'

'…left the room…'

'…said he's coming back…'

Snippets of conversation spread around Scott. Bodies knelt beside him, his rucksack shifted in the melee, shoved aside by impatient hands to sit underneath his desk. He pulled the bag onto his lap, drew his feet up to his chair, wrapped his arms around his knees and waited.

11

Sara
Now

Sara woke early. A glance at the clock told her she'd had just under three hours' sleep. The silent special chicken dinner had been fleeting and unfulfilling.

Scott had agreed to go with her to the Centre and check out some of Travis's classes. For a moment at the worn pine table, she had been hopeful. His interaction with her, however brief and singularly worded, had been *something*. He had eaten a piece of the chicken. He hadn't gone so far as to compliment the meal, or her, but he had eaten it. She was sure he had reached for another piece, but by then her mind had turned to her younger son. As it always did. He wasn't what he used to be.

What had he been? Boisterous, cheeky, free with hugs and affection for his mother, though only when nobody had been watching. Vocal and smart and well liked. So well liked.

In the last year, like all of them, Ryan had... faded. It was the only word that came to mind. He sat in corners, he stood in shadows. Ever so slowly he was becoming unreachable.

He came to the Centre with her most days, but he didn't participate. She would catch a glimpse of him through the windows as she cleaned her way around the property. A flash of his T-shirt among the trees, a brush of golden hair in the long grass. That was fine by her. She didn't want him in a classroom. Out there, in the near wilderness, he was free. Should something – someone – come, he could run to safety. Four walls were not conducive to keeping a kid safe.

Introspectively, she wondered why was she so keen to have Scott within the boundaries of the Centre, but not Ryan? She dismissed the musing before it could land as a fully-fledged thought by throwing the thin sheet off her body.

Not quite seven a.m. and the heat was already upon her.

She slipped into the bathroom, stood under an icy shower and ran her hands over the ribs that protruded from her body.

Had she eaten any chicken last night? She couldn't remember. Cutting off the water, she wrapped a towel around herself and made her way downstairs.

The buffet-style dinner still sat out on the table. The chicken congealing on the plate, the potatoes beside it, greasy and shiny and untouched. One less piece of meat than she had cooked.

So, neither she nor Ryan had eaten after all.

She stood and stared at the abandoned food. A creak from upstairs pulled her to attention.

'Get up,' she called as she hurried back up the stairs to her bedroom. 'Scott, you're coming in with me today, don't forget. Ready to leave in half an hour.'

She dressed and dragged a brush through her hair, pulling it back into her everyday ponytail. Staring in the mirror, she tugged the band free, let her hair fall around her face.

The tendrils, damp from the shower, curled on her cheeks. He had loved her hair. Ran his hands through it as they lay side by side in those cheap pay-by-the-hour hotels. The exertion from their sex had made her skin damp, and the curls had come out then too.

'You should wear it like this,' he said as he clutched handfuls of it.

Like she always did, she turned her head away from him. But the next day, knowing she would see him pass through the bar at lunchtime, she had worn it down and curly. He had smiled at her, his eyes narrow and shining, thrilled that she had done it for him.

She had feigned sickness to her boss. He'd not gone back to work. They had not gone to a hotel; they had gone to his car and driven to an industrial estate, right down the far end, where the units were empty.

Later, she had returned home to the house in darkness. Mack was in his chair.

'Work called, wanting to know if you felt better,' he said in a monotone. 'Want to know if you'll be well enough tomorrow, or they'll find someone to cover your shift.'

She had felt the heat in her face, but because he didn't look at her these days, he didn't see it.

A door opened and closed. Sara sat up, startled.

'I'm ready,' said Scott from the landing.

Swallowing, she stood up and smoothed down her shirt.

'Coming,' she said.

One last glance in the mirror. Her reflection stared back, pale and drawn and gaunt. She felt her lip curl with distaste as she snatched up the band and pulled her hair back into a ponytail.

–

'Travis knows you were at the... school, but he doesn't know... what happened.' The words were painful to say, almost impossible to get out. Her voice was so low she wondered if Scott even heard her.

He angled his head to the side, a sign that he was listening.

Up ahead, she caught a glimpse of Ryan, before he rounded the corner and disappeared from sight. For a split second she sped up, almost broke into a run, before pulling herself back.

This lane, this hill that led to the Centre, was not dangerous. A car would not come hurtling around the corner and smash into Ryan. Gunmen did not hide in the trees that lined the verge.

'Don't...' She stopped short, took a breath and tried again. 'He's not there to talk to you, you're just going to be... I don't know, drawing, painting and stuff. He doesn't need to know stuff about us, about our family.'

She looked sideways at Scott. His head hung low as he walked beside her, so slowly that every few steps he fell behind her, just out of view.

'Like what stuff?' he murmured.

'Personal stuff.'

'Isn't that his job, to be nosy?'

In answer to his question came the words she really wanted to say: 'You're just going to be drawing. He doesn't need to know everything.'

She stopped walking; he did too, and for a long moment they stared at each other. Something passed between them, and to Sara, there was more truth in that single mutual stare than had been spoken in the entire last year.

Scott swallowed. She watched as his Adam's apple nudged against his slender white throat. When had he become an adult, her boy? The answer was lightning quick, scathing in its speed: a year ago.

Scott broke eye contact and looked down the road. Sara followed his gaze. Ryan had long since vanished. She felt a pulse throb in her neck.

'Come on,' she said, and she set off at a half-jog towards the Centre.

–

'Morning, Sara!' Gordon, the Head, greeted her cheerfully as always. His eyebrows, bushy and grey, betraying his years, bobbed up and down as he looked at Scott behind her. 'Hi, you've come to join us today?'

When no reply was forthcoming from her son, Sara forced a smile. 'He's going to check out some classes. Travis invited him.'

Gordon nodded; thoughtfully, it seemed to Sara.

'Excellent, that's good to hear.' His frown didn't quite match the joviality of his tone. 'I'm heading over to Travis's room now, why don't I escort…?' He tailed off, waiting for an introduction.

Sara moved a step back and put an arm around Scott's shoulders. The proximity of his body sent little shock waves through her, reminding her of just how long it had been since she had touched him.

Almost one year ago. Twice. The first time, when he had emerged from Farenden, dazed and bloodied. She

68

had grabbed his shoulders and pulled him to her, buried her face in his neck, pulling him, pulling him, closer and closer until she had thought she could bring him back inside her like a foetus, where he was safe and nothing could hurt him.

The second time, exactly a week later, she had grabbed his shoulders again. That contact had been nothing like the ferocious hug of the previous week. That time, she had shaken him, hearing his teeth click together, over and over again, until she felt it in her own limbs. She had pushed him away when she was spent and retreated to the other side of the room until her back had come into contact with the wall. She had slid down it, her mouth agape in a silent scream that never emerged. He had balled himself up in the opposite corner, ironically curled foetus-like.

Almost a year had passed. She hadn't touched him since.

12

Travis
Now

Travis stood at the window, looking out to the forest borders. Inside his left boot he scrunched up his toes. Something had cut him last night, when he was wandering barefoot. He had been disappointed when he saw the blood on his sole. The forest floor was soft with mulch composted over the seasons. He couldn't remember the last time he came home from a back-to-nature-walk with a graze. Somehow he felt that the forest had turned against him.

Silly thoughts, he told himself. Equally as ridiculous was the fact that he had got spooked. So a twig had snapped somewhere. Sound carried far in the trees; it probably wasn't anything that was even close to him. It probably wasn't a person.

Still, it had left him slightly shaken. Usually when he opened his eyes each morning, his stomach churned with the promise of a brand-new day and everything it could bring. Today had been different. The faces he had looked at on the computer before the walk had been the catalyst, culminating in the way he was feeling now. Off balance.

Shake it off.

He took a deep breath and thought about going to refill his coffee. It was going to be a big caffeine day. And that was okay. If a few more mugs than usual were what it took to get him over this strange little blip, then that's what he would do.

He had no group sessions until ten a.m. He had an hour to gather himself.

'Travis!'

The Headmaster's voice boomed from the corridor. Travis winced before hastily arranging a smile on his face.

'Hi, Gordon.' His eyes widened slightly at the sight of the boy behind the Head. 'Scott, good to see you, pal.'

Travis kept the smile in place as Scott stared blankly over his shoulder. For a long moment the three of them stood in a strange silence. Gordon Bridge locked eyes with him. Travis was determined not to look away first.

Travis won.

'I'll leave you here, Scott, enjoy your day,' said Gordon. With one last, lingering look, the Head raised a hand in a half-wave and turned back the way he had come.

Travis turned his attention to Scott. 'Come in. I don't have a group session for another hour. You're welcome to join in, but in the meantime, what would you like to do?' He gestured to the far wall, where the supplies were stacked neatly on the shelves. Clay, acrylic paints and watercolours, pencils, canvases and brushes jostled for position on the overloaded unit.

Travis waited a beat before picking up his mug and draining it. He held it aloft and said, 'I need a refill. Why don't you check out the stuff, see what you feel like doing? Nothing's off limits, help yourself.' When Scott made no reply, Travis nodded and edged past him in the doorway. 'I'll be right back.'

He made to move off, but something in Scott's face made him pull up short.

'You okay?' he asked.

Scott's face was steady, but Travis could see it was an enormous effort. Suddenly he realised his error. Those words he had just said. He had read them last night, during the mammoth task of bringing himself up to speed on the Farenden massacre. It was what the kid, the shooter, had said, according to a survivor. *I'll be right back.* Travis swallowed, wondering if Scott had been there when those chilling words had been spoken.

It wasn't the time to broach the subject. Not yet, not when the lad hadn't even made it inside the classroom.

'Won't be long,' he said, kicking himself over his faux pas, and clutching his mug, he made off at speed towards the kitchen.

He took his time in the kitchen, mulling over what he was going to do about Scott. The boy never spoke. Twice now he had interacted with him, and there had been only a handful of words. Travis thought back to the first time he'd seen the kid, at the water, and the attempt he'd made at striking up conversation by warning Scott about the people who'd got lost there after dark. Scott had wanted to know if the lost people had died. And when Travis had encouraged the boy to walk home with him, Scott had made a reference to Travis being a pervert. Two exchanges; one an unhealthy interest in death, the other regarding paedophilia.

It was interesting, on the therapy side of things, and Travis made a mental note to study whatever words Scott might deign to say today. He would try to insert Sara into the conversation, glean more knowledge about the boy's delicious mother.

He could procrastinate no more, he told himself sternly as he picked up a cafetière and two clean mugs and made his way back to the room.

'I brought you coffee. Don't know if you drink it, but if not, I will, so don't worry.' His voice was cheery as he entered the room.

He stood, mugs dangling loosely from his hand as he surveyed the empty room.

The kid's done a runner, he thought.

Then he heard the unmistakable sound of rubber soles squeaking on the parquet floor.

There he was, stationed behind an easel that was so big it concealed him entirely. Travis placed the mugs and coffee on his desk and leaned against it.

'You got started, that's great stuff,' he said. 'What's your medium?'

He waited for the inevitable question that normally came from beginners, about what a medium was. To his surprise, Scott glanced up at him, stretching up to see him over the easel.

'Charcoal,' he said.

'Awesome,' replied Travis. 'Mind if I check it out? Alternatively, if you want to work on it a little longer...' It was important to give a choice to the kids he worked with. Children and teenagers struggled with their lack of options, which was why so many of them acted out by kicking back.

A few seconds of silence before Scott spoke up. 'Okay,' he muttered.

Travis picked up the mugs and the cafetière and walked with them across the room to where the boy was stationed. He made a show of pouring coffee, slowly. He had the impression that Scott either didn't like or wasn't used to the limelight. Like the kid's mother, it was important not to spook him.

'Coffee's there if you want some. So, let's see what you're...' He tailed off as he turned to study Scott's work.

It was astounding in its clarity. A boy's face, technically sketched – Travis could see the outlines of hastily drawn grids.

'Shit, Scott,' he said, smiling – the kids liked it when he swore sometimes, it put him on their level – 'this is... really good.'

He glanced at the boy next to him. Not really a boy, as the sunshine streaming through the windows highlighted the hair on Scott's jawline, not soft and downy, but real dark stubble. With the things he'd seen or heard in Farenden, with the classmates he'd lost, he had grown up fast.

'Yeah?' Scott stood back and studied the canvas critically. 'It's all right, is it?'

He was pleased, realised Travis. Happy to hear a compliment, cheered to have someone look at his ability with awe. An unlikely occurrence, probably. In the last year, he would have received looks and murmurs of pity, of sympathy, and been stifled by those adults who couldn't protect the kids in the school and were unconsciously making up for it by smothering him now.

He thought of Sara when she'd come to the door after he'd found Scott on the moors. She hadn't come across as suffocating with her love. She hadn't seemed to realise he was even gone.

He stored away that thought to muse on later and turned his attention back to Scott.

'Good doesn't do it justice. Really, it's not just that it's a good drawing. It's… almost professional.' He stood back and tilted his head to one side. 'Do you have training?'

Scott shook his head.

'A natural ability.' Travis felt his mouth twitching. 'The technicality of this is really something.'

Scott glanced down, rolling the piece of charcoal between his fingers. 'Cool,' he whispered.

Anxious not to overdo it by fawning over the lad, Travis retreated to a safe distance. 'Carry on,' he said.

A thought occurred to him as Scott got back to work. He craned his head to watch him unobtrusively. 'Who is the boy in the drawing?' he asked.

Scott swept the charcoal over the canvas, smudging and blending like a pro. The silence stretched on for so long, Travis thought he might not get a reply.

Then, at last, he stopped and looked up.

'It's my brother,' he said.

And to Travis's horror, Scott began to cry.

13

Sara
Before

'Elaine Fleecy has been shot.'

They were almost at the community centre now, and at Jojo's words, Sara looked up at him.

'*What?*' she said. 'Where did you hear that?'

He waggled his phone at her in response. Even as he held it in her view, she saw the screen lighting up with half a dozen notifications.

She pulled hers out of her bag and stared at the blank screen.

'It's the Year 9 WhatsApp group,' he explained. 'I know you're not in it.'

She blinked and stared straight ahead. How did he know she wasn't in it? Had he scrolled through the members looking for her name?

School-gate parent politics. The other mothers didn't like her. Didn't like the mistake she'd made all those years ago that they'd never let her forget. Didn't like that she was young and widowed and attractive. She wasn't blowing her own trumpet, but the long stares and sideway glances at her told her everything she needed to know.

And she didn't care, *hadn't* cared, wouldn't have wanted her phone to ping at all hours with stupid comments and requests about PE kits and teacher-training days. But now, today, she was missing out on all the information.

'Add me, please,' she asked.

He scrolled up to the top of the screen. 'Kathy Driver is admin. I'll ask her to do it,' he said, stabbing at the phone as they walked.

Kathy Driver.

Sara let out an involuntary shudder. She reached out and put her hand on Jojo's wrist.

'Don't,' she said. 'It's okay. You can tell me if there's anything important.'

He stared at her fingers as though they were burning him through the material of his shirt. Sara withdrew her hand. He put his phone in his pocket and they walked on in silence.

She had created a problem now, because asking him to keep her in the loop meant they were going to stick together once they got to the community centre. She'd studiously avoided the man for the last fourteen years, and now here they were, her clinging to him like a limpet, no regard for the promises she had made herself all those years ago.

She recalled the first time she'd seen him after the event. Scott had been in his pram, asleep for once, and she and Mack had taken him for a walk.

Mack had stopped to peruse the window of a hardware shop. Sara had continued walking.

'Hi, Sara.' Jojo had popped up out of nowhere.

Newly single Jojo. His wife had divorced him, whether because of Sara or not, she didn't know.

She'd frozen as he moved around the pram and stared at the sleeping child.

Don't wake up, she'd pleaded silently. *Don't open your eyes.* Because once Jojo saw Scott's eyes, the magical, clover-like green hue of them…

She'd kept her own eyes on Jojo's face as he looked at the baby before meeting her gaze.

'Sara, is he…?' His words, soft and sombre, a tone she'd never heard from him before, trailed away. Her heart had banged painfully in her chest.

'Mack is just there,' she'd interrupted him before he could say any more. 'We're in a hurry.'

One last stare passed between them. Sara moved on, hoping that everything unsaid had been conveyed in that look.

That he was happy for her little family. That he accepted and understood. That he would never utter the unasked question that he'd seemed about to.

Now, consciously, she widened the gap between them as they walked.

–

Sara didn't know what she had expected when she'd walked into the community centre. Screams and tears perhaps. Silence, deathly and far worse than hysterics, hadn't been it.

Chairs had been hastily set out, initially in rows, but groups of people who knew each other well enough, or friends and families, had pulled them into clusters. Talk was in hushed whispers. Sara stood in the doorway, looking around in disbelief. Her eyes settled on a witchy-looking woman. Kathy Driver, admin of the cliquey WhatsApp group that Sara would never be invited to join. Surrounding her, the other mothers in her friendship circle. Women who were... gobby, for want of a better word. They had been at the top of the pecking order during their own school years and had grown into women with the same traits. Sara hadn't quite fitted in with them as a young girl, much less so an adult. But now these women were quiet and cowed.

It led on to another thought. The children of these women were much like their mothers, bolshie and confident. Were they now mimicking their parents as they sat in the classroom being threatened by a gunman? She thought of Ryan. He was bold and self-assured. What was he doing at this very minute? Was he bravely standing up to the man who held a life-shattering, life-ending weapon at his face?

Dear God, she hoped not. She hoped he was copying his older brother, staying small and silent and *safe*.

She pulled out her useless, empty phone again and stared at the blank screen. No notifications, no texts or missed calls. With a motion that spoke of anger, she shoved it back in her pocket.

'Anything more?' she asked Jojo as he scrolled through an endless stream of messages.

'Nothing from Jaden. Phone's off,' he said.

His mouth was a grim straight line. Only once before had she seen it that way, his lips devoid of that ready smile.

She was about to speak again, suggest that they move away from that horrible woman Kathy Driver, whose eyes she could feel burning into her, when a noise started up.

Mobile phone notifications, pinging all around the room, resonating, echoing. *Haunting*.

Sara pulled out her own phone again. Nothing. But Jojo was reading his. He turned to her, and she shied away in dismay at the horror in his eyes.

'It's a kid,' he said. 'It's a kid with a gun. It's Noah Miller.'

14

Travis
Now

Scott's tears stopped almost as soon as they'd started. In fact, Travis noted, they didn't even really begin. It was over in seconds. His face had screwed up, his eyes popped red and watery, but the most chilling noise was the groan he had let out, one that seemed to come from deep within him.

'You okay?' Travis asked, as casually as he could manage.

Scott nodded and wiped a hand across his face.

'I didn't realise you had a brother. I thought it was just you and your mum.' A thought occurred to him. He wondered how best to phrase it. 'Does he live with your dad?'

Scott shook his head. 'My dad's dead.'

So that meant Sara was a widow. Travis fought hard to keep the smile from his face. A widow! He couldn't believe his luck.

He cleared his throat and focused on the boy. 'Sorry to hear that, pal. How—'

'Cancer,' Scott interrupted him. 'Years ago.' He flapped his hand as though it was long in the past, therefore no big deal.

It was a big deal, though.

Travis thought of his own father, taken suddenly while his twenty-year-old son was studying abroad, in dark, snowy Georgia. Travis was in the middle of his trip, and nobody had thought to make contact with him until it was far too late for him to go home.

Eventually, as the camps got further and further apart, and they neared the end of the trip, crossing from Georgia into Turkey, there was a note.

Call home when you can.

Casual, like nothing major had happened. Like it didn't really matter if he called or not. No big deal.

By then, not only had the death come and gone, but the funeral had too. Travis had never returned to his family. He didn't forget them, though, and he had sent regular notes and letters, until the police made contact with him and told him he couldn't do that any more.

Soon after that, he had turned his attentions away from them. If he couldn't help his blood relatives see the error of their ways, he would help others instead. There were plenty of hurting souls in the world who needed to be fixed; who were crying out for the attention of a man like Travis.

He pushed away the sudden talk of dead fathers and smiled brightly at Scott.

'So, your brother lives here with you guys? Does he come to the Centre?'

'He doesn't like classrooms. He prefers it out there,' said Scott. He jerked his head towards the window.

Travis looked outside. The sky was azure blue, cloudless. He didn't blame anyone who preferred to spend time there.

He looked back to Scott, motionless now at his easel. 'Do you want to go out, take some sketchbooks?'

Scott shrugged. 'Okay.'

Travis gathered up charcoal sticks and pencils and placed two brand-new sketchbooks in his old canvas bag. As he collected the items he thought they might need, he kept one eye on Scott.

The boy was standing in front of the charcoal sketch he had done of a brother Travis hadn't known about. Carefully he reached over the easel and put the cover in place, concealing the drawing.

Travis pretended not to notice and picked up the bag. 'Ready?' he asked.

Scott nodded, just once, and followed Travis to the door.

'Doesn't your brother do any classes here?' asked Travis as they made their way over the lawn, crispy and slightly yellowed thanks to the hot summer. 'What's his name?'

'Ryan. He's two years younger than me.'

'Do you get along together?'

'Suppose. He's not too bad, not really.' Scott's voice dropped to a whisper.

'I'm sorry about your dad. Would you like to talk about him?' asked Travis.

'No.' Scott kept his eyes firmly fixed on the ground in front of them as they walked side by side.

'No worries. What about… Farenden? I understand you went to that school. It must have been hard.' Travis spoke cautiously.

Scott muttered something too quiet for him to hear.

'What's that?' he asked.

Scott stopped walking and turned to face him. His hands clenched into fists at his sides, so tightly gripped that Travis could see the whites of his knuckles.

'Now you see me,' said Scott. His left eye developed a sudden tic, and he blinked rapidly, as if trying to dispel it. 'That's what he said to us, "Now you see me."'

Travis had read that phrase. Even though he knew the answer he asked, 'Who?'

The tic increased in speed. Scott put a hand to his face and pulled at his eyelid. 'Noah Miller,' he said. 'The one who shot everybody.'

Travis searched his memory for where to go next with the conversation. They had stopped walking, were standing, both looking awkward, Scott wringing his hands, Travis clutching the bag of art supplies.

'Why don't we sit?' He nodded to a wooden table, set close to the border of trees that separated the forest from the Centre. As Scott walked obediently ahead of him, Travis said, 'Did you ever speak to anyone – a counsellor, or any services that were offered to you?'

Scott shook his head. 'We were supposed to, they were sorting something out, the school, I mean. But then we left, we came here.'

Movement in the corner of Travis's eye. He glanced over, and for the very first time was disappointed to see Sara heading their way.

He raised his hand in greeting. Sara, around twenty feet away, seemed to falter. Her hands were stuffed deep in her pockets, and instead of returning his wave, she gave a brief nod.

'It's your mum,' said Travis as he turned back to face Scott.

Scott too was looking towards Sara. Travis watched as his eyes narrowed before he turned away to stare out at the trees. 'Yeah,' he said.

The boy seemed to fold into himself, shoulders hunched, head lowered. Then came the transformation. He raised his chin, turned his head at an angle to look directly at Travis and jerked his head towards Sara.

'Now *she* sees me,' he said.

His mouth flickered; whether it was a half-smile or the facial tic of before, Travis couldn't tell. It didn't matter. It wasn't how Scott looked; it was the words he'd spoken that chilled him to his very core.

The same words Noah Miller had said before he took the lives of nineteen innocent victims.

15

Scott
Before

'Why aren't we doing anything? Why aren't we *running*?' spat the voice of Beth Cage.

'You run, then,' shot back Iozif.

'He's just one person.' Chase, a football star, stood up. 'We can take him.' He looked firm and strong and angry, but his voice broke in the middle of his sentence.

Murmurs of assent from a few people.

There might be more than just Noah, thought Scott.

'He might not be doing this on his own,' said Emily.

He glanced at her, astonished that she seemed to have read his thoughts. She looked unseeingly through him. Scott looped his arms through the straps of his backpack, trying not to look at the stains, dark brown against the black material. Emily gazed curiously at him and he felt his face redden. Armour, he was thinking, but he didn't say it, because bullets would punch through his bag as though it were made of paper. Instead, he averted his eyes and looked at the others.

Jessie, a red-haired girl from Emily and Beth's popular clan, had stationed herself by the door. A brave move, it occurred to Scott.

Now she turned and ran in a crouch back to the far side of the classroom. 'He's coming back!' she hissed.

Phones went down, slid into pockets, pushed into the sleeves of oversized jerseys that were not needed on this roaring summer's day but were an essential fashion accessory.

Noah had left silently and smoothly, but his return was different. A heavy boot kicked open the door. It bounced against the wall; its trajectory stopped by his palm before it could fly back in his face.

He held something in his left hand. A phone, thought Scott at first, but as Noah kicked the door closed behind him and walked into the room, he saw it was a walkie-talkie. In his ears he wore a set of wireless buds. Turning his back on the class, he muttered something unintelligible into the handset. It crackled in response.

Scott's blood ran cold.

'Told you,' Emily whispered from behind him. 'I said he wasn't working alone.'

Scott was certain she wasn't talking to him, so he ignored her. Another thought caught at him as he watched Noah hunch over the walkie-talkie. How confident was this boy that he would turn his back on an entire class? He clearly knew they were not going to retaliate. But that cockiness could be used. They could behave, they could comply with him, do whatever he wanted, go wherever he told them. Then, when it was least expected, they could tackle him.

He looked around the room at the sports stars, at his fellow classmates who looked more like men than boys. They could do it, he thought. Surely they could. All that bravado couldn't be just for show.

But it could. It was, or they'd have done it by now.

'We're going to the main hall.' Noah's voice broke through his thoughts.

Scott waited for one of the boys – or girls, he supposed, looking at Beth – to speak up. Their heads were lowered, staring at the floor; all of them, even mouthy Beth, even gobby Chase. Scott felt a flicker of anger that he couldn't decipher.

Crash. The walkie-talkie slammed down on the desk nearest to where Noah stood. 'NOW!' Noah shouted.

Motion, movement, a Mexican wave of bodies as they stood as one and unconsciously huddled together. Scott, on the fringes, narrowed his eyes.

None of them wanted to lead. None of them wanted to be at the back. They all swarmed for the middle.

For the safe place, where the outer bodies could shield them.

Still nobody made to leave the classroom.

Noah studied them, sweeping his gaze over each face.

If he touches them, one of them will snap, thought Scott.

And just like Emily had, Noah seemed to read Scott's mind. He moved towards them. The crowd of students shimmied in response, pressing close to each other as he approached. But he kept going, past them to the other side of the classroom. In the corner was a pole with a hook on the end, eight feet in length, used to open and close the upper windows. He took hold of it and returned to the group. Holding it out in front of him horizontally, he pushed the end of the pole towards the group.

'Walk now,' he said. He prodded it forward a little more and the people at the outer edge of the group staggered back a little. 'That's right,' he said. 'Walk now.'

They shuffled, Scott included. A shiver ran through him as he realised he was on the edge of the group. Subtly he tried to wedge himself in, wanting to be at least two- or three-deep in the throng. The other kids wanted to live, though, they didn't want to give up their spots for him, and elbows jabbed at him, silent weapons of an intent to survive.

Inexplicable tears sprang to his eyes. This group wouldn't let him in their midst on any day, at any time. Today, right now, with breath and heartbeats at stake, he didn't stand a chance.

He stopped nudging and allowed himself to stand alone. On the outskirts looking in.

Noah, confident with the long pole now, wielded it in one hand. He used it like a boundary, almost a fence, and herded the tight-knit group towards the door.

'The main hall,' he said, bringing up the rear. 'Just keep moving.'

Suddenly he stopped and juggled the pole down and back, so he was holding it near the hooked end. Carefully, squinting in concentration, he manoeuvred the hook to catch in the hood of Emily's jacket.

She felt the backwards pull. Her arms came up around her head, fingers seeking for the obstacle. She turned her face, saw how close she was to their tormentor.

Scott watched as she panicked.

Screams that she couldn't control poured out of her, chest hitching, head tipped back. She struggled, spinning this way and that, trying to get away from the hook, from the pole, from *him*. Trying to get back to the safe centre.

Noah shuffled the pole again so she was on a long lead. Restrained, but room to kick out. He put his other hand on it, used all his strength to navigate her away from the herd.

'Keep moving,' he cried to the others.

Scott trembled. Noah's cry wasn't one of fear, of losing control. It was excitement, pure and simple.

'Not you, you stay.'

A hand grasped Scott's sleeve. He heard an audible gasp, realised it came from himself. He looked down at Noah's long, thin fingers wrapped around his wrist.

'You stay here.' Noah smiled, chillingly. 'Because you see me now too, don't you?'

16

Sara
Now

She'd done her work, got it all finished in double time. It was good to do this job. All automatic; just scrubbing, wiping, sweeping, emptying. She often thanked her lucky stars that she had money coming in from a job where she didn't have to think. Didn't have to be careful about making errors in spreadsheets or with large sums of money that put others at risk. She wouldn't be able to do that.

She had once, though, in the pub. Barmaid was far from her only role. She was good with numbers. Or she had been, back then. Loren, the owner and landlord, had seen her totting up the large rounds of drinks for the crowds that came in at lunchtime. All in her head, not stabbing at the till to keep a running total.

Impressed, he'd asked her to do the accounts each month, offered her another two hundred quid in her pay packet. And with Mack still sitting in his chair, lights off, both inside the house and in his head, missing days of work here and there, an extra couple of hundred came in very, very handy.

These days, that aptitude for figures and numbers had deserted her. All gone. She didn't even try to keep track any more. Just spent the bare minimum to keep them in food. Topping up the gas and electricity when the meter finally started blinking at her.

Numbers and figures and the joy of an awestruck glance regarding her mathematical skills mattered not a jot now. Neither did money, not really.

She moved over to the window that looked out onto the forest and blinked.

They were out there, talking. Her son and that Mr Travis. No, she corrected herself absent-mindedly, not Mr Travis, Travis was his first name. It was different here. Less formal than Farenden had been. There, in that slightly stuffy London school, even the parents were encouraged to call the teachers Mr and Mrs, or Miss. Mr So-and-So, Mrs Fleecy.

She dropped the kitchen roll at the sudden thought of dead Mrs Fleecy. It bounced and rolled under the desks, unfurling as it went.

She remembered Mrs Fleecy's name. She wasn't sure if it was because she'd been the first victim, or because *he* had been the one to impart the news to her. Jojo, his face, his words, grim and serious, so unlike the man she once knew. *Elaine Fleecy has been shot.* If he hadn't told her, she wouldn't remember the woman's name today. But somehow, things that Jojo said to her were right there in the forefront of her memory. Impossible to block.

She pulled herself back to the present and moved along the floor, wrapping the kitchen roll back up and shoving it in her trolley before looking back out of the window.

Were they supposed to be talking? Hadn't Travis promised to get Scott to come out of himself by using art? She hadn't wanted an actual talking therapist. They'd offered them all that back in London and she'd declined. No, she hadn't actually said no. She had simply packed up and left. She had run away.

She left the trolley of cleaning products in the middle of Drama Room 3 and walked outside.

Travis's face betrayed nothing as she approached them. The red clay of the path gave way to grass. The summer had scorched it, and it crunched underfoot.

'Hi,' she said, keeping her eyes on him as she spoke. 'How's it all going?'

He turned to look at her directly, and now she saw it in his face. He was a professional, but not good enough to hide it from her. What the hell had Scott said to him?

She looked at her son. He ignored her gaze. When she glanced back to Travis, he had cleverly rearranged his features.

'We've had a good start. Sara, you didn't tell me that Scott is a natural artist!' he said.

The pulse in her neck that she was sure he could see slowed a little. 'Oh,' she said.

So there had been art. That was good. Very good.

An awkward silence as her instincts deserted her. She groped around for what she was supposed to say before finally grasping it.

'Can I see what you did?'

Scott looked at her. Was she wrong, or was that surprise in his face?

Another long moment of silence, broken by Travis. 'Ah, that is the artist's choice,' he said. His voice falsely jovial, as though he could sense the tension present.

Of course he could sense it. She felt it, always felt it when in the presence of her elder son. Like an electric fence between them, shimmering with something unseen, a shock given if one tried to reach out to the other.

Scott shrugged. 'If you want,' he said.

Together they crunched their way over the grass back towards the classrooms, Travis stopping to pick up mugs and a cafetière.

'A real natural talent,' he was saying, 'and I'm not exaggerating. His skill is really rather wonderful.' He uttered a little laugh as he fell into step beside Sara. 'To be honest, I'm actually envious.'

Sara raised her eyebrows. 'He always got good grades in art. I didn't realise...' She trailed off.

I didn't realise it was a real talent. What parent didn't know that? She thought of Ryan's achievements. She could list them all. She had pushed him, her and Mack both. All the shining gold trophies, hardly any bronze or silver. All those medals and cups and shields. Pride of place on the unit in the lounge in London, now lined up on the fireplace here in Kielder. Jostling for position, there were so many of them.

If Scott was such a damn fine artist, where was the proof of that? Why were his paintings not adorning the walls of her home, past or present?

She didn't want to think about the answer to that.

Instead, she watched as he walked ahead. He never walked ahead. He loitered behind, quiet and still and silent.

Something new pinched at her heart. She put her hand on her chest, unused to this sensation. She was full of tics and shakes and tremors, full of worry and anxiety, empty inside yet bursting with a love she yearned to give him.

He had emotions that manifested into physical issues too, she knew. She saw him when he thought she wasn't looking. When he clutched at random pains in his stomach or lower back, his eyelids doing the same dance of horror as hers, as tics grew and abounded from some place of trauma that sprang up at inopportune moments.

We are damaged, she thought now, as she walked through the door into the art room.

'...in charcoal too, which is a very hard medium to work with.' Travis was speaking, she realised, and she bared her teeth in a pretend smile and moved her head up and down in agreement.

There was an easel at the end of the otherwise neat and tidy room. Charcoal stubs lay on the table next to it. Scott was already there, peeling back the pages of the larger-than-life sketching pad.

Tension surrounded her, that electric fence again, and she clenched her fists.

'I'm going to get a fresh brew.'

She turned at the sound of Travis's voice. He stood behind her, mugs and cafetière held aloft.

She shoved her hands in her pockets and stared at him. The tension, the awful sudden feeling, was coming from *him*.

She managed a nod as he walked quickly from the room, then turned back to Scott.

Dear God, what had he drawn?

She moved quickly to the easel, needing to get it done now, needing to see for herself. It wasn't what she was thinking, she told herself as she approached; it couldn't be as bad as she imagined, wouldn't be fire and brimstone or the visions that filled her own head when she lay awake in the hours of darkness.

Scott moved away to lean against the wall.

Sara raised her head and looked at the picture.

No words; instead, it was all physical. Fists closed again, within her pockets. She felt the heat leave her face, her entire body cold as ice. Beyond Scott, the door they had entered through was still ajar. The open air, hot as a desert, beckoned her.

She lowered her head, not looking at him as she passed him, not speaking, not hesitating as she pushed the door wide open and stepped outside.

Halfway across the red clay path, he called to her.

'Mum.'

In her pockets, her nails dug painfully into the fleshy bit of her palms. She wanted to scream. Instead, she turned around, forced a hand from her pocket and lifted it to shade her eyes.

'It's really good, love,' she said. She peeled back her lips again in a mockery of a smile and somehow gave a thumbs-up. 'See you at home later. I've got to catch up with work, so don't wait for me.'

He stood in the doorway, and with each word she spoke, his eyes grew smaller and smaller.

17

Travis
Now

The fresh coffee was an excuse. He'd actually had way over the quota he allowed himself daily, and it was still early. Even now, as Travis stood in the kitchen and rinsed out the mugs, he knew that tonight would be both a beer and spirits evening. He would take a bottle out into the woods, barefoot, and he'd let nature envelop him until he was able to think clearly.

As if in reminder, his foot throbbed where he had cut it last night in the forest. He curled his toes and dismissed the niggling pain.

His own discomfort was nothing compared to the agony those two were in. It was stifled, buried deep, he could see that. But it was there, between them.

He wondered about the second son. He should like to meet him, get his outlook on the family dynamic. From what he had gleaned, the younger lad was carefree, standing apart from mother and elder son. And what was it that was so torn between the two of them?

Was it the trauma of the father's untimely death, or the aftershock of the Farenden massacre?

Both, surely. A double whammy.

As he stood, tap running, mugs still in hand, he allowed himself a daydream. That he would swoop in and make it all better. Not only for Sara, but for Scott. He could nurture Scott's natural talent. He could be there for the other lad, for Ryan. Briefly he wondered if he too was an artist. But no, if he were, he would be in here, in the classes, excelling. What was it that Scott had said about his brother? He preferred being outside.

Excitement grew. Maybe he was an outdoorsman like Travis. Maybe he enjoyed nature and trees and wildlife.

A ready-made family, Travis's for the taking.

He turned the tap off and put the mugs on the side. No more coffee. Later, there would be beer. Not spirits – no need for them, not now he had a semblance of a plan in his mind.

Later still, weeks or months from now, there would be champagne.

–

'Where's your mum?' Travis asked.

Scott was standing by the open door. He turned at the sound of Travis's voice.

'She had to get back to work.'

Travis was disappointed.

'Did she like your drawing?' He nodded towards the easel.

Scott shrugged. 'Yeah.'

Like pulling teeth. Travis rubbed at his brow as the squeak of soles and high-pitched chatter filled the hallway. 'I've got the Sunday morning class starting soon. You can hang around if you like.'

Scott nodded, just once, a single jerk of his head. The sound of the oncoming students must have reached his ears, as he hurriedly pulled down the cover on the easel to hide his work.

Before Travis could say anything else, the kids piled in. He turned his attention to them, greeting a few with high-fives – only those he knew well, and only if they initiated the contact. With the children, he played by the rules.

He wondered what they would think of the new boy, and he waited to see their reaction. These were mostly good kids, kind, welcoming, funny, talented. Just what Scott needed.

He turned, ready with an introduction. It would be cool, casual, nothing that would overwhelm the skittish kid.

The students flowed around him, picking their favourite spots, hands already digging into the trays at the back of the room, grabbing at the paints, the chalks, the pencils.

Travis frowned at the empty easel where Scott had stood only moments before.

'Guys, set up your workstations and select your equipment. Back in a second.'

Outside, the forest border greeted him, silent and still. He walked to the edge, closed his eyes and listened. It was all forest here, lining the Centre. It was the perfect place for a solitary boy to hide, or vanish altogether.

Travis waited, and when there was no sound from within the trees, he sighed and returned to the classroom.

The kids were enthusiastic, the room was loud. It was the sort of class that levitated him to a state of excitement. This was what it was all about. These guys here, in the most influential years of their life, and it was Travis who was guiding them.

All social classes mingled here. They had regular slots for looked-after kids; those who came here with their foster parents or support groups or newly blended families looking to bond. Then there were the increasingly rare 2.4-kid families. In theory, they were all treated the same. In practice, Travis made it his job to read every single application and subsequent file that came in before term started. He knew what had happened and to whom, what their triggers might be, what activities might aid their mental health. The result was classes that simply worked, for him, for the kids, for the parents.

Because that way, at the end of the day, once all the walls and the divisions were removed, they could be exactly who they were: children.

If only Scott had stayed. If only Scott would give this place a chance.

Travis tuned out the racket of the kids and pursed his lips, deep in thought.

He had faced it all here. As far as he was aware, he had fixed them all. Every single one of the children who came through the door.

Scott would be no different.

Neither would Sara.

But there was a missing link that needed to be located and examined.

Ryan.

Scott and Sara proclaimed the unknown boy to be easy-going, laid-back, satisfied with sourcing his own means of entertainment.

Entertainment that didn't involve the Centre, a place where, as far as Travis knew, Ryan had never been.

He stayed outside, played outside. He caused no trouble and was content with his own company.

Travis felt a stirring of anticipation. He could have used those words to describe himself, and he knew the forest as well as he knew his art and therapy – better, perhaps.

Ryan would be his way into the Doyle family.

—

He was walking home at the end of the day, the hill stretching on, the treetops of Kielder glorious in the distance. The cabin was here, the high hedge that bordered it frustrating as always, concealing the family within.

When he reached it, he bobbed up and down, catching barely a glimpse of the windows of Sara's home, where she lived with her boys. At the gateway, he stopped. The cabin stood empty. Devoid of anything, the windows in shadow betraying no movement beyond.

He moved up the path, walking quickly to shrug off the hesitancy that crept around him like the black-berry brambles that trailed the forest floor. With a quick glance around, he reached out, twisted the doorknob and pushed. The door swung open, revealing the gloomy interior, silent, cold. Empty.

There wasn't much in here. No trinkets or ornaments or those cough-inducing candles that women seemed to be so fond of. The only thing that separated this from a show home was a jacket draped over the back of the sofa.

Quietly, Travis walked towards it.

A cream trim: a woman's garment then. He picked it up and held it to his nose, inhaled. Bursts of delight vibrated through him. Pulses that began as a flush to his face wound around his limbs. He moved the jacket, still scrunched in his hands, to his crotch.

'Who's there?'

The voice was sharp, but also coated with fear.

Travis dropped the jacket and spun around.

Footsteps on the stairs, coming down, a split second for Travis to compose himself.

'Scott!' he exclaimed. 'It's me, Travis. Your door was wide open. I wanted to make sure everything was okay.'

Scott came into view, his gaze not on Travis, but on the door itself.

Travis saw his mistake. This family knew about tragedy from an intruder. No way would any of them leave the front door open.

He raised his chin. 'Your door was open,' he said again. His stance dared Scott to defy him.

'Mum's not here.'

He smothered a smile. He'd had a narrow escape.

'Oh, that's all right. I was wondering if you'd like to come to a barbecue next weekend, at my place?'

Silence.

'All of you, I mean. You and your mum and your brother.' He paused, checked himself. Did he detect a hint of desperation in his own voice? The thought made him falter, and he raised a hand in farewell and backed up to the door. 'Think about it, or not. Whatever.'

Jesus Christ, now he sounded like one of the kids.

He sighed, pushed out the last of his speech. 'My place is off the next track; you follow it down and you'll see my house. If you hit the deer or the pit caves, you've gone too far. Ha ha.' He finished on a lame laugh and wanted to curl up and die. 'See you, then.'

'Caves?' Scott's voice was small but alert.

'Yes, the pit caves.' Travis smiled gently. 'You should check them out one day, they're really interesting.' A frown crossed his brow as he hurried on. 'But dangerous, you shouldn't go alone.'

'How will I find them?'

The door was open now, the late-afternoon sun only serving to accentuate the gloom inside the chalet.

'I can show you, if you like. Saturday? We'll go check out the caves, then I'll put the barbecue on.'

Scott nodded, a ghost of a smile on his lips.

'Tell your mother and brother. Come over around midday.'

'Okay.'

Travis stepped outside, closing the door softly behind him. He waited by the gate for a few minutes before a grin broke out on his face.

A barbecue, beer and wine with Sara and a chance to show off his forest to the boys.

He turned and continued up the track, a bounce in his step, the smile still wide on his lips.

18

Sara
Before

Noah Miller. Noah Miller. She searched her recollection for mentions of his name and found none.

'How old is he?' she asked Jojo.

'Same year as Jaden, and… Scott.'

'How did he get a *gun*?' Her hand was on Jojo's arm now, fingers twisting the skin on his wrist. With a conscious effort she removed it and asked her question again. 'Where'd he get a gun?'

Jojo didn't answer and she didn't press him. How would he know? They were both – all of them, actually – in the same boat. In the dark, on the outside unable to look in. Snippets of vital information pinging on random phones through fucking WhatsApp.

She looked at her own phone again. The blank screen mocked her.

'I need to know where the boys are,' she said.

'Me too,' said Jojo.

Sara glanced at him, saw the colour rise in his face.

'Jaden, I mean.' He looked away from her, around the community hall. 'I'm going to ask some of his mates' parents. Who do Scott and Ryan hang around with?'

Ryan was friends with everyone. Scott never mentioned any names.

'I don't know.' It was the easiest answer.

'Let's see if we can get any more info.' Jojo moved off, towards the cluster of women that included Kathy Driver.

Sara caught his arm again. 'Not her,' she murmured.

He gave her a questioning look. Sara remembered: he wasn't aware that Kathy Driver *knew*.

She let her hand drop once more. 'You go, I'll wait here for you.'

'I'll ask about your boys,' he promised.

Her thank-you dried up in her throat.

Was it her imagination, or were everyone's eyes on her? She lowered her head. Of *course* they weren't. Their kids were in a school with a madman with a gun. Mad kid, rather. Their teacher had been shot.

Nobody was looking at her.

Nobody was whispering about her.

Nobody gave a toss.

Nonetheless, she looked over at Jojo. Head bent close to Kathy's. A stir of something shivered through her veins. What was Kathy saying?

'Nothing, it's nothing,' she told herself.

'You all right, love?'

Belatedly she realised she had spoken out loud. She looked up into the watery blue eyes of an elderly gentleman.

'Silly question,' he said as he scooted his chair closer to her. 'Never did I think I'd be sitting here like this, hearing all this...' His liquid eyes shimmered.

Sara stared in horror as a single tear tracked a path down his face. Who was he? Who was he here for? A grandchild? And yet she couldn't comfort him, couldn't lay a hand on his arm in a gesture that was useless but that told him *we're in this together*. Words wouldn't form; even breathing was difficult.

Instead, she averted her eyes, crossed her arms and waited for Jojo to return.

–

He was on his way back to her, weaving through the people who stood motionless in his path. Chairs were empty now, bar a few, as if the occupants couldn't bear to sit in relative comfort while they waited for news.

Jojo nodded at her as he approached. Sara's heart thudded. What did he know? What had he found out?

'They're together, your son and Jaden,' he said as he reached her.

Sickness replaced the battering of her heart. 'Jaden's with… Scott?'

He shook his head. 'With Ryan.'

The sickness dissipated somewhat. Ryan and Jaden.

'They're… okay?' Her voice rose to a pitch she'd never heard before.

'So far. They're holed up with Max. Max's mum got a text.'

One son accounted for.

She heaved out such a heavy breath it was audible in the otherwise quiet room.

One more to find.

'Scott?' she asked. That pitch was there again, the name of her son almost a strangled cry.

106

'Nothing yet. What lesson did he have?'

She closed her eyes, thought about the timetable on the fridge. Ryan would have been in maths. On Scott's movements for the morning she drew a guilty blank.

'WHAT THE F—'

The roar shuddered through them all, a tsunami in its volume, the power behind the words shifting the entire hall as shoulders bumped and people jumped in terror.

'What... what is it?' Sara heard her own voice, saw her own body instinctively moving close to Jojo.

A man was up over the far side of the room, his chair clattering to the floor with the force of his movement. Other fathers instinctively surged forward, fists raised at the threat that Sara couldn't yet see.

Not just the men. She saw that much. Some of the mothers were barrelling across the room, swearing, screaming, arms flailing.

'Fuck, it's Noah's mum and dad,' said Jojo. His voice was awestruck; some unconscious part of Sara's mind thought it was like he'd spotted a bloody celebrity or something. 'They can't come in here!' Outrage now, and in a single beat Jojo turned from a calm, organised, caring man into one of the others, impulse and intuition taking over.

She saw their faces then, the father pale and drawn, eyes stony. Noah's mother, a petite woman, put her hands to her face. Sara saw the jagged hole of her mouth before her fingers covered it.

A split second of something like sympathy. Sara knew what it was to be stared at, gawked at, talked about and silently hated.

The empathy fizzed away. So she had cheated on her dying husband. She had paid for it for years and years;

she'd done her penance. She hadn't murdered anybody. Unlike the son of the couple at the other side of the hall.

The police folded in then, forming a human barricade between the haters and the hated.

The Millers were surrounded and eased back out through the double doors.

'They have to speak to them!' said Sara. She moved forward, her feet walking automatically, headed towards the doors, towards the police, towards the hateful parents who must have failed so badly for their son to do this.

Arms circled her, a broad chest at her back. 'They will,' said Jojo.

The tension didn't fade, but there was a definite softening. She let it go as she leaned against him. Fuck those looking. Fuck what they all thought.

Across the room, Kathy Driver watched her with eyes narrowed to slits.

—

'His guns are missing.' Jojo, again with information, knowing everything it seemed while Sara was in constant darkness.

She dragged her eyes up to his. 'Whose guns?'

'Mr Miller. He's missing handguns.'

It made no sense. This was England. Sure, there were hunts and shooting ranges, clay pigeon, but even she knew they were all rifles. She wasn't sure why that mattered; a gun was a gun no matter the shape.

'Why does he have handguns?'

'He's some sort of diplomat, or foreign affairs or something. They're all registered, all legal.'

'How many?'

He looked up from his phone screen long enough to give her a questioning gaze. 'Huh?'

'You said he was missing *some*. How many?'

He shrugged and went back to his phone. Moments later, his face turned granite and cold.

'What?' asked Sara. 'What is it?'

'There's another kid in on it. At least one, maybe more.'

The tremors returned, icy cold along with them. 'Oh God,' she muttered.

She imagined them. A handful of kids, long black trench coats, guns concealed inside, heavy silver jewellery, black hair, black eyes and big black boots. Such a cliché, but it was the vision that formed.

She looked up and across the hall. It wasn't so silent now. People were antsy, muttering, louder now, words no longer quiet or muted. Impatience bounced from person to person until they were all infected.

Sara stood up. 'I'm going back to the school,' she said. 'I can't just sit here. The police aren't telling us *anything*.'

Oh, damn this helplessness. Twice in her life she had felt like this. The first time when she sat in that awful beige office with Mack and listened as the consultant's words pierced her like bullets. The sentences hadn't registered, just a smattering of words and phrases: inoperable... terminal... months... palliative care... All the words she heard on that day could be condensed into just one: hopeless.

They were reeling from that – both of them, even though he'd already known – when the second piece of bad news came. But *they* didn't reel from that one. No, that second horror show she kept to herself, carried it alone. Still did, in fact.

Now, all those years later, sitting in a hall while kids with guns flew around her sons' school, that second blow flitted into her mind.

Punishment.

She stiffened as the word was whispered in her ear by the part of her that hated herself.

It was a new word, and the taste of it was even more bitter than any of the others she had hurled at herself over the years.

'Don't try and stop me,' she said to Jojo now as she slung her bag over her shoulder.

'I won't,' he said. His face did that thing again, stony and hard. 'I'm coming with you.'

—

Sitting in a fucking community centre while her children were under threat. What the hell was wrong with her, with all of them? Sara's thoughts were angry, a red rage that boiled over as she stalked down the road, not waiting for Jojo, shouldering past the police who attempted to talk to her in soothing, irritating tones, telling her it was best to wait, best to stay put, best to—

'Leave me alone!' She barged the arm of a woman constable, a young girl, too young for this job.

Echoing cries from behind her, and when she'd got through the throng of uniforms, she risked a glance over her shoulder. She wasn't the only one on this impromptu march. Jojo was there, long strides catching up with her. Behind him, a dozen more mums and dads trickled out, barking at the police, who cajoled them into sitting like good boys and girls in the community centre.

Kathy Driver too, one of the last to emerge, batting away the police officers' concerns.

Sara turned back the way she was going, grim determination on her face now, no longer worried about behaving for the authorities. Fuck them. If they were going to bring out her boys in body bags, she would be right there at the gates. Not sitting like a lamb in the slaughterhouse.

The vision was deadly. She would have thought it impossible to imagine, but it came all too clearly. Black bags, small ones, because these dead people were just kids; no need for adult-sized ones.

She broke into a jog as the first dry sob erupted.

19

Travis
Now

Travis stood in the city centre and breathed deeply. The noise assaulted his ears: cars and chatter, roadworks there by the main square, distant sirens wailing.

He smiled.

He came here on occasion, maybe once a month, simply so he could return home and appreciate all that his forest offered him. When he'd been on his enforced break, he'd come here a lot at first. He hadn't liked it. Hadn't liked the noise, the polluted air, the fact that he was just one face in a sea of thousands.

It was special in the forest. There were no sirens there, not many cars, never any roadworks, and few people, all of whom he knew and who pretty much left him alone, and none of whom screeched and yelled like the families who passed him now, herding their caterwauling kids towards the parade of shops.

The loudest sound in the forest was the rapid-fire magpie's call, or the incessant shriek of the blackbird that sang all day. Occasionally, foxes began their mating ritual near his cabin, vocalising their joy with deep, sharp barks that sounded like a person dying.

None of those sounds was as offensive as what he stood in the middle of right now.

Time to go home.

Time to go home and spend some time trying not to daydream about the impending barbecue. It was Thursday today, a half-day at the Centre, and the day after tomorrow, at around this time, Travis would be sitting on the bench on the porch of his cabin, Sara next to him, her boys... well, they would be off exploring the forest. He would show them the pit caves as he'd promised, then they could go off and have their own fun. He felt no guilt that her sons didn't figure quite so much when he imagined how Saturday would pan out. They were kids; lovey-dovey stuff would only serve to make them squirm uncomfortably. They would be there on the periphery, because they were part of Sara, therefore almost as important as she was. Almost, but not quite.

An ear-splitting wail from a buggy-contained toddler shattered his vision.

Definitely time to go.

He started the walk back to the train station. Normally, if he didn't have all day to spare, he came here on his motorcycle or in his car, but he preferred the train. At this time of year it was sticky and hot and raucous. It only served to remind him of how lucky he was when he disembarked at the other end.

As he walked jauntily down the street, skipping smartly out of the way of sprinting kids, cycling adults and the seemingly ever-increasing number of drive-on mobility scooters, the health shop, largely ignored by the residents and visitors here, caught his eye.

They had a little vegan section, one he'd treated himself to bits from before, and he thought now that it was just what he needed. Some gloriously healthy snacks to purge the badness of the city and the darkness of the memories that threatened.

He ducked inside, tipping a nod to the bored-looking woman behind the counter, and breathed in the slightly plasticky scent of the rumbling air conditioning. Picking up a basket, he roamed the aisles, taking his time, beginning the soothing motions of winding down from the city before even leaving it.

A sample of hand cream stood on the end of a row. He squeezed a small amount onto his palm and rubbed it in, lifting his hand to sniff at it.

Freesia. Clean, like linen, a similar scent to the jacket of Sara's that he'd manhandled.

The skin on his neck tingled, and he glanced up to see that the woman behind the till was watching him. No longer looking bored, she had a half-smirk on her face. Despite constantly telling himself that other people's reactions to his odd little nuances didn't matter, he felt himself flush with anger.

He averted his eyes and put the bottle back on the shelf. The perfume lingered, circling him, the fragrance trailing after him.

It would smell amazing on Sara.

He smiled to himself at the thought, looked longingly back at the hand cream. He couldn't buy it for her, it was too soon. But one day...

The basket was heavy, and it was only when he tried to put two bottles of organic ginger beer in it and almost dropped it that he realised it was time to go. He had to carry all this stuff, and that wouldn't make for the pleasant stroll up the hill to his home that he'd been looking forward to.

He moved on to the till, the scent of freesia still following him, and put his basket on the counter.

The woman was back to her original stance, leaning on the wall, staring outside. With an aura of heaviness she sighed, attempted a smile, and began ringing up his stuff.

Usually, here, at the pit stop of the after-shop, Travis was a talker. But her attitude of only moments ago, the smirk at his enjoyment of a woman's lotion, had irritated him. He punished her by staring through the window as she scanned his goods.

A vision floated past. He stood up straighter. The freesia pounded in his senses.

Sara.

As if he'd conjured her up, as if that lovely hand cream that he'd associated with her had drawn her here, to the city.

It was a definite sign.

He blinked, just in case it was a daydream, because that had happened before. He moved closer to the window. It *was* her, but part of what he'd seen was incorrect. He'd thought she was floating, a gentle stroll, the way he intended to when he got off the train at the other end.

But she was slouching, shuffling, head down, walking as though she were wading through concrete.

There was a reluctance to her movements, as though she didn't want to be here.

An appointment, he thought, as he watched her move past the top of the road into the main square. The doctor, perhaps, or even the dentist. He knew that some appointments caused stress and anxiety, though he was lucky enough not to suffer with such afflictions.

He drew in a deep breath, an idea forming in his mind. He could help her! All his various therapies, all the tricks of the trade, the cognitive tips that he'd learned for a moment just like this.

He moved to the doorway, eager now not to lose sight of her. As he craned around the entrance to the shop, he saw her, blonde head weaving in and out of the scooters and bikes that Travis himself had negotiated just a few minutes earlier.

'Hey, mister,' called the woman behind the till.

He raised a hand without looking at her. 'Sorry,' he said as he darted out of the shop and made his way at a jog back up the street.

As he dodged the clusters of pedestrians, he kept his head up, panic rolling through him as he realised he could no longer see her.

He emerged into the square, moving quickly to the centre. There, he turned in a full circle, his eyes scanning slowly, the myriad of shoppers seeming to have tripled.

'What a blow,' he muttered to himself. And then, because that didn't seem quite violent enough to match his disappointment, 'Damn!'

He sighed, looking back to the side road he'd come from. He couldn't continue on to the station that way, not past the wide-open windows of the health store. The woman would be there; she would see him and express her chagrin about the huge basket of goods that she'd put through the till and he had run out on.

He shrugged. No matter, there were other routes, luckily none of which would take him too far out of his way.

He walked to the edge of the square, down a pedestrianised alley, lamenting the loss of the basket of nice things. It had been worth it, though, losing them, because he'd seen her. Even if it had been just for a few seconds, and even if she had looked weary and slouchy and... sad.

It heartened him. It proved that what he'd felt was correct: that he was the man to help her, to heal her, even if she didn't know it yet.

He felt his steps quicken as he made his way along the slight incline, picking up speed, his thoughts already back at home, back in the forest... And that was when he saw her again.

Right there. At the end of the little street, outside a bank of three telephone boxes. She was motionless, staring ahead at... Travis glanced to the right. Staring at nothing.

People moved around her, going so far as to jostle her. She stumbled, just a little, but didn't look around.

The freesia had gone, to be replaced by something that smelled like a foul drain. The sun, previously blazing in a flawless blue sky, had dipped behind a lone cloud. The alley slipped into sudden gloom.

What was she *doing*?

Travis moved three steps to the right, to duck into a doorway, and watched intently.

Sara was psyching herself up, but for what? He looked in the direction she was staring, apparently unseeingly.

The phone boxes.

But that seemed silly. Who used a phone box these days?

He let his body slide down the wall and came to rest on the doorstep.

He was going to be in for a long wait.

But if Travis was good at anything, it was waiting.

He had plenty of patience.

It turned out that the wait wasn't actually that long. After twenty minutes, Sara took a deep breath. Travis could tell from the way her chest hitched up that it was a huge inhalation. Then she brought her small, pale hands up to cover her face.

Slowly, cautiously, thinking again of that deer and how it mustn't be spooked, he stood up.

At the far end of the street, she shook her head, very slightly, before lowering her hands to her sides. Then mechanically, she turned to her left and shuffled away. Within seconds, the crowd had swallowed her up.

Travis swallowed against the angst that had lodged in his throat. He inserted himself into the flow of human traffic and began to follow her.

20

Sara
Now

Saturday dawned dry and sunny, a blue sky that promised a scorching day. A day that would stretch on and on into a warm evening and even hotter night.

Today Sara had to go to town again. The city. Newcastle. Just over an hour on the bus or the train, another hour back home. It was a trip she made every couple of months, and in her opinion, it was pointless, a waste of time. But unfortunately, it was necessary. She had tried to go on Thursday. Indeed, she had made it there. But she'd been unable to do what she needed, so today she would have to try again.

'Mum?' A small voice, timid and quiet, outside her bedroom door.

She sighed. 'Yes, Scott?'

She watched the door creak open. Her elder son stood behind it, one half of his face in shadow, his eyes glinting at her.

'Are we going to the barbecue today?'

'What barbecue?'

'Mr Samuel… Travis, he invited us to a barbecue at his place. Said he'd show me the pit caves and the deer in the forest.' He shuffled his feet, stared down at the carpet and swallowed before looking back up. He didn't look at her, rather over her shoulder, out of the window at the bright blue day. 'He said we're all invited.'

'Jesus.' She said it under her breath, turned her head away so he couldn't read her lips.

This was the problem. This was what happened when you gave someone just a small piece of information. They were never happy with what they were given. They wanted more. More and more and more until they knew every single part of your life and there were no more secrets and no more privacy.

Was it time to move on? To pick up and leave in the middle of the night? But no, there would be other people, other do-gooders, other nosy parkers who wanted to know who they were, where they'd come from, what had happened to the husband, what, where, why?

It was her own fault. She knew that. She'd invited this Travis in. Thought it would be good for Scott to open up.

Open up a little, but not too much. Not all of it.

She shuddered at the thought.

'So, can we go?' Scott's voice broke into her thoughts, and she studied him.

He didn't ask for much. He didn't ask for anything, ever. He didn't badger her for meals out or fancy clothes, or computer games or Wi-Fi access – all the things the other lads crowed about at the Centre.

'Who else is going?'

He blinked at her through the gap in the door. 'Just us, I think.'

'And what do you mean, he invited all of us?'

She heard the intake of breath. Saw his foot knocking against the door, pushing it closed, hooking it open, repeating the motion time and time again.

'He… wants to meet all of us. He thinks…' He didn't finish the sentence.

Sara spun around again to face the window so her son wouldn't see her face.

'I'd like to go.' Scott's voice again, more determined than she'd ever heard it.

He never asks for anything. He doesn't demand or create a fuss or act like a spoiled brat.

'What time?' she asked, her back still to him.

'Midday.'

'I have to go to the city, I won't be back by midday.'

She could, easily. It was not even nine yet.

She thought of him again, Travis. His kind face. She thought of her husband, serious and dependable. The solid, mountainous mass of him, before the illness took hold. She thought of Jojo, the opposite of Mack, slim and wiry and happy-go-lucky.

Travis was neither of them. Or he was somewhere in between.

She thought of how long it had been since either Mack or Jojo, and something deep in her belly shivered at the thought of another man, whether with desire or revulsion, she wasn't sure. Then the guilt came, because this man, this teacher Travis, was for Scott, not her. She deserved nothing. She deserved no happiness or moments of frivolity or passion.

Or did she?

Did Scott, come to think of it?

The gentle sound of boy breaths told her he was still there, waiting for an answer.

'Go then, if you want. I might see you there if I get back in time.'

A moment's pause, and then, 'It would be nice if you came, Mum.'

She heard the intake of her own breath at his words. He didn't say things like that to her. They didn't say things like that to each other. The word 'nice' was never exchanged in conversation. Not that they fought. Rather, they circled each other warily, and spent their time in different parts of the house so the chances of running into each other were minimal.

'I'll try,' she said when she could speak again, but Scott had already gone.

She wouldn't try. She knew that. By the time her business in the city was done, she would be drained and emotional, and all she would want to do would be to turn off all the lights in the little cabin, open a bottle of wine and drink it until she was once again numb inside.

It would be easier, she concluded, if Scott wasn't at home. She could have her semi-regular breakdown in peace and quiet. It would be a novelty not to have to stifle her sobs.

When she finally made it downstairs, the house was quiet. The cabin was devoid of anyone but her, and the silence hung thick and heavy.

In the kitchen, she opened the cupboard next to the sink and perused the alcohol. Two bottles of red, and a white chilling in the fridge. It was enough, more than enough.

In the living room, she picked up her jacket from the floor behind the sofa, where it had lain for the last couple of days. Slinging her bag across her body, she slipped out of the cabin and began the long walk up the hill to the bus stop.

In a window seat she rested her head against the glass and closed her eyes. The bus was more than half empty, and knowing she was going all the way to the end of the line, she allowed the sleep that wouldn't come at night to swamp her.

Her dreams were as they always were. Black and smoke-filled, the pungent scent of burning flesh in her nostrils and throat, choking her with a phlegm-packed hacking cough.

Hands on her back, soothing her. Mack's meaty fist alongside Jojo's gentle caress. The smoke cleared, and finally she could see. She looked down at her enormously pregnant stomach. The men in her life were in front of her now, gazing at her with accusing stares. Then she was holding her babies, both of them, and she knew it was a dream, because though they had never been babies at the same time, here in the nightmare they were identical.

She could tell the difference, though, she knew which one was Scott, because he would reach out a chubby fist, his fingers would transform into razor-sharp claws and he would swipe at his brother's face—

She awoke as she always did, with a scream that died in her throat.

The few passengers on the bus turned in their seats and stared at her with disdain.

Drugs, they were thinking, or drink. Perhaps she was homeless, suffering with mental health issues.

Soon enough they would turn back.

Show's over.

She put a hand to her head and tried to smooth her hair. It felt like silk under her fingers, and she started, surprised, before remembering that she had washed it last night. A rarity for her these days, self-care.

Maybe she didn't look homeless then, just like an addict, perhaps.

In order to dispel the nightmare from her mind she thought about the trip ahead. It would be hard and awful; surely she deserved something for making this godforsaken journey every couple of months? What she needed was a treat, a prize, a *reward*.

A pack of tobacco, she decided on a whim, remembering the other day outside the shop, how she had nearly turned back and bought some cigarettes. Not tailor-made, though. She would buy rolling tobacco, the same kind that both Mack and Jojo had enjoyed. It would bring her closer to the men she had loved. To the men who were gone.

–

At the end of the line, she alighted from the bus with as much dignity as she could muster, and walked through the bus station, out the other side and up into the main square before slipping down one of the walkways that branched off it. Not the same one as Thursday, because that hadn't worked, but one on the opposite side of the square.

There, she paused and studied the bank of telephone boxes that lined the wall of the now-defunct post office. Six of them in all. Half a dozen bygone treasures that she was fairly certain only she used. Even now, among the whirl of chatter and the irritating idling of a motorbike engine that seemed to have been present ever since she stepped off the bus, the sounds of people chatting into mobile phones surrounded her.

She didn't have a mobile for various reasons. They seemed to be the number one way for people to be found, though that wasn't really it. After *that* day, all those phones going off, all the terrible, horrific messages coming through, she never wanted so much as to look at a mobile again.

The boys had had them, back then. She assumed they were still around. After she had removed the batteries and SIM cards, she couldn't remember what she'd done with them. Besides, she'd not paid the bills on them; they would have been cut off months and months ago.

Therefore, a phone box it was, for the semi-regular calls she made.

Taking a deep breath, she pulled open the door and stepped inside.

It held a faint aroma of urine, a faded scent of weed alongside stale smoke. She dropped her coins in and dialled the number she knew off by heart, then turned and studied the newsagent opposite.

Mustn't forget to buy tobacco.

'Hello?' The voice came down the line and Sara jerked upright.

'Hi, Mum,' she said. 'It's me.'

'Are you okay?' Her mother's voice was quick and urgent – well, as urgent as it ever could be for a woman who had always been so cool. 'You're doing all right?'

'Yes. Yes, we're all good.'

A long pause at the other end before her mother spoke again. 'Both. You're *both* good?'

Sara swallowed. 'Mum…'

'All right.' The word was sharp and impatient, more like the woman she actually was rather than the woman she'd pretended to be in the last year. 'What are you doing?'

'What do you mean?'

'I mean, are you still working? Where are you living? How's—'

'Yes, working, living, whatever.' Sara leaned her head against the filthy glass of the phone box. How could she explain to her mother that these calls were for one purpose only: to let her know that she was still alive? There was no need for anything else; they had dispensed with pleasantries a long time ago. This was a duty call, but she wasn't sure why she still made it.

Because if you didn't, she'd hire every private detective under the sun to track you down.

'Sara, I'd like to see you. I'm… worried about you. You're not handling things very well, are you?'

Sara held the phone slightly away from her ear. How easy it would be to replace the receiver. How easy it would be never to make this call again. But she didn't hang up, even though every fibre of her being told her that any second now her mother was going to say the words she didn't want to hear.

'I'm fine,' she managed to say. 'We're fine.'

'I've been speaking to Dr Kim. He thinks—'

'Jesus, Mum!'

'He thinks you need help. You're not over this, you can't even begin to get over this until you accept the facts of what happened.'

'What happened? You don't even know what happened!'

'I do. I was there when they brought them out, I was there that day, that night, all night, all the next week…' Mary trailed off, her words fading to nothing.

Inside the cramped phone box, Sara heard a strange noise. She stiffened, glanced around her. Outside, the world walked on.

The noise was her, her own breathing, she realised. Not just inhalations, but like something had cracked inside her. A hole had opened up in her breastbone, and the darkness that she had concealed for so long spilled out, loathsome in its velocity.

Oh God, it was happening, now, here.

A wail, also from herself, and she pressed her lips to the filthy mouthpiece in an attempt to stifle it.

'Muuuuum…' It was a pitiful sound, one she never made, especially not to the cold woman on the other end of the line.

'Sara, SARA,' Mary barked down the phone.

It was now or never, and it was outrageous that although this was something she already knew, it was like hearing it for the first time. She'd pushed it down with booze, Mack's old pills and sheer bloody willpower. Now it was emerging, escaping, and she was sure it was going to be the end. She would hear the truth, the wicked words, she would remember all over again, and she would have to choose whether to walk out of this phone box and go to the Tyne Bridge and fling herself off, or go home to this bloody barbecue, where she would have to pretend to be normal and not act like her heart and her world had just been smashed to pieces.

'Mum,' she said. A rare and terrifying moment of something – strength? – pulsated within her, and she pushed on, breathless now. 'Mum, tell me.'

An inhalation at the other end of the line. Outside, the world seemed to fall silent.

'Ryan died,' said Mary. 'Your son is dead.'

21

Scott

Before

Just the two of them. Scott and Emily, her standing against the window, him on the opposite wall. All he could hear was the harsh, heavy sound of her breathing.

Plenty of times he had sat in class looking at the back of her head, or her profile, and thought about being alone with her. Never in any of his daydreams had she looked the way she looked now.

Ashen to the point that her skin was grey.

Actually, not just the two of them. The inert form of Mrs Fleecy lay between them. Her leaking blood had stopped along with her heartbeat. The red puddle was no longer spreading across the floor. He was glad she had fallen face down. He didn't want to see the damage done to her. He could imagine it, though: a jagged red hole, ripped skin matching her torn, bullet-shredded top.

He cleared his throat and looked at Emily.

'You should move away from the window,' he said.

She looked up, her eyes wide, as though shocked to see him there. 'Why?' she asked.

Her voice was a whine. It was unlike her normal speaking tone. He didn't like it. Emily was self-assured and confident, without being loud-mouthed or vociferous like most of her friends.

The fact that she was speaking to him, looking at him, had him scrubbing his sleeve over his face. He glanced past her, through the window, to the high wall that surrounded the school grounds.

'When they send the police in, they won't see you properly. They might just see a shadow, a figure. They might not realise it's you and not... him.'

He watched her pale throat as she swallowed.

'Like... snipers?'

He nodded and then forced an awkward laugh. 'I don't know how it works. It's just the sort of thing... It just occurred to me. Like, a possibility.' He was rambling. Soon she would lose interest. Her eyes would glaze and she would stare right through him.

To his surprise, she dropped to the floor and crawled towards him. She made a wide arc around Mrs Fleecy, keeping her eyes on Scott as she slid along on her hands and knees.

'What should we do?'

He resisted the urge to look behind him to see who she was talking to.

Him. For the first time, probably the only time, she was speaking to him.

Get her out.

He closed his eyes and thought of the layout of the school. Noah was taking the others to the main hall. Out of this classroom, down the corridor, bypassing the library, the language units, the science labs. It was a five-minute walk. It was a two-minute run.

But what would he do when he got there? Would he deposit them in the hall and expect them just to sit in there and wait while he came back here and did who knows what to Scott and Emily?

Scott looked back to the windows. Only the fanlights opened, way up at the top. The lower ones were slightly tinted, toughened glass with no openings.

This school was a good one. They had air conditioning. No need for actual fresh air, floating inside and bringing allergens and pollen.

'The main door, before the assembly hall,' whispered Emily.

'Yes.' He nodded, too much time gone already.

The one good thing about her plan was that the hallway was long and straight. If Noah decided to come back, they would see him coming. The good was also bad: Noah would be able to see them as well.

'Come on.' Her tone was low and urgent.

Scott looked up to see she was already by the door, peering through the small glass section.

He nodded again.

They ducked out of the classroom, trying to remain silent, shoes squeaking nonetheless on the floor. Scott was struck by how quiet the school was.

It was like nobody was alive anywhere in the building.

They reached the main door.

'I can't believe we did it,' he murmured. Warmth spread in his chest, the afterglow of survival. Even as he spoke, he knew he should be sad. Because Mrs Fleecy hadn't made it, and maybe there would be others not as lucky as him and Emily. But right now, relief was the only thing there.

'No,' Emily breathed, the single syllable loaded with pain.

'What?'

She reached out a hand and touched a finger to the heavy chain that was wrapped around the handles of the double door.

He stared at it, at the injustice and awfulness that the chain signified. 'Shit,' he swore quietly.

Emily's chest hitched, her breathing grew rapid, and Scott's heart beat faster. She couldn't lose it, not here, not now; neither of them could, not when *he* could come marching down the hallway any minute.

He stood back and looked at the door. The chain was padlocked. No key, no chance of getting these doors open.

How had Noah done this? Were all the other doors chained closed? If so, how had he come into school with chains and guns and walkie-talkies, and not only that, but *when* had he done this?

He'd been late for English. Not just by minutes like some of the students, trickling in as the echoes of the last bell rang. He had been *late* late.

Scott breathed out. Happiness and relief gone.

'Don't you have a brother here?' Emily's question pulled him back to the present.

He glanced at her and frowned. 'You know Ryan?'

She nodded. 'If we could find him… he might help.'

He felt his eyes bug out. How could Ryan help? Ryan was two years younger than him.

'I mean, if we can get enough people together. People like Ryan, Chase, that Zimbabwean kid who does the weightlifting competitions…' She rattled off more names. Names of the talented, the strong, the brave.

Scott noticed she didn't include him in her list.

Happiness long gone. The fear was fading. Irritation and that slow-burning anger that came so often when Ryan was singled out were at the forefront now.

He ignored Emily and stared at the doors, scanning the frame, the side panels, the reinforced glass, the fanlight above, cranked open slightly…

'The window!'

'What?'

He moved in for a closer look. The fanlight, like the others in the classroom, was six feet up. A small opening. He glanced at Emily. She was slim, slight of build.

Behind them, way down the hall, came the sound of a door opening.

Scott placed his hip against the door and interlocked his fingers. 'Come on,' he said. 'Step on my hands.'

She'd heard the door too. She didn't waste time with questions. She walked right up to him, put her hands on his shoulders and placed the sole of her left foot into his palms.

There was a moment, not long, no more than a second, when she looked into his eyes.

Footsteps now, echoing, the sound of somebody marching with intent.

'Go,' he whispered, and he heaved her up, his breath juddering as she flung her hands out, scrabbling for purchase on the ledge, pushing the fanlight wide with her forehead.

No room for manoeuvre; she would have to topple out head first. It would be painful; she might sprain her wrists or knock herself out. Again, in an awesome moment of synchronicity, she seemed to be on his wavelength.

'I'm going to fall,' she hissed over her shoulder. 'I can't turn around up here.'

Something flared in his chest. Not happiness or fear or fury, but a sense of urgency.

'You'd prefer the alternative?' he spat back at her. 'You want to end up like Mrs Fleecy?'

His words and the tone that accompanied them were harsh and cruel, but they were needed. And they worked. With a last shove, he pushed on the soles of her feet. She squealed and toppled through the window.

Scott waited until she'd unfolded from the heap she had landed in. She staggered to her feet and turned to look at him through the glass.

Go. He mouthed the word. Eye contact again, a millisecond, before she beckoned to him.

Come on.

He looked up. He could reach that window. If he wanted to live, he could reach it.

He raised a leg, awkwardly, muscles complaining, and hooked a foot into the chain.

Beyond him, the footsteps approached.

He prepared to jump, to claw, to stretch his way up. Outside, Emily had turned away and was running, blonde ponytail bouncing, arms pumping. He watched her for a moment. Happiness back again.

A thought popped into his head, unbidden, of his mother and her favourite son.

Ryan.

He stared at the chain, at his foot, at the jump for freedom that he could make.

Across the playground, Emily was just a dot in the distance.

He wondered if Ryan would turn back for him.

It was the uncertainty, ironically, that made his mind up.

He hated himself for it, and he hated Ryan, and even his mother a little bit.

The footsteps had reached him. Reluctantly, he turned around.

In the hallway, Noah stood silent and motionless, gazing at Scott, a question in his eyes and the gun in his hand.

22

Sara
Now

The air felt thick as soup as Sara got off the bus. It was good, she decided, that the heat gave the atmosphere this quality. It held her up. It enabled her to stagger down the hill to her cabin.

As she walked, she couldn't help but think of the phone call. She had known it was coming, the words that she'd practically forced her mother to say. There was a familiarity in it, like a recurring nightmare or a sense of impending doom. She had no doubt that today wasn't the first time she'd made her mother have that conversation.

How many times before? How deep was her grief that she needed to be reminded of the cause of it?

She slowed her steps as the cabin came into sight. She had been gone for almost a year. She called her mother every couple of months, but surely the conversation that had taken place today didn't happen every time. Because she was certain that if it did, it would take another two months to get over the heavy leaden weight that was currently settled deep down in her belly.

She turned in through her gate, up the path that led to the door, pausing as she always did at the white rose bush. Every time she saw it, she wanted to plunge her bare hands

135

into it, regardless of the thorns, and tear it up by the roots. Sometimes she would go so far as to pull a blossom off it and crush it, either in her fingers or underfoot. Every morning she swore she would destroy it. Every afternoon it was still there.

She understood now why the rose bush remained. Why she never went through with her mental threat to annihilate it. It was her daily reminder. The thing that kept what had happened buried somewhere deep in her mind, without her having to relive it by actually thinking about it.

If she thought about it, she would break.

So instead, she ignored it.

She kicked out at the bush now, suddenly, sending a shower of blooms to the path. She stood on them, slowly and deliberately, a sad, strange dance, until all that was left was crushed white powder.

The bush would survive the assault.

Whether she would was another question.

Inside, the cabin was cool and quiet. Scott wasn't home. She slid the lock across on the door and dropped her bag to the floor.

She didn't wonder where he was. Instead, she found herself musing upon what he made of her refusal to think or talk about what had happened to Ryan.

Did it worry him? Or did it fill him with joy that finally he had his mother all to himself, with nobody else to share her?

Saliva flooded her mouth. She clapped her hands to her lips as she lurched over to the sink. Black coffee and not much else bounced off the stainless steel. A flashback, a thought, and she bowed her head.

I've been here before.

She leaned her forearms on the sink and stared out of the window.

That time before, the glass had been a mirror, the sink had been ceramic. That time, there had been a hand on her back, ever-increasing circles, starting in a tiny motion at the centre of her spine, moving outwards to graze the sides of her breasts, fuller and heavier than normal.

'You ate something bad?' His Irish lilt, his tender tone.

He doesn't realise, she had thought.

She didn't know how she knew. She had never been pregnant before, but along with the vomit came knowledge, clarity, an explanation for how rubbish she'd been feeling lately without being able to pinpoint the cause or effect.

She'd been unable to meet Jojo's eyes in the mirror, nor look at her own reflection. She'd muttered something about dodgy chicken, a day or two out of date, and making her excuses, she'd left the rented-by-the-hour hotel room and raced home.

There, she expected to find peace and solitude. Mack had actually gone to work this morning, and she could sit down in the living room that held the scent of his current state of staleness, and think, and maybe even vomit some more. But the sanctuary she'd expected wasn't to be found. He was there, the curtains were closed once again, the mustiness hung heavy in the air.

It was time to face facts. Mack didn't love her any more – what else could possibly be making him so unhappy? She felt a little fury then. It was his attitude that had sent her into Jojo's arms. Now look at what had happened. Pregnant by her lover.

She raised her head high. If Mack wanted a way out and didn't know how to say the words, she'd done it for him.

'Mack,' she said, 'we need to talk.'

He snapped his head up as if he hadn't even heard her arrival, then he winced and rubbed the back of his neck.

'Look,' she said, 'I know you're not happy. You don't love me any more.' Saying it out loud paved the way for the hurt and rejection she felt. She pushed on through the pain. 'If you want to call it a day...' Her words faded to nothing as, through the tiniest crack in the curtain, the sun cast a thin strip of light on his face.

There, in among the stubble and the sad, sagging skin, she saw tears.

He spoke then, for the first time in months. As if a dam had been opened, his words poured forth, a torrent of misery, bleak, black reasons for the hostility and despair that had all but consumed both of them. She didn't hear full sentences, just random, terrible words that pierced her ears. 'Inoperable... palliative care... matter of months...' Later, his consultant would repeat the same words. Then, like now, she would only hear snatches of them.

He hadn't fallen out of love with her. He was dying. The awfulness of her own actions in taking a lover felt like a punch in her newly pregnant stomach. In the gloom of the room, she pressed her face to Mack's, and her mouth to his mouth, to stop him talking as much as to give comfort. The burden of the last while, the pit of blackness, the moody, silent nights fell away with each tear they shed.

No more words, because there were none to be spoken. Carefully, she peeled away his clothes, covering his lips with her own each time he half-heartedly protested, aghast to see the crêpe-like skin and the protruding bones, so long it had been since she had seen him naked.

He rose to the occasion, by some terrible miracle, and already she was thinking of a way out of this mess she had created. There would be a baby, someone to carry on his name, a parting gift to make his departure from this world a little easier, a bit less senseless than it actually was. It would save her own soul in the process. Mack would never know, never find out that the child was already inside her, and that although it would carry his name, it would never be of his bloodline. Nobody would ever need to know the truth.

The affair had been such a cliché, she realised. She had thought Mack had fallen out of love with her, but that, nice guy that he was, he couldn't find the words to tell her. But it wasn't about her at all, his depression. Jojo's face floated in front of her. Not just an affair; possibly love, definitely more than lust, but it didn't matter now.

He had rallied, Mack had, going on for years more than the doctors had estimated. Long enough to have another child, and to live a normal life for a while. At times, Sara had tried to look at Scott and be thankful and grateful that his presence had given Mack those extra years. She had failed. All she saw when she looked at him was Jojo's eyes.

This was payback, she thought now, as she stood at the sink of a home 300 miles away from the house she used to live in, and a million miles from that past life. A punishment from God for that awful, unforgivable lie she had created all those years ago. He'd not forgotten. He had watched her, lulling her into a false sense of security. Then, when she had least expected it, *bam*, here came the forked lightning, to strike down and take away not the one she had lied about, but the innocent one. Taking Abel, leaving her with Cain.

She dry-heaved again, sickened by the feelings that arose when she thought of her elder son.

She fought against it, the feeling of horror. She loved Scott, always and ferociously and forever.

She wiped her mouth with the dish cloth and stared unseeingly out towards the forest.

She loved him, she just needed to learn to *like* him. To understand him. But as much as she tried, because of what he had done, it was a seemingly impossible task.

Through her tears, through the glass, she saw a now-familiar head bobbing along the hedgerow.

Just keep walking, she begged silently.

A knock came at the door, resounding around the silent cabin.

'It's just me, it's Travis!' The call was accompanied by the letter-box flap rattling.

In mounting horror, Sara watched as the doorknob twisted. Why was he trying her *door*? She had locked it, she saw now, and she recalled stumbling in after the rose bush fight, intending to head for the alcohol and having the foresight to slide the lock across, lest Scott walk in and find her on her knees, drinking straight from the bottle.

The door handle clicked back into place. There was a slight pause before Travis called her name once more. His voice was falsely jovial, tinged with a merriment that made Sara want to open the door and smash her fist into his helpful, friendly face.

Instead, she gripped the sink tighter and bit her lip.

'Sara?'

A low moan came from her. She buried her mouth in her shoulder to stifle it.

Why couldn't he just go away? Why was he always there, probing, head tilted to one side, listening and watching?

'I've got some stuff for the barbecue, I'm going to light it up soon, get it going. Scott might already be headed to mine, so... if you're in, join us when you're ready.'

Barbecue! She thought of what she had learned – relearned – that morning, and her knees buckled. How could he talk of such things when this had happened to her?

He doesn't know, the remaining rational part of her brain told her.

Slowly, she straightened up. Travis didn't know, but what about Scott? Surely he remembered? After all, he couldn't be suffering from the same... *denial* as her, could he? Or could he? She'd heard about such things; living in close quarters, closeted, claustrophobic atmospheres with secrets unsaid. They could manifest themselves onto someone else.

Then, like a wave upon a shore, pain crashed at her again and again. Real, visceral jolts of visions and memories.

Scott remembered. He remembered everything.

Her hands clenched into fists as she swept them along the draining board. Her wrist connected with a glass, the dregs of days-old wine staining it claret. She picked it up by the stem and cracked it against the sink.

It shattered, satisfyingly, and she held up the remaining piece, brought it down on the worktop, hitting it again and again, until nothing was left apart from tiny shards. The scratches on her palms bled a bright pink. She held them up to face her, reminded of the time another girl had shown her her hands, scratched and filled with dirt, her face stained with somebody else's blood.

The letter box clanged shut. Outside the window, Travis bobbed his way from the porch. His shoulders slumped as he sidestepped to walk a wide circle around the crushed roses on the path.

23

Scott
Before

'I tried to stop her, but she ran anyway,' blurted Scott. It was an awful lie, but that instinct had risen again.

Do what you need to do. Say what you need to say. *Survive.*

Noah tilted his head. 'Who?'

Scott swallowed. 'Emily,' he said weakly.

Noah looked past him, through the glass, and surveyed the empty playground. 'You tried to keep her for me?'

Scott felt a tremor in the base of his spine. He shrugged. 'Yeah,' he said softly.

Noah grinned, one side of his mouth lifting. But his eyes narrowed, scrutinising, judging... wondering.

Then he raised the hand holding the gun and gestured. 'Come on,' he said.

Scott cast a last glance out of the doors. The playground, the border of poplar trees, the cars and people beyond. He wondered where Emily was now. Had she run into the arms of waiting policemen? Or was her mother there, beckoned by the desperate calls and texts of the students that had passed from parent to parent? Were they all there? Was his own mother there?

The walkie-talkie flashed into his mind. It wasn't just Noah on his own. There were others.

He thought of Emily again, sprinting for her life away from the building, running into the arms not of an officer or her mum, but another boy in a long black coat. Another boy with a silver gun and a mind that had gone to another place entirely outside the bounds of normal civilisation.

No.

He would not think like that. She had escaped, and right now she was sitting on the roadside, surrounded by people in uniforms. She was giving them all the information she had. She would remember the important details, like the gun and the silencer, and the name of their persecutor, and the fact that he wasn't working alone. She would tell them about Mrs Fleecy. She would tell them about Scott and how he had saved her life.

He scanned the empty playground once more.

Outside. Freedom. Safety.

The tremor in his back turned into a vice, gripping his kidneys. He winced, crossed his arms and looked back to Noah.

The boy with the gun was still waiting, that strange half-smile on his face.

'Come on,' he said again. Then he turned and walked off back towards the assembly hall.

The pain in Scott's sides cramped once, badly, before fading away. He raised his chin. Twice now his classmate with the gun had turned his back on him. The very next time he did it, Scott vowed he would take his chance.

The back pain flared, as though in shock at his brave notion. It disabled him, momentarily, before dimming.

He took a deep breath and followed Noah to the hall.

The assembly hall held an air of terror that Scott had never felt before in his life. There were maybe forty or fifty people in there, more than double the number that had been in the classroom. They sat on the cold, hard floor, teachers and students alike, though the kids far outweighed the adults.

He had trailed behind Noah on the walk down the long corridor, looking left, right, up and in front of him, eyes darting everywhere for an escape route, a door that hadn't been chained, a weapon. Next to the hall doors, he saw a fire extinguisher. Briefly he considered grabbing it and smashing it down on Noah's head. But he'd never held one before. Didn't know the weight of it, didn't know if it was actually really light and would do nothing but glance off Noah's skull. The kid would then be furious. He would raise that arm that held the gun so casually. He would aim it, pull the trigger, and Scott's chest would bloom red just like Mrs Fleecy's.

Scott exhaled in frustration. No to the fire extinguisher.

He would have to wait, bide his time, and not make a move until he was really, really sure of success.

'Inside,' Noah said. His voice wasn't so friendly any longer, and the strange smile had vanished altogether.

Scott felt his face fall. Noah had seemed to trust him, especially after the lie he'd told about Emily, about how he had tried to prevent her escape.

Now there was nothing. Noah wasn't even angry. He was blank.

Scott did as he was told and edged past Noah into the big room. All eyes turned to stare at him. Was it him, or did their glare hold a note of accusation? Why? he wondered. Because he'd not escaped, not raised the alarm or managed to disable Noah?

Fuck you, he thought. Nobody here ever even so much as looked at him, and now they wanted him to be their saviour? Besides, hadn't he already done more than was expected of him, by pushing Emily out of the window to freedom?

He felt his face twist in a scowl as he caught the open stares of those who had been in the classroom with him. Beth, Chase, Jessie, Amir and Iozif were all looking at him rather than the man with the gun.

They were wondering where Emily was, he realised. And with a small degree of shame, and for reasons he couldn't explain, instead of making his way to be among them, he thought: let them wonder. Let them wonder about their friend. Let them think she's back in the classroom, in the same condition as Mrs Fleecy. He slumped down, his back to the wall, to sit on the floor near the door.

Alone, as always. Glancing up at Noah, he wondered what the boy would do next. Noah stared back at him, something else on his face now.

He was intrigued, realised Scott. He wondered why Scott had not joined his classmates. Scott held eye contact with him. He didn't look away when his heart began to thump, nor when another sudden pain flared up in his stomach.

-

The boy with the gun walked the perimeter of the hall. Each cluster of students he approached wedged themselves tighter together, moving inwards until the groups of friends were no more and they were just one big crush of bodies.

Scott scanned the hall for the teachers. He saw just two of them: Mr Khan and Miss Dolby. They sat together, in the middle of the students. He squinted at them. They were not talking; they were not moving. No hushed whispers of a plan being formed.

They were the adults. Why weren't they *doing* something? And… where were the rest of the school? There were two hundred students at Farenden, probably a hundred adults, including the teaching assistants. Were they somewhere else, held captive by another kid on Noah's team? Or had they escaped at the first hint of trouble?

Or, Scott gulped, were they dead, lying stretched out in a red puddle, just like Mrs Fleecy?

Ryan.

His brother's name crashed into his head like a freight train. Ryan, the reason he had hesitated, the reason why he wasn't already out there on the roadside next to Emily.

He braced his back against the wall, pressed the soles of his feet into the floor and rose to get a better look at all the people here. He ran his eye over each head, dismissing any dark-haired kids, pausing to scrutinise the blondes.

Footsteps to his right. Noah, completing yet another circuit of the room. His shadow fell over Scott. Scott inched his way back down the wall.

Noah grinned. 'Who're you looking for?' he asked.

24

Travis
Now

Travis kicked off his shoes and walked the few metres to the edge of the forest. Under the shade of a Norway spruce, he moved his right foot around in the loose, cool soil. It was how he listened to the world encapsulated by the woods. He heard through his toes, sensed vibrations through the soles of his feet. At the height of the day, the forest was quiet, nowhere near as busy as it was at dawn or dusk. It wasn't deserted, though. Intrigued, Travis made his way into the woods.

His heart pulsed in his chest. Here, shoeless, with no compass or guide, he was at his most alive. He'd tried to explain it to a colleague once, under the false impression that because the woman lived here, she would also be at one with nature. He'd told her – Frances, her name was – about walking out of his cabin and into the woods with nothing. No water, no survival or first aid kit. No shoes, just his wits.

'No shoes?' She had been aghast, though Travis had mistaken it for admiration.

He'd nodded eagerly, talked about the goodness of the earth, and how the bottom of the foot was where all the vitality entered and all the badness flowed out.

He'd thought he sounded insightful, spiritual, even, and was pleased to have left the usually talkative – and, admittedly, attractive – Frances speechless. He'd hoped she would think about the new world he had opened up to her, fully expected her to come back to him asking to join in on one of his trail walks. It was entirely possible that underneath her confident exterior, she was in need of a man like Travis. She could very well be the one in need of saving that he'd been looking for.

Later, he'd been outside the kitchen and had heard her talking about the woods on their very doorstep, and all that they had to offer. Travis had felt a jolt of worry: what if all the staff wanted to come out with him on a walk? He shuddered. The invitation was for her and her only. The forest wasn't made for man. Not great hordes of them, anyway.

He needn't have worried. As Frances' retelling of the story went on, it soon became clear she was taking the piss.

He wasn't embarrassed, or mortified, just angry. He was self-assured enough to know that when certain people didn't understand something, it was deeply engrained in them to mock that thing. It wasn't a personal slight, or an attack against him. He tried to take it as a lesson learned about who to invite into his life, and who not to.

He had, however, been deeply disappointed that the woman he'd been so sure of had been no different from all the rest.

The memory reminded him why he was out here, and he kept his head up and his eyes open as he walked sound-lessly over the mulch, decades' worth of natural composite squishing between his bare toes.

He looked down occasionally, seeking tracks of boots or trainers, or recently snapped branches along the narrow pathways, seldom travelled.

Then he stopped, tilted his face up to the sky and inhaled deeply.

Cigarette smoke. Unmistakable.

He followed the scent.

Smoke curled out of a pit cave. The deepest one Travis knew of. He approached, alarm and excitement mingling.

The sun was almost at its highest point, though you wouldn't know it here under the thick covering of trees. The caves, with their short, winding entrance tunnels, were almost always in constant darkness, save for very late summer evenings when the setting sun cast an eerie glow over the shafts.

'Hello?' he said, as he crept close to the entrance. 'Is someone in there?'

There was no reply. Listening keenly, his hearing finely tuned over the years, he heard a tiny fizz as the cigarette was put out.

He went with his gut. 'Scott? I'm coming in.'

He took a deep breath and braced himself. He didn't often go into this particular cave, simply because once you were in, it was a nightmare to get out of. In fact, he'd never gone into it without ropes to aid his ascent. But at this time of the year, with no mudslides, it wasn't as bad as it could have been. Still, he reckoned it would be a struggle to exit. And Travis thought of himself as an expert. For Scott – if it was him in there – it would be practically impossible without assistance.

Unless he was with his brother. Two could manage it easier than one. Three, he considered, would be even better.

He gripped the caked sides of the cave and allowed himself to slither in. It was no mean feat. To slide in without tumbling and breaking a limb, he had to brace his hands and feet firmly against the sides. He felt something sharp slice his left foot, and he swore internally. There were some positives to wearing boots or shoes.

He landed in a springing crouch at the bottom, his eyes narrowed to slits, allowing them to adjust to the gloom. The smell of smoke was far stronger in here, and when he opened his eyes fully, he gasped. A small fire was alight in the furthest corner.

'Shit!' He said it out loud this time, and looked around the remainder of the cave. In the deepest shadow, head down, hood up, was Scott.

'Put the fire out, Scott,' he said. His words came out sharply, sterner than he could ever recall his voice being. He tried again. 'Please, just stamp on it, there's a lad.'

For the longest moment, they locked eyes. Travis felt his heart beating faster underneath his thin shirt. The strangest thought crossed his mind.

This boy looks like he could kill me. Looking into his eyes is like looking in a mirror.

It was as terrifying as it was ridiculous.

When Scott made no move to put out the smoking fire, Travis cast around for something to do the job himself. As he bent down, about to pick up some dirt that had slid from one of the walls, Scott moved.

Travis felt himself cringe at the sudden action. He relaxed in an instant as Scott walked the few steps to the fire and kicked the loose soil over it.

The flames diminished, suddenly and with no drama, and Travis felt rather foolish for his internal overreaction. Now that the fear was gone, irritation returned.

'You can't do that, buddy; don't you know the dangers of setting fires in enclosed spaces like this?' He pushed on, not waiting for Scott to reply. 'This stuff down here, the old branches and the leaves, they get swept in here every autumn. They're so dry this whole place could go up in flames.'

'I contained it, see?' Scott spoke for the first time, surprising Travis into silence.

He looked to where the boy was pointing. It was harder to see now the fire had gone out, but Scott was right. Large rocks in a ring around the fire pit. He couldn't help but be impressed, but now wasn't the time for praise. He hadn't finished chastising him.

'I see, but it's not just that. Fumes from fires can be poisonous, deadly even.'

The atmosphere changed.

Scott looked him in the eye. 'I know,' he said.

The air, acrid now with foul-smelling smoke, stung Travis's eyes. 'Let's get out of here,' he said. To his relief, Scott nodded his agreement.

At the mouth of the cave, peering up to the trees swaying gently above them, Travis set his body firmly against the wall and made a step with his hands.

'Push yourself up,' he said. 'Okay?'

Scott backed up a little and stared at Travis's hands before slowly bringing his gaze up to look him in the face.

'It's all right, it'll be fine. I won't let you fall back.'

The boy shook his head. 'It's not that. It's just a… a memory. It reminded me of something… before.'

'Oh.' Travis flexed his fingers and looked at him doubtfully. 'You want to do it the other way round; you boost me up, I'll pull you out?'

'No, it's fine.' Scott tugged up the bottom of his T-shirt and swiped at his face. The shirt came away striped with dirt, soot and... tears?

'You okay?' Travis asked.

Scott blew his lips out and scowled. 'Let's just do this, yeah?'

He stepped forward, put his hands on Travis's shoulders and his left foot in Travis's clasped hands.

'One... two... three... go!' Travis cried. Up his hands went. Puffing at the same time as trying to hold his breath, he prayed it would work. For his age, he knew he was fit and strong, but though Scott's frame was slight, he was still a teenage boy, and heavier than Travis had anticipated.

Loose soil, twigs and leaves cascaded down. Travis ducked his head and closed his eyes. Suddenly, the weight left his hands. He stilled for a moment, half expecting Scott to come tumbling back down. When nothing happened, he looked up cautiously.

'You okay, are you out?' he called.

He waited in the gloom, listening for a response.

He waited, and waited, his pulse beginning to fly again, panic rising.

Above him, in his forest, the only reply was the machine-gun shriek of a lone magpie.

In the cave, it seemed like time had stopped. Travis had been in dangerous situations before. He had travelled the world, been on the fringes of war zones and in perilous climates. He had trekked mountain paths at midnight, experienced critical outdoor temperatures at both ends of the scale. The number one lifesaver in any circumstance was not to panic. Panic overrode everything, and nothing good ever came of it.

Still, it was also the body's natural response. It could hardly be fought against, so he let it in.

He set the timer on his wristwatch for thirty seconds. At the first beep, he allowed himself to moan. He let his heart do what it needed to, and whatever thoughts entered his head, he granted them entry. All of this time, his eyes were tightly screwed shut.

When the second alarm sounded, signalling the end of his allotted panic time, he opened his eyes and assessed the situation.

He needed to get out, and it was going to be difficult. He couldn't stay here, because he had no water, food or shoes. He couldn't wait for someone to pass, because this was way off the beaten track.

Other thoughts tried to crowd into his mind. He should have left the cave first. Scott wouldn't have been able to get out on his own. Dreamily, he imagined the scenario. Sara would need him more than anything if something happened to her son…

He shook his head.

He couldn't waste time on pointless fantasies. Scott was out, Travis wasn't.

Getting out of the cave was the priority now.

Concentrate.

He looked at the edges of the shaft that led to the open air above. More than six feet, a bad fall if he misjudged anything, but it was doable. He needed footholds, for one thing. He looked mournfully at his bare feet. This look was fine for wandering through the forest, but not so much for climbing. But shoes were not an option.

No room for wishful thinking here, he told himself sternly.

He curled his hands into fists and, without pausing to think about it, pummelled the right-hand side of the heavy clay wall. Heartened to see it denting slightly, he carried on.

The grey clay turned red as his knuckles grazed and split. He switched off the pain, closed his eyes and punched harder.

He knew that he would need more than one foothold. He realised that he would have to do this three or four more times. It was the wrong thing, to think. It allowed the pain to enter.

He cried out and sank to his knees.

'Scott?' he shouted, and then, louder, 'SCOTT!'

Something hit him on the back of the neck. He jumped, whipped his hands up, allowed another moan to escape.

He thought of Scott above him, a collection of bricks and heavy stones by his feet. There were rocks around these parts, shards that had split off from the Girdle Stone – a monument shrouded in history and legend – in the recent bad storms. Scattered like so many hailstones or raindrops. Travis thought of those slender artist's hands curling around them, aiming them down into the cave; he thought of Scott listening to the sound they made as they struck Travis's head. The blood that would follow, pooling around him. How long did it take to die from death by stoning?

A second rock struck him, on the shoulder this time, shocking him to his feet. Instinctively he moved to the side of the cave.

'Why are you doing this?' he cried, his voice low and heavy with misery and shock.

He looked at the rocks, his eyes slowly becoming accustomed to the gloom. Slowly, more far slowly than it should have, his mind reworked them into the objects they actually were.

Boots.

He had barely registered that when a third item came hurtling down into the cave.

A rope.

He fell on them as though they were floats in a sea that he was drowning in. Relief and gratitude spun to anger in an instant.

The climb to the exit was over in seconds. What a difference a length of rope and a pair of shoes made. When Travis's head emerged, he tipped his face back and gulped in the air.

He went into a crouch, noticing that his legs were shaking. Adrenaline pumped through him, lighting up his veins and nerve endings with an energy he no longer needed.

He let himself sink to a sitting position. Across from him, a few feet away, Scott stood at the entrance to the pit cave, winding the rope back into a circle.

He swallowed as if choking back the fury. 'You... you scared me, Scott,' he said.

Scott stopped looping the rope around his shoulder and looked down. 'Did I?' he asked.

'Where did you get these?' Travis was looking at the boots, now on his feet. His own boots, he realised belatedly. And the rope that Scott was tying in an efficient bowline knot.

'Your house,' said Scott.

'You... you know where I live?' Travis frowned.

'You told me. You invited me round. We were going to have a barbecue, remember?' Scott let the circle of rope fall from his shoulder. He held it in his hands, his knuckles suddenly bone white as they clutched it. 'Or did you mean for just my *mother* to come to your little camp-out?'

There was something about the way he said the word 'mother'. Almost, but not quite, spitting the two syllables.

Travis flailed. He rarely felt lost, hardly ever in front of his subordinates, never, ever in front of kids.

It was all unravelling. He floundered for a moment, seeking to gain back some control. If Scott didn't like him, it would hardly encourage Sara into his life.

'Gosh, I'm sorry, mate. I'm just a bit discombobulated...' He gestured to the yawning mouth of the cave. 'It got me thrown, if I'm honest.' He shuddered, deliberately and dramatically.

Scott said nothing, though he relaxed his grip on the rope. The skin of his fingers flushed, red and normal, as the blood flowed back to the joints.

'Come on,' said Travis. 'Let's get this party started.'

25

Sara
Now

By some miracle, Sara hadn't reached for the booze or the pills. The pills were still there, half empty now. The first bundle she had been fed every day in that first week by her mother.

Fragmented memories came at her. Mary, stern but almost kind, tipping her only daughter's head back, pushing two pills in, then clamping Sara's mouth closed and holding a glass of water to her dry lips. Water that Sara had no choice but to accept, because the pills were lodged halfway down her throat.

One day, maybe only hours after the massacre, or perhaps three or four days, or a week or so after it had happened, the pills got stuck as usual, and Sara considered grabbing the glass from her mother's hand, smashing it so all the water escaped and choking to death.

Mary had pre-empted that; she'd clasped Sara's hands together with surprising strength and got a good half of the pint glass down her throat.

The next morning, Sara had picked up the razor, Mack's razor, from the cupboard. It was rusty now, three years after his death, but still she kept it.

She'd thought she just wanted to look at it, to hold it and touch it, because it still held pieces of him. Stubble and skin and possibly the smallest bit of blood from where he'd nicked himself shaving. In fact, the razor was very old. He hadn't had any hair to shave during that last year. The razor was almost a talisman, a reminder of a time when he'd been briefly cancer-free, and life had been all right.

Mary had come in, snatched the blade away and tossed it in the bin.

'No,' she'd said, sharply, her tone stinging more than the razor would have. 'You seem to be forgetting that you've still got a boy there, one who needs his mother.' She had shaken Sara, just once. 'It's the funeral in a couple of days,' she'd said.

So soon, too soon. She wasn't ready for that.

She was ready to curl up with Mack's razor and take a good handful of Mary's pills.

Later, that night, she sat on the end of the bed in her darkened room. Eyes gazed at her from the hallway.

'Scott,' she croaked.

He blinked once, then was gone.

She had cried then, her arms aching for her boys. One of them gone forever, one just out of reach.

She promised to do better by Scott.

But that was before she knew what he'd done.

Now, it wasn't just her arms that ached, but her very core. A pain that radiated from her toes, snake bites and venom in her spine, branching out and up to her head.

She wished the pain away, opened her eyes wide and dragged her tired body upstairs, into her bedroom.

A barbecue. She was supposed to be at a barbecue at the home of the man who was helping her son.

Could he help him?

It was the burning question now, the only question, the one important thing.

Well, there was the other thing, the need to stay hidden. She had worked on that for practically a year, and she thought she'd accomplished it. There had been no knock at the door, no strange phone calls, simply because there was no telephone to ring.

She gazed at the wardrobe, where the box was concealed on the top shelf. It still held her mobile, switched off for almost a year now, SIM card removed, stored in her bedside table.

There were photos on it, pictures of her and Mack and Ryan and Scott.

She had thought the temptation to switch it on and devour the images of her life lost would be strong by now. It was; but the fear of being found was stronger. But because today seemed to be self-flagellation day, she opened the wardrobe door and reached up for the box.

It was a Timberland box, boots she'd purchased for Mack before he died, when it looked like the years of sickness and the radiation and pills and chemo might just be behind them.

New boots for a new start. He'd said that, his thin face creasing into a smile.

Sara had smiled with him, daring to hope that the thing she'd done had been forgiven by those who handed out retribution and punishment.

It hadn't. Payback waited in the wings, patient as a saint before it struck.

She put the box back without opening it. She pulled out a pair of cut-off jeans, a short-sleeved black shirt. She thought of her trips to the city and who might have seen her there, knowing even as she thought it that nobody knew who she was, but pulling on a black baseball cap anyway.

She slammed the wardrobe door closed, took half a Tramadol to quell the paranoia. Not from the pack she'd been prescribed after Farenden, but from the stash that Mack had barely started. Then she headed out of the cabin.

She didn't know exactly where Travis lived, but she knew it was in the forest, not far from her own home. She shoved her hands in her pockets, put her head down and started to walk.

As she scuffed along, she thought about how it made her feel, knowing he was so close to her.

Uncomfortable was the best she could come up with, though she wasn't sure why.

She pushed the thought from her mind and pressed on, leaving the path and stepping into the woods when she spied a gap in the hedge.

Ahead, the scent of smoke; along with it, laughter.

She was close.

It wasn't Scott who was laughing, he didn't do that. She recognised the sound as Travis, and just like the very presence of him, it was overly loud, compensating no doubt for her son's silence.

She came upon the barbecue unexpectedly. One minute she was traipsing through the forest, the next she found herself in Travis's garden.

Not a garden, not really, for there were no boundaries or fences here. The forest was part of his home, she saw now; he had made it deliberately so.

They hadn't seen her, so she took a step to her right and positioned herself behind one of the large trees that bordered his modest cabin.

On the porch, Travis leaned on the railing, a bottle of beer held loosely in his hand. He lifted it, called out an instruction, and then laughed again.

Sara looked to where he'd gestured.

Her son, Scott, yards away on the… lawn area, if you could call it that. Standing over the barbecue, poking at the grille with a pair of tongs. He seemed to give up, looked over at Travis.

'It's gone.' His voice was loaded with mock disappointment. The look on his face was pure Mack, his gentle comedy that once upon a time had had both her and the boys in stitches. Learned behaviour, no genetics at play here.

Travis, on the porch, tipped back his head and roared with laughter.

Another giggle joined in. Sara, forgetting her subterfuge, forgetting her son, who in that moment was a dead ringer for the man who wasn't his father, looked around, panicked at the thought of a third person joining them.

Nobody in sight. Her hand flew to her lips. This time, it *was* Scott laughing.

He saw her then, Travis did, or rather, the motion she'd made, and as he looked up at her, she understood. He'd known she was there, probably as soon as she approached. After all, living in a place like this, she supposed one would become attuned to the sounds of the forest, no matter how slight.

He'd wanted to show her this sight. This vision of her son, happy, normal, *laughing*.

As she nodded to him and approached the cabin, she realised that she might have underestimated this man. Travis Samuel understood far more than she had given him credit for.

26

Sara
Before

The school gates were in view when Sara felt her phone vibrate in her pocket. She pulled it out, gasping, realising she was swearing, fumbling and almost dropping it.

Ryan's name flashed up on the screen.

'Oh Jesus, Ryan, Ryan!'

Sweat on her hands as she swiped, and it didn't connect the call. She screamed, short and sharp in frustration, swiping, swiping, stabbing at the screen. Jojo was at her back now, and something radiated off him, covering her, calming her.

She took a deep breath, slicked her thumb down her shirt, which felt equally as damp as her hands, and slid it on the screen again.

'Ryan, Ryan!'

She held onto the phone, held onto her breath until he spoke.

'Mum!'

An eruption like a blast within her core. She nodded frantically into the phone, didn't care when she saw snot and tears and frothy spit fly from her mouth. She dragged her sleeve across her lips, suddenly so dry, and barked his name.

'Ryan! Ryan!'

Calm yourself. She tried, some part of her dimly aware that since answering the phone, all she'd done was call his name. She needed to establish things, she needed to reassure him, assess him for damage, gather information that could get him out of this godawful state of affairs.

'Ryan.' She said his name once more, and drew in a great jagged breath of frustration at her own inability.

A hand on her arm, cool and calm.

Jojo.

'Are you okay?' The first question came out, and it made sense, and she sounded like a mother.

'Yes, yeah, we're all right,' said Ryan at the other end.

He sounded so small and quiet, and she realised he was whispering. He was hiding, then.

'Are you safe, hiding somewhere?'

'Yeah, the science lab stock room.'

'How many of you are in there? Are you all uninjured?'

A beat, as though he were counting the cupboard's other occupants and verifying there were no injuries.

'Three of us, me and Max and Jaden.'

A dip in her chest. She sucked in breath, blew it out. *Don't lose it now, not yet.*

'Have you seen your brother?'

'No. Mum?'

'Yes, my darling?'

'Do you reckon he's okay?'

'Your brother?' She thought of Scott, also hiding, but without the support of others. He would be alone, scared. She swallowed. 'Of course he is, my darling.'

Something – some*one* – hissed at the other end of the phone. Hushed conversation in whispers before Ryan came back on the line: 'Mum, someone's coming, I'll ring you back.'

'Keep your phone on,' Sara whispered back, but she spoke to nothing but dead air.

'Sara?' Jojo leaned in to her, stooping a little to see her face.

'It was Ryan. He's in the science lab stock room, he's with Jaden and Max. They're all okay.'

The last three words broke her and she bent over, winded.

They're all okay.

'They're all okay,' she whispered.

Jojo, unknowingly, unwittingly, ruined it. 'So we just need to locate Scott, and hope they all stay hidden until this is over.'

With a great effort, she straightened up and staggered the last few feet to the gates. The relief left her. It wasn't over: she still had one son whose whereabouts were unknown.

Police officers, a handful of them, plus a couple of PCSOs, stood in a line across the locked gates. Sara ignored them and sank onto a low wall beside them. Jojo came to join her.

'Where's Scott?' she asked.

'Try him again.' Gently but firmly, Jojo took her phone out of her hands. 'Here, let me.' He scrolled through the numbers, pressed dial.

'Voicemail,' he said, hanging up.

'Someone was coming,' she said.

Jojo glanced around. Sara shook her head impatiently.

'Ryan said he had to go, someone was coming. What if it was…?'

'Don't.' He stopped her and shook his head. 'Just… don't.'

His son was in the same cupboard, she remembered. 'Sorry,' she whispered.

He shrugged, nodded, scrubbed at his face with his fists. His hands were large and gnarled and hard-working. They were also tender and kind and skilled.

Sara twisted away from him and vomited down the other side of the wall.

'How many of them are there?' she asked as she swiped her wrist across her mouth. 'You said earlier he wasn't working alone. Who else is it?'

'We don't know yet. Hold on…' Jojo pulled out his own phone and tapped onto the WhatsApp group, scrolled through, notifications pinging up even as he read.

'They're trying to account for people, for students. They're going round all the families, checking who has heard from who.'

Sara frowned. That would be an obvious move. She wasn't sure why this was news. Jojo, always so intuitive, sensed her confusion. He lowered his eyes to his phone screen.

'I guess whoever is left, whoever hasn't made contact, might be an accomplice. Or… you know.'

Or dead. That was what he meant.

Sara shivered. She felt a thought try to form in her mind. It was too awful even to let in, so she pushed it away, took her own phone back from Jojo and dialled Scott's number.

Again, nothing.

She pushed her hair back and blew out a breath, staring uselessly at the phone in her hand. Willing it to ring, praying for Ryan or Scott or… or even her mum.

She and her mother weren't close. They never had been. Mary had lost her husband, Sara's father, when Sara was only five. It had only been the two of them, but it hadn't drawn them together. Mary was poised and brittle, unemotional and closed off. Dutiful yet distant.

What had happened to Mack should have filled the void between them, but instead, the distance had only grown.

It was a rare event that made Sara long for Mary, but now was one of those times.

She stabbed at her phone again and lifted it to her ear.

It rang just once before Mary's voice came down the line.

'Sara?'

'Mum.' Only the one word would come. Just like when Ryan had answered his phone. Speech had deserted her, and she wondered if she would spend her lifetime just repeating names, over and over.

'Yes, dear. Are you all right?'

She didn't know, hadn't heard. Sara closed her eyes briefly.

'Mum, there's been a shooting at the school. The boys are still inside.'

A silence, brief but palpable, before Mary spoke. 'I'm coming now.' The line went dead. Sara stared dumbly at the phone in her hand.

'Your mother's coming?' Jojo's voice brought her back to the present.

'Yes.'

She looked around the street. It seemed like everyone was here now – parents, friends, extended families, people who lived in the houses surrounding the school. The police moved in and out of them all, walkie-talkies crackling, phones ringing and pinging constantly. Cars had been abandoned haphazardly on the no-parking cross hatches.

'She hadn't heard?'

Sara shook her head, wilted a bit inside. How had Mary not heard? The whole city seemed to have congregated outside the school gates.

The old man, the one who had cried back in the community centre, came to Sara's mind. What must it be like to have a parent like that?

And yet, she herself was no better, not really. She kept her emotions in check, held herself ramrod straight, like a human being glazed with iron cladding. What little affection she showed all went to one person.

Ryan.

A sob escaped and she covered her mouth.

Ryan had been her second chance, her and Mack's second chance. And for a very short while it had been almost perfect.

Think of something else.

She sat up a little straighter and looked back to the road. The police were moving, forming something that looked almost like a human chain, trying to press people back from the fence, directing them to the other side of the street.

They seemed to have given up on the community centre plan.

'Do you think they're still in there?' she asked suddenly.

Jojo looked towards the deathly quiet school building.

Sara shook her head. 'No, I mean the Millers, Noah's parents. Do you think they're in the community centre?'

His face darkened, suddenly and without warning. His nostrils flared, his jaw ground tightly into itself. From his chest came a tremor. He pushed himself up off the wall and gave her a single glance. 'Wait here,' he said.

She watched as he moved at speed through the crowd, back towards the community centre, breaking into a jog as he reached the end of the street.

Without him she felt tiny and small and… unprotected. She felt… *watched*.

Sure enough, when she dared to glance up, her breath snagged in her throat at Kathy Driver's approach.

'Sara, did you hear anything from the boys?'

Unconsciously, Sara inched away slightly as Kathy sat beside her. 'I got through to Ryan. He's… okay, he's staying safe.'

For now.

Neither woman said the words, but Sara was sure they were both thinking it.

She cleared her throat.

'Um, did you hear from… yours?' The name of Kathy's daughter escaped her. She knew it, or had once known it, back when the kids were all little and before Sara became the most hated woman in Farenden.

'Louise is at home,' Kathy said. She offered Sara a pinched smile. 'She was sick this morning, so I didn't send her in. She said she had a headache, period pains.'

Sara felt her mouth fall open. Kathy's child wasn't even here, wasn't at the school, wasn't in danger from the threat of kids with guns. Why wasn't the woman at home, holding her daughter close, thanking her lucky stars?

'Why… why are you here?'

'Excuse me?'

Sara stared at her. 'Why are you here? If your girl is okay, if she's safe at home, then why the hell would you be here?'

Kathy sniffed and raised her chin. 'I'm on the committee, it's part of my duty. I'm here to support people, help in whatever way I can.'

'Bullshit.' The word slipped out in a hiss.

'Excuse me?' Kathy said again, hand on chest now, playing the wounded victim to the hilt.

'You're here for the info, the intel, the gossip. My God, Kathy, this is real life, these are children's lives. This isn't water-cooler chit-chat, or a whiff of scandal! This isn't like…' Sara trailed off and squeezed her lips together.

Kathy's eyes flashed, just once, as she stood up again. 'Isn't like someone sleeping with someone else's husband? Someone who is a wife herself, someone whose husband is—'

Crack!

Sara's palm across Kathy's cheek made a sound like a gunshot.

Kathy put her hand to her face, already blooming red. From between her fingers, Sara saw the glimmer of a smile, satisfied and smug.

'Leave me alone.' Sara's voice was hoarse and ragged. She slumped back down to sit on the wall, ignoring the gaze of the gaggle of mothers nearby.

Kathy dropped her hand and raised her chin to ensure that those gathered got a good look at the red mark.

Sara put her head in her hands and tried to block out the increasing sound of the whispers around her.

27

Sara
Now

As she walked up to the porch where Travis stood, the atmosphere changed. Not from Travis's perspective. He grinned at her, wide open, his feelings, his joy on view. She felt a twist in her gut, envy that he could show himself, that he seemed to have nothing to hide.

No, the mood swing came from her right, where smoke billowed like clouds, obscuring her son's face. She didn't have to see his face. She knew what his expression would be: part fear, part hate, one third love and devotion.

A poisonous, toxic combination.

She fixed her eyes on Travis.

'Sara, you came!'

She shrugged, willed herself to say something, something normal. Failing, floundering, she simply shoved her hands deeper into her pockets and gave him what she hoped passed for a smile.

A short, sharp breeze filtered through the scattered tree trunks. The smoke from the barbecue cleared.

'Hey, Mum,' said Scott. He held the tongs in one hand, charred bits of something stuck to the ends. In his other hand he held a bottle, matching the one Travis brandished.

'Is that... beer?' she asked, shooting Travis a look.

He was quick to shake his head. Leaning over, he pulled another one out of a cooler by his side. 'Ginger beer,' he said. 'Would you like one?'

She blinked at him. Ginger beer. What was this, The Famous bloody Five?

Her eyes drifted towards his cabin, imagining a bar inside. Whisky or wine, anything but sodding ginger beer.

She sighed. The half-a-Tramadol was wearing off. She needed... *something*. Something to ease the pain that the day had already been, something to soothe what this night could become.

'Something stronger,' Travis stated, like he could see her need on her face.

Like he could read her mind. And just like the closeness of his home to hers, the thought made her squirm.

She took a deep breath. 'Yes, please, that would be lovely.'

He nodded, pushed himself upright and made his way in through the open door. It was only as he walked past her that she noticed he was barefoot, and that his feet seemed to be streaked with something... something that she didn't even want to try to identify.

'He walks barefoot in the forest.'

The voice, directly behind her, made her jump a mile.

Sara spun, hand on chest, to come face to face with Scott.

'Wh-what?' she asked, pulse pounding, skin ablaze. She brought up her other hand to cover her chest, so sure that her son could see her skin twitching and jumping with the drumbeat of her heart.

'I had to rescue him earlier,' Scott said. He didn't look at her when he spoke, but past her, to the open doorway Travis had disappeared through.

The fear of facing her son vanished. Sara leaped back in time, to almost a year before, when anger had overtaken everything.

Like she had back then, she grabbed him now, her hands digging into his thin shoulders. 'What do you mean, rescue him?' She resisted the visceral urge to shake him. Instead, she held onto him, his bones sharp underneath her fingertips. 'What did you *do*?'

'Nothing!' Scott's voice was a whining cry, a sound one would expect from a much younger boy. Almost as though he realised what he had sounded like, he coughed, looked down to the side before bringing his eyes up to meet hers. 'I rescued him!'

It was more of a shout this time, more in keeping with the age he was. A normal teenage boy's battle cry.

Sara drew in a shaky breath. The silence stretched on.

Eventually, behind her, she heard Travis step through the door. She glanced at him; anywhere rather than stare into her son's eyes. He'd put his boots on, she saw now.

Timberlands. Just like the ones Mack had once treated himself to but had barely had a chance to wear.

'Cocktail time!' He came down the stairs, held out a glass to Sara.

She took it, raised it to her lips without asking what it was, and sipped at it.

Bacardi.

She nodded, sipped some more. Bacardi was as good as anything.

The couple of mouthfuls soothed her, as instant as a pill.

She smiled, tilted the glass at Travis and moved her head to include Scott in her salutation. 'So, what's all this about a rescue?'

There was a strange moment, something indistinguishable passing between man and boy. She caught it, bit her lip, and took another long swallow from her glass.

Time pushed on, pulsing through the trees that surrounded her. Sara felt her eyes fill with tears. She blinked them back, not wanting either Scott or Travis to see them.

'Scott said he rescued you.' Her words were desperate, a plea for him to corroborate her son's story.

Travis, clever, sensitive, slightly weird Travis, nodded as he looked at her.

'That's right, I... I got trapped in a pit cave.' He uttered a laugh, and for the very first time since she'd started taking notice of him, it didn't seem genuine.

Now, despite her pushing, she found she didn't want to know. It was easier, always, to pretend otherwise. It was how she'd got through the last year.

By pretending.

'A pit cave?' She changed the subject quickly, eagerly, as she took another long swallow of her drink.

'That's right. The pit caves are a bit of a phenomenon around these parts, man-made – or machinery-made, if you will. Then, across the decades, nature took over...'

He was so happy, Sara saw, telling the history of the forest that he seemed to have claimed for his own. Scott, clearly having heard this tale before, moved back to the barbecue. She heard the slap of meat, saw the subsequent smoke at the fresh offering on the grill.

It obscured him once more. Knowing that they couldn't see each other, Sara relaxed.

She tuned out Travis's story but kept her eyes on him as she sipped and swallowed until her glass was empty.

He had finished speaking.

The realisation gave her a jolt. She hadn't commented. Hadn't even made the listening noises that she had taught herself to do over the last year. Now, he stared at her, an intense look, not pissed off or annoyed, simply a... Travis look.

'Are you ready for some food?' he asked.

She knew that tone. It was the sort of thing her mother would say. What he really meant was, do you think you should eat to soak up some of the alcohol you've been drinking as though it's water?

But she'd only had one glass, the one he'd mixed for her, hadn't she?

Wrong.

The bottle of Bacardi was in her grip, and it was less than half full. She felt a tremor in her stomach. Had she got up, gone into his house and helped herself to it? Or, seeing her glass empty, had Travis refreshed her drink and left the bottle?

The second option, surely.

'Not a bad little mixer, is it?' He gestured with his own glass towards the bottle.

She smiled, not a real one, because she couldn't remember how to do that, but one that would hopefully pass for something genuine.

'Scott, how's that food coming along?' he called over his shoulder.

The smoke had cleared. The knowledge that she could see her son clearly caused the inane grin to slip from her face.

Travis got up and limped over to the barbecue. Sara frowned, remembering the thing that had looked a lot like blood on his feet when she had first arrived. Now he was limping.

Pit caves.

Scott had rescued him.

Scott had tried to harm him.

She shook her head to banish the thought.

If anything untoward had happened, surely Scott – and most likely herself – wouldn't be welcome here?

Both of them came towards her now, plates of meat in hand, fresh food on the grille as the smoke poured up and around again.

Sara blinked at a hard substance beneath her elbows.

Picnic table.

She was seated at a table on the porch, and yet when Travis had started telling his boring story, and she had commenced drinking, they had been standing on the grass, in the little clearing between the trees.

She shivered, even though the summer was still in full force.

How could she not know how she'd got from there to here?

The half-a-Tramadol, she reassured herself. It did that. It had done it before, caused gaps in her memory, and no doubt would again. She wondered if she could cut down on the crutches she used. They had made her forget. No, not really forget, but they had dulled both pain and memories. She needed to face them, once and for all.

She put the bottle back on the table as Travis and Scott reached her, before changing her mind and pouring just one more glass of Bacardi, hoping they didn't notice that she failed to add the mixer.

Nobody said anything, and the meat and the salad and the brioche rolls that had sat out too long were served.

The meat was burned and charred, the peppers blackened sticks of charcoal, the bread had dried in the sun. Sara pushed it all methodically down her throat.

The taste didn't matter.

Nothing that used to be a pleasure mattered any more.

–

After the night she'd found out about Mack's terminal diagnosis, she'd arranged to meet Jojo one last time. She'd insisted on going further afield and had taken a tube to Hammersmith, the last stop on the line.

When she was above ground, her phone had pinged with a message. He was in the Palais restaurant, did she want her usual white wine or something else?

Neither, she wrote back, before deleting it and requesting a large white. Even back then, with an unborn child in her belly, she'd needed a crutch.

He had booked a room in the adjoining hotel. Her heart had plummeted before soaring for joy. Could it hurt? Just one last time?

She took a sip of wine as Jojo perused the menu, one hand on her face, his eyes moving from the menu to her. His thumb stroked her lip, the touch sending pulses of pleasure through her, in spite of what she had come here to do. She shifted her chair back, out of his reach.

'Mack has cancer,' she said. 'I can't see you any more.'

He had been horrified, sympathetic, full of questions. Genuinely concerned and sorry, because Jojo was – despite sleeping with a married woman – a nice guy. He didn't hate Mack. Just like Sara didn't hate Jojo's wife.

He reached a hand across the table, a comforting gesture. Sara stared at it in horror, knowing that if he touched her again, they would be in the pre-booked room before they'd even ordered a meal.

She wrapped both hands around the stem of her glass and drained it.

He was still talking, platitudes and empty gestures of support, when she stood up, grabbing her bag off the back of her chair.

'You need to stay away from me,' she'd said, voice shaking.

It was only then that she noticed Kathy Driver, sitting with another woman Sara didn't know, only two tables over. Kathy didn't greet her, but she watched very carefully, her mouth a circle of shock, as Sara walked out of the restaurant, out of Hammersmith, out of Jojo's life.

Back to Mack, taking with her the baby that was growing inside her but wasn't her husband's.

–

It was Mack's food sensitivity that had unconsciously caused her own aversion to eating, she thought now. She'd been starving through the pregnancy, right from the off, but it was oh-so-hard to enjoy food while Mack moved on to the liquid supplements, and it was impossible when even they were abandoned and a feeding tube was fitted.

She'd never quite managed to retrieve her lust for food, not even in the years when Mack made a comeback and was well. Even less so now.

'Delicious,' she said, when it seemed like nobody had spoken for a really long time.

Beyond the trees, the sun blazed scarlet in the sky. Quietly, Travis cleared the plates. Scott remained on the bench in front of her. Soon, the scent of freshly brewed coffee wafted out of the cabin.

Sara leaned back against the wall of the house and closed her eyes.

Coffee was something – maybe the only thing – that was a pleasure. It was also a necessity, like cigarettes and alcohol and the occasional pill.

As the sun dipped even lower and grey twilight approached, Scott got up and walked to the treeline.

If he were Ryan, she would have called to him. *Don't wander too far.*

But he wasn't, and she didn't call to him.

Ryan.

His name… his name… the memory of before, of the again-realisation of today.

And then, as she heard Travis's boots clumping across the wooden floor towards the porch, another thought.

Scott had said they were all invited to this barbecue today.

His roundabout way of saying that Travis would also be expecting Sara's younger son to be here.

And yet he hadn't enquired as to his whereabouts.

Knowing Travis, even as little as she did, it was something he would certainly ask.

She opened her eyes at the sound of the coffee pot being placed on the table. Looked at him full on for the first time.

There was knowledge in his face. Travis knew now that Ryan was dead.

28

Scott
Before

In one hand Noah held a bag, larger than an average rucksack. The gun ever-present in the other.

He squatted in front of Scott. Scott drew his knees up to his chest and dug his fingers in. Noah, that half-smile back, tapped the barrel of the gun on Scott's leg.

'Who're you looking for?' he asked again.

'My brother.'

As Noah regarded him, Scott wondered why a lie had come to him so easily to protect Emily, yet when asked about his brother, the truth had fallen out with the same ease.

'Ryan, right?'

Scott resisted an eye-roll. Nobody knew *his* name, but everybody knew exactly who good old Ryan was.

'Huh.' Noah sat down and looked out at the students. In response, they all averted their eyes. Some looked at the floor, some at each other. Scott looked at Noah.

The silence stretched on, broken occasionally by the sound of someone weeping.

Finally, Noah stood up and looked down at Scott.

He lifted the left side of his shirt. A second handgun was tucked into the waistband of his trousers. He smiled, a full one this time, showing his teeth as he said to Scott, 'You want to find your brother?'

Two guns. One silver, one black, both equally deadly.

Nobody else had heard his question to Scott. Scott was on the outside looking in, as always.

He answered instantly. 'Yes,' he said.

Noah nodded. 'Wait a second.' And without turning around, he swept his right hand up and out, firing three shots into the group crushed together in the middle of the assembly hall.

As one they all screamed. Not at the noise – there was still a silencer on the gun after all – but purely at the action.

When the hubbub dimmed and hushed, further wails carried on. Somebody, maybe more than one person, had been hit. Scott couldn't tell who, but as he clambered to his feet, he saw the group separate, scattering in places. The middle was no longer a safe place to be. They headed for the corners of the room, grabbing onto people, no matter if they were friends or not now. Instinct had kicked in. Bodies were now shields.

Always, this hall that doubled as a gymnasium smelled of teenage bodies, overly perfumed girls, chewing gum and floor polish. Now, a heavier aroma settled in to mingle with the palpable panic. A metallic tang of blood, so visceral Scott could taste it; a burning smell, heat from Noah's weapons and the scent of the gun smoke that curled upwards like blown-out birthday candles. Sweet sweat and pure fear.

'Go,' said Noah. He jerked his head towards the doors.

Scott moved, keeping his back to the wall, watching the carnage unfold in front of him. Surely now it would be over. Surely now the police would burst in with weapons of their own. But the heavy doors remained locked.

Behind him, Noah removed the chains and yanked one open.

'Come on,' he said.

With one last look at the assembly hall and the panic that flailed within it, Scott slipped out of the room.

'You know what it is not to be seen, right?' asked Noah conversationally as they walked side by side down the hall.

Scott glanced at him. The gun in the waistband of his trousers, the one he held oh-so-casually in his hand. He had on a black hoodie with deep pockets. From the left-hand one, copper-coloured wires poked out. Scott stared. What were they, parts of a bomb? How many more weapons of destruction did this kid have? And where was he planning to use them?

Something ice-cold ran through his body and he shivered with something that felt strangely like excitement.

'Yeah,' he said softly. 'Nobody sees me either.'

Noah stopped walking and stared intently at him, for so long that the ice-cold thrill turned dark and hot.

Finally, he nodded, seemingly satisfied with Scott's answer.

'Come on then,' he said. And in a chilling move, he patted the gun in his waistband, gave a tight smile and strode on.

They walked for an age, for what seemed like hours but would only have been minutes. Time had stopped. The bells signalling the start and end of classes no longer rang out. The school was silent. The alarm and subsequent announcement that should have denoted an intruder, and the scale of danger, hadn't come.

Corridors looped around the assembly hall, branching off into smaller hallways, departments and classrooms.

Scott fell behind Noah, risking a look into every window. Noah did no such thing. He moved onward, never looking left or right, not seeming to care that at any moment the police could – surely *would* – burst in and take him down with their own firearms.

They passed the library, Noah so far ahead now that Scott stopped for a moment and peered through the glass window of the door.

A kid, one he didn't know, moved across the room in a hunched sprint, arms up over his head, quick as lightning, to disappear behind a row of bookshelves.

'Someone in there?' Noah's voice pulled Scott back to where he was, on the outside looking in. The place where he always was. A familiar place.

He chewed his lip and looked once more into the library. He didn't know the kid. He'd never wronged him. Then again, he'd never righted him either.

'No,' he said. 'It's empty.'

'Come on, then.'

'Who doesn't see you?' Scott dared to ask as they continued their never-ending patrol of the corridors.

It was the one thing Noah had repeated, over and over, this talk about seeing, how nobody saw him, how now everybody would.

They walked on for so long, turning two corners to end up back at the doors they'd exited from, that Scott thought Noah wasn't going to answer.

'They're going to ask why, you know. They're going to investigate every part of my life, from birth until now. They're going to look at my parents and wonder where they went wrong. Abuse, they'll think. They're lazy like that.'

Scott suddenly realised he had lost all the feeling in his hands. He clenched his fingers, rubbed the tips together. They were ice-cold while the rest of him sweated.

He didn't ask who the 'they' were that Noah referred to. He doubted that the boy with the gun had been abused, by his parents or anyone. That wasn't what this was. They could interview Noah and people like him for years and never discover what it was.

The why wasn't even important. It was already too late for that question. It was too late the instant Noah pulled the trigger and sent the bullet into Mrs Fleecy's chest.

'Do you want to get out of this?' Noah, leaning against the padlocked door of the assembly hall, opened the rucksack that Scott had noticed before. From it, he pulled a pouch of rolling tobacco, some papers, and a handful of loose bullets.

Scott focused on the question he'd been asked. He wasn't sure what Noah meant. Was he asking if Scott wanted to get out of this school with his life intact? Or – the option Scott suspected he meant – did he want to get out of this... *partnership* that he seemed to now be entwined in?

For a few long seconds they eyeballed each other. Scott felt his heart thudding, a pulse in his throat that he was sure Noah could see, the skin there thin and fragile, covering vital veins with nothing thicker than gossamer.

He didn't ask for clarification. 'No,' he whispered.

Noah swallowed. His face betrayed no emotion until he smiled, bright and white and chilling. 'Need a signal.' He held up the walkie-talkie. 'I'll be right back.'

Those words again.

Scott nodded obediently.

Noah cocked his head. 'Wait here,' he said. Then he was gone, a flash of long black coat in a tailwind. The double doors that led to the eastern side of the school.

Scott looked at the bag that Noah had left by the door to the hall. Behind it, a set of bolt cutters was propped against the wall. The flap of the bag was still open. Scott hefted his own rucksack higher on his back before darting over to it and peering inside. Knives, dozens and dozens of bullets, empty casings, rope and wire. A lighter, red and cheap, sat among some papers, screwed-up notebook pages, scrawled with writing.

He realised his error immediately. He was standing by the glassed section of the doors. Inside the assembly hall, a face caught his eye: Matty Cranshaw. Scott blinked and stepped away from the glass. Matty was older than Scott, and wouldn't know his name to identify him. Nobody knew his name. But he could pick him out of a line-up.

One of the panes of glass was cracked, a tiny circle in the centre that led out to spider's-web fractures. A bullet must have caught it when Noah had fired into the group earlier.

Scott glanced through the doors where Noah had vanished. The corridor was empty, deserted. Leaning to his right, he picked up the bolt cutters and tested their weight.

There was power in the seemingly innocent tool. They possessed something that could make him a hero or a villain. He could perform heroics in a two-fold scenario. He could snip the chain off the doors and free the assembly hall occupants. If Noah came back, he could club him over the head with his new heavy weapon.

Or he could leave them where they were and continue to follow Noah on his strange, seemingly disorganised journey through the labyrinth of Farenden.

He stared once more into the hall, thinking about it. Matty Cranshaw was watching him, his face white. He looked half furious, half scared.

Scott raised his chin.

'Now you see me,' he said, more to himself than to Matty.

He propped the bolt cutters up against the glass and hurried out of the door that Noah had left by.

29

Sara
Before

Murmurs, growing in volume, and a sense of unease rippled through the crowd.

Sara, who had kept her head down since the altercation with Kathy Driver, looked up reluctantly. Scared of what she might see, of what this new, fresh atmosphere meant. The crowd surged forward, blocking her view.

Unsteadily, Sara stood up.

An angry shout, and she drew in her breath shakily.

What was it? Body bags? Walking wounded?

She pushed her elbows out and made her way through the throng. Finally, on the front line, she felt herself deflate.

It was just Jojo, coming back towards the school, flanked by two police officers.

Beside him, a young adult skipped along backwards, his head bent close to Jojo's. The youth jogged over towards the gates where Sara was, his face flushed with the excitement of breaking news.

'Jojo confronted the Millers. Apparently they were just sitting in the hall, they weren't being questioned or anything! Jojo threw a punch, and now *he's* been arrested!'

He had indeed, saw Sara now, as the officers paused by one of the police vehicles and steadied him against it. Jojo's face was fear intensified. Yet another expression she'd never seen from him. Using her elbows as weapons once more, she hurried over to him.

'You can't *arrest* him!' she said. 'His son is in there.' She jerked her head towards the school, heat in her face, fury and anger boiling inside her to simmer alongside helplessness. It wasn't a heroic move on her part; more that if they took Jojo away, she would be totally and utterly alone.

One of the officers, the younger of the two, faltered. Sara saw it, grabbed onto it. 'Please,' she begged. 'We... we need to stick together, all of us. We need each other.'

The officer looked to his superior. Sara looked at Jojo, who said nothing.

She understood. He would beg nobody for anything, except maybe the gunman inside for the life of his son. There it would end. He had too much pride to plead the way she was doing now. After all, with all his suspicions back then, he'd never begged her either.

'You've got better things to be doing, lads,' said Jojo finally. He held up his hands, which Sara now saw were cuffed.

She averted her eyes as the officer took out a small key and released him. 'Stay here, and no talking to anyone. Like you said yourself, we've got enough to deal with.'

They drifted away, not far, just to stand by the gates, their hands resting on their radios, which were disturbingly silent. Or maybe it was a good thing, thought Sara as she watched them. No news was good news.

'What happened?' she asked Jojo. 'What did you find out?'

He clenched his fists and rubbed at the place where the handcuffs had been. 'They were just *sitting* there, just like everyone else, all the other normal people, like they were the same, like they're like us!' He hissed out his words, reminding Sara of herself moments earlier with Kathy.

'They told me fuck all,' he continued. 'The kid's dad, he just sat there, wouldn't even look at me. The ma's crying, pleading, "Not my boy, not my boy."' He broke off and rubbed his palm across his face. 'Maybe it's not their boy. What do we actually know?'

'But... but the WhatsApp, it said his name, didn't it?' Sara glanced at her phone, glued to her sticky hands now, but Jojo was right. What did *she* actually know? She wasn't on the WhatsApp group, was she?

'That kid over there,' she pointed to the youth who seemed to have declared himself the news broadcaster to those at the gates, 'he said you punched Mr Miller?'

'I'm not proud of it.' Jojo took a deep breath, his mouth settling into a tight, pinched line. 'But I'm not sorry either.'

Later, she would always think of that moment as the first lightning strike. The words spoken, the expression, the mannerisms, the folding of the arms and the grim, stony face.

It spoke volumes, more than any DNA test could ever do.

She couldn't look at him for one second longer. Even though minutes ago she had pleaded for him to be allowed to stay, she had to get away.

'Sara!' Her name cut through the crowd, the voice authoritative and in control.

Sara turned. For the first time ever, she was thankful to see her mother, winding her way through the clusters of people towards her.

Mary Carter stood out among the others. The mothers and fathers, the grandparents and friends and aunts and uncles had left their houses in whatever state they'd been in when they heard the news. Pyjama bottoms, bare feet, suit trousers along with hastily pulled-on trainers. The hair of some of the older women still in rollers, men with half-shaved faces. Mary Carter would never be seen like that, no matter what the emergency.

It wasn't just that she was dressed, thought Sara as she approached; she was perfectly coiffed, not a hair out of place. Even Sara, who had been out and about in a respectable manner, now felt hot, sweaty, dishevelled and dirty.

If Mary stayed for longer than half an hour, perhaps she might fit in.

Sara stifled a giggle that she recognised as bordering on hysteria.

'What do you know?' Mary asked as she reached her.

Sara felt herself moulding, folding and relaxing, ready to be drawn into her mother's arms. As if sensing this anomaly, Mary put one arm out and gripped her shoulder. The outstretched arm locked, holding Sara a good foot away from her body.

Sara blinked and attempted to recalibrate herself.

'Nothing,' she said, 'not yet.'

Mary shook her head and clicked her tongue. 'Well, what have you *heard*?' she asked.

'Two boys, guns that one of them took from his father. Mrs Fleecy has been killed.' Three pieces of information, the echo of them resounding back at her, filling her mouth with bile. Desperately, unconsciously, she searched around for something better, something heartening to share. 'Ryan's okay right now, he's staying safe.'

'And Scott?'

Sara glanced at the phone, the screen smudged and slick with sweat. 'Nothing yet.'

'When did you last try him?' Mary asked.

Sara drew a breath. Why did her mother's questions seem so forceful? And what was the answer? Minutes ago, hours, never? While she scrambled around for something to say, Mary tutted again and pulled out her own phone.

Sara glanced over her mother's shoulder. Jojo was still standing by the police car. He shaded his eyes and tilted his head at her.

Sara sent him a silent message. *Stay there, don't come over.*

'No answer,' announced Mary. 'I'll try again.'

Sara shook her head, frustration tipping the balance from the uselessness she always felt around her mother. 'He won't answer; the phone isn't even switched on.'

Mary paused mid-dial, glancing to her right. Sara followed her gaze, saw that Jojo had pushed himself off the car, was heading their way.

'Christ,' she muttered. Cornered, trapped now. Was this how the students in the school felt? Were the two-or-more boys doing just this to them? Stalking their prey, grouping them in, the net closing until it was smaller, smaller, too small.

'Ugh.' Mary slipped her phone in her bag and clamped a hand to the nape of Sara's neck. 'That's the last thing you need. Come on.'

Sara allowed herself to be led away from Jojo's approach, ending up back at the low wall she'd been sitting on earlier. In what felt like a state of shock, she managed to disengage her mother's heavy hand from her spine.

'Wait, what… what are you doing?'

'People talk, people listen, people watch,' said Mary out of the corner of her mouth. 'This isn't the time or the place for that.'

Confused, Sara looked back towards the gates. Jojo had turned, blended back into the crowd. 'What… what are you *talking* about?'

Mary lowered her head and spoke into the collar of her expensive coat. 'It took years for all that to be forgotten; don't go giving it cause to rear its ugly head again. Not here, not today.'

Sara fell back to sit on the wall. Her *mother* knew. Her mother knew about Jojo, about the affair?

'You… you…' *You knew?* she wanted to say, but it would validate it, confirm it, and she didn't want to do that. Couldn't admit it, not even to herself, really. 'You heard that rumour?' she managed eventually.

Mary laughed, a tinkling sound so out of keeping with the shrouded atmosphere of misery that Sara winced.

'Silly girl' were the words she said. *Everybody knew* were the words she mercifully didn't say but actually meant.

A thought, horrifying and heartbreaking, one that Sara voiced without thinking. 'Did Mack—'

'No! Goodness. Now, let me try Scott again.'

Irritation now, but from experience Sara knew it would soon be replaced by a bone-tired weariness. Thus was the cycle of any time spent with Mary.

'He won't answer, his phone is switched—'

Mary, phone clamped to her ear, held up her hand to silence her daughter. 'Scott, darling,' she said, 'it's Nanny. Are you okay?'

Travis
Now

Travis had been shocked but happy when Sara appeared at the non-border of his home. Although happy didn't really cut it. He was ecstatic, filled with joy that only trebled when he thought of how he had witnessed her when she'd been in the city.

She looked cautious and nervous and he'd offered her a ginger beer, which had been stupid, juvenile. Why couldn't he ever get it quite right? He had retreated inside for the harder stuff, reaching for the Bacardi, hoping fervently it would do. He would make it fancy, he decided, with a mixer, some ice. Perhaps a glacé cherry or a slice of lemon. There was a jar of olives in the back of the cupboard, a leftover from his last date, a woman working temporarily at the Centre. By the way she dressed and spoke, he'd suspected she was the sort of woman who enjoyed the tasteless, soulless snack.

The jar hadn't been opened. She'd never made it as far as his cabin in the woods.

He stood on tiptoe, his bruised and bloodied feet protesting against the motion.

He looked down at them, wondering if Sara had noticed, hoping against hope that she hadn't.

It was the downward glance that led to the discovery. It put him off balance, his thighs jostling the desk. The mouse sprang into life, the computer screen lit up, the names of all those victims blazed out at him.

One more prominent than the others. Buried in among the Nicoles and the Iozifs and the Chloes.

Ryan.

He glanced outside, saw Sara and Scott together. He had time.

He pulled out his chair and slipped into it, speed-reading now. It surely wasn't Sara's son. Ryan was a common name; out of a school of however-many-hundred were at Farenden, there would likely be two, three – a dozen Ryans.

Ryan Fuller.

The kid's name was Ryan Fuller.

He breathed out – Fuller wasn't Sara and Scott's name – exhaling air he didn't know he had been holding, and carried on reading further down the article.

Ryan is survived by his older brother, Scott, and their mother, Sara. In a twist of awful fate, the Fuller brothers also lost their father, Mack, a few years…

His hand shot out and switched off the computer screen. He didn't need any more information.

His excitement grew. He'd been right. This family needed saving, rescuing, *healing*.

The Bacardi bottle sat to his right, beside the treacherous computer mouse. He unscrewed the cap, swigged straight from the bottle and put it back, gasping.

The Doyles had come to the right place. Travis could help them.

There was so much to fathom here. Ryan had been a victim, yet both Scott and Sara spoke as though he was still alive. *Was* he still alive? Had the newspaper article been wrong?

He looked out of the window again; mother and son were still standing close together. Scott looked… well, almost happy, something close to animated as he spoke to his mother.

Travis blinked and the vision in front of him shifted.

The smile on Scott's face was gone. Sara had a hold of him now. Through the open door he heard her words: 'What did you *do*?'

Scott's voice in reply, shrill and unhappy: 'I rescued him!'

Him. They were talking about Travis, about the earlier part of the day, the bit that he hadn't even attempted to unravel yet. How sinister it had seemed at the time. How he was sure he was going to meet his death in that cave.

Scott's words were true. He *had* rescued Travis. But only after he'd lured him down there in the first place.

Lured.

It was a strange turn of events. It was Travis who usually lured people – women – mostly unsuccessfully, to his forest haven.

Taking a deep breath to gather himself, he pulled his boots on and went back outside.

'Scott said he rescued you,' Sara said, accepting the drink that he handed her.

He paused before answering. Something fizzed between the two people in front of him; a sorrowful atmosphere hung in the air. It sparked something inside Travis. He needed to play this right.

'That's right,' he said, 'I… I got trapped in a pit cave.'

Was it his imagination, or did Scott throw him a grateful look, before the lad wandered back to the ever-smoking barbecue?

Sara raised her eyes at him, as though not at all surprised that he'd got himself into a pickle in a cave. He wanted to tell her then, about his survival techniques, places he'd been, things he'd witnessed, so he didn't come across as such a dork. She had no idea of how brilliant he was, in so many ways.

She looked confused now, and he realised she probably had no idea what the pit caves were.

He told her, trying not to show his irritation about the fact that she clearly wasn't listening, a little concerned by the way she gulped the Bacardi. He held the bottle in his hands, watching as she eyed it greedily. He topped up her glass.

Sara's inhibitions would be lowered, and that could lead to all sorts of things. With this thought swirling around his already churning mind, he handed her the bottle and led her to the table.

There was no talk, no chatter, just the draining of the bottle. It went down at such an alarming rate, Travis knew he had to step in.

Lack of inhibitions was good, but complete inebriation would mean the entire day had been a waste. After all, he couldn't make love to her if she were unconscious.

Could he?

He swiped at his face, sure that his thoughts were readable there, and was about to offer to pop to the shop to pick up another bottle of something when he noticed her eyes were closed.

He looked at Scott, still seated on the bench opposite his mother, looking out across the grass towards the trees. The boy's feet tapped on the decking.

For once, Travis could think of nothing to say.

Scott got up and moved quietly to the edge of the trees. Gently, so as not to wake Sara, Travis stacked the plates, grateful at least that the food had been eaten.

As he crept past her into the cabin, she slept on.

He abandoned the plates by the sink. He didn't own a dishwasher. He didn't want one, either. One of the pleasures of his day was standing at the sink, watching the sun set, humming a tune while he rinsed the plates by hand.

Tonight, although it was a truly wonderful sunset, all he could watch out of the window was Sara.

He brewed coffee, his gaze travelling to her unmoving form, to that of her son. Scott was by the trees still, but further into the woods.

Twilight was fast approaching. For a newbie, the forest wasn't the place to be in the dark. The pit cave entrances were concealed; it was easy to stumble into one. He should warn the boy, really. But he wouldn't.

He poured the coffee into the jug, put two mugs on a tray. No milk, no sugar. A small bottle of brandy sat at the back of the cupboard, and after a moment's thought, he added it to the tray. A little snifter. Keep the party going.

He carried the tray outside, pausing on the threshold to watch her.

Sleep brought her no peace, he noticed as he looked at her in her slumber. Her mouth was downturned, her eyelids twitching as though experiencing some fast-paced dream.

Or a nightmare.

Or more likely a memory.

He walked to the table, deliberately making his footsteps heard.

'Coffee,' he announced. He tried for a smile, smooth, moving proceedings along, but it wasn't as polished as normal.

She caught it, the change in him. He knew it, and he also saw now that she hadn't been sleeping at all.

It felt wrong to shy away from his new-found knowledge. As a therapist, as a friend, as a potential... something.

He was in charge here. He was in control. Both things she needed, both natural for him.

He glanced to the trees that bordered the forest. There was no sign of Scott any longer. He scanned the horizon for the boy, and without looking at Sara, he said, 'I'm so sorry about your son. I really am sorry.'

He slipped into the seat opposite her that had been vacated by Scott.

She reached her hand across the table, not for him, not even for the coffee, but for the brandy bottle.

Unscrewing the cap, she drank from it, before placing it back on the table.

It was okay, he told himself. One day she would depend on him rather than the alcohol. In the meantime, he could let her little flaws go.

'You're sorry, yeah?' she said, her words quiet but loaded. Finally, she raised her eyes to meet his. 'Which son are you sorry about?'

31

Travis
Now

She was belligerent and full of attitude. Just like some of his students. Again, he let that slide, because things were moving along, and one day in the not-too-distant future she would be grateful and beholden.

'I'm sorry about Ryan, and I'm sorry for the impact it must have had on Scott,' he said. He was pleased at how steady his voice sounded, and he pressed on. 'You had already lost your husband when you... when it happened?'

She nodded and crossed her arms across her chest.

She is so closed off, thought Travis. A family of four shot down – literally in one case – to just two people. And nobody to talk to about it. Nobody to vent to, or to cry on. Nobody to even just hold her in a simple embrace.

But where was everybody? Nobody reached middle age without storing at least a small collection of friends and relatives for support.

You've not got anyone, the voice he tried not to listen to piped up.

Shut up, he told it.

He focused back on Sara and narrowed his eyes. Travis saw the parents at the Centre. Strangers on the first day, bosom buddies by the time school was out that very night. Even the ones he deemed unlikeable. They simply sought out similar personalities.

And Sara was very definitely not unlikeable. She was beautiful, without being over the top.

'Would you tell me about Ryan?' he asked.

It was a risky question. She was so obviously teetering on the edge of a precipice. It might be too soon. However, Travis liked to think he was good at gauging people, and he would bet Sara hadn't spoken about her dead son to anyone for a very long time.

She sipped her coffee. He breathed out, congratulating himself on his clever manoeuvre. She needed him; the fact that she hadn't thrown the drink over him for having the audacity to probe where nobody else had proved that he was right.

'Oh, Travis…'

He stilled. His name on her lips… it was magical, remarkable. He blinked very slowly, and for a second, they were in his bed, and she was saying his name just like that. *Oh, Travis.*

'He was… brilliant.'

Trying not to feel disappointed as her words disrupted his dreams, he leaned back against the railing of the porch and assumed his friendly therapist expression.

'I can tell, just by the look on your face.' He smiled gently. 'What did he enjoy? What were his hobbies?'

Sara shook her head and laughed. An actual laugh, not a drunken one, nor one that would dissolve into sobs. A real laugh.

'Everything! He was brilliant at everything. Football, school, karate, cricket. Languages, even. He'd been learning French, was picking it up like he was a natural.'

She shook her head, lost in the wonder of him. 'Don't know how. Mack and I could barely manage the Queen's English.'

Don't do that, he wanted to say to her. *Don't put yourself down. You created this boy you speak so lovingly about. You had a hand in all his achievements.*

But therapists never told people what they should say, or how they should think. They simply stored away the little tics and nuances so they could manipulate their thoughts on the patient later, using them as a knowledge guide.

'He was brave, too,' Sara said. She leaned towards him, as if confiding in him. 'That day, he saved a girl. A fellow student. He got her out, he… he saved her. He saved her instead of himself.'

In the ten seconds it took for her to say the sentence, her demeanour changed. She'd been proud of the hero he had been, the selflessness he'd shown. By the time she'd finished speaking, though, her mouth was twisted.

'Sometimes I *hate* her.'

She picked up the Bacardi bottle, slammed it down again when she realised it was empty and made a grab for the brandy.

'Why didn't he save himself? Why did he have to be the hero?' She was mournful now, the glitter in her eye drowned in an instant as she plummeted back to her normal cloak of despair. Even her anger at the injustice of the girl who had lived instead of her son had vanished. She was back to… Sara. Quiet, closeted, closed off.

'It's who he was. Some people are just born kind and good. Or it's an instinct. To help, to protect. For some people it's natural. Your son was a hero, Sara. Hold on to that.'

'Do you want to sleep with me?'

The question made no sense for a long, long moment. Travis remained motionless, replaying it. Had he misheard? It sounded like she'd just offered herself up on a platter to him. What if he had heard wrong, what if she'd said something else, and his teenage-horny middle-aged brain had turned her words into what he *wished* she would ask?

'What?' he asked, stupidly.

He was slightly irritated, because it should have been *him* leading *her*, offering comfort and a pair of strong, loving arms. But at the end of the day, it *was* the endgame. Did it really matter the journey it took to get her from porch to bedroom?

'I would, very much.'

There were no more words, only a silent acceptance on both sides.

He couldn't let her lead, though. There had to be a semblance of control, of being in charge. So he took her hand and guided her inside.

She removed her clothes, in much the same mechanical manner that she'd eaten her dinner, he realised. Had he been someone else, any other man, she would have done the same thing. Tonight, it didn't matter to her who he was.

It was okay, though. He understood that her need wasn't due to an overwhelming attraction she had for him. She sought comfort, the closeness of a body. For this night, she was looking to forget.

He could handle that. Sometimes love bloomed slowly, especially in those who had suffered.

It was hard and fast. At first he held her like she was a precious thing, to be handled with care, before it became clear to him that that was not what she desired. She urged him on not with words, but with motions, hands, legs and nails. He altered his stance, closed his eyes and pretended to be someone he wasn't in order to fulfil her needs.

Later, she slept deeply. He knelt on the bed and peered at her face. She looked peaceful for the first time since he'd known her, and he smiled, pleased with his work.

Now it was done, his thoughts were back. Haywire and tangling in his mind. The worries returned too, along with the discoveries he hadn't even started to process.

Leaving his boots where he'd kicked them off in the kitchen area, he left the cabin barefoot and made his way to the road.

The lane was in darkness, no street lights here, and he didn't have to venture far along the hill to see the glow of a single light in what he presumed was Scott's room in the cabin he shared with Sara.

He let his mind wander. What if there hadn't been a light on, or if there wasn't a son left for her? If it had been Scott stranded in the pit cave, rather than himself? Just the two of them left, Travis and Sara. She really would lean on him in that scenario.

Silently, as stealthy as a fox stalking a rabbit, he made his way back through the trees. In comparison to Sara's small home, his own cabin blazed with lights. The porch glowed, the kitchen area, the whole house. How Sara could sleep with all the lights on was beyond him.

The Bacardi might have helped, and the brandy, alongside anything else she'd taken before she arrived for the barbecue. The coffee, he noticed as he stepped up onto the porch, had gone mostly untouched.

It was okay. A dependency on something made her pliable, easier to mould.

Moving back into the cabin, he switched the porch lights off, and the ones that lit the kitchen. As he closed the door onto the forest, he pulled off his shirt. Hope sprang within him that she would wake up – if not straight away, then later, early in the morning – and want him again.

He paused, his back still to the room, wondering if he should shower. After all, he'd been in the cave, covered with mud and silt; the smoke of both the fire Scott had set and the subsequent barbecue clung to his clothes, hair and skin. His foot was still crusted with blood. After the cave, when he'd been sitting at the computer, discovering that the son he'd expected to show up today was actually dead, he'd sweated profusely.

He wrinkled his nose. Decided a shower wasn't a bad idea at all.

Desire curled up inside him, a half-thought that if Sara heard the running water, she might be inclined to come and join him in the shower.

He felt his own smile and looked over at the bed.

He stopped, in the act of unbuckling his belt.

The bed was empty.

Sara had gone.

32

Scott

Before

'Who else is doing this?'

Scott came across Noah at the far end of the hall, outside the science labs. The boy in the trench coat was motionless, staring at nothing on a wall in front of him. In his fingers, a hand-rolled cigarette burned down; a teetering line of ash threatened to drop to the scuff-marked floor.

Noah's head jerked up at the sound of Scott's voice. 'I told you to wait,' he said, but he didn't seem overly annoyed.

Not mad enough to raise his right hand, which still held the silver gun, and aim it at Scott.

It made him braver. Or perhaps the dawning know-ledge that Noah now saw him as being on his team lent him the edge he needed to form words and questions.

'Nobody you need to worry about. You'll know what you need to know.' Noah's tone was placid and cool, something to it that troubled Scott.

It hit him before the thought was even fully formed.

Noah's anger was missing. Everything had been done with a calmness that was unnerving. Matty Cranshaw back in the main hall had looked ten times angrier than Noah had during this whole situation.

There had been one instant, when he had returned to the classroom, entering by smashing the door open with his boot. There had been violence in that kick, but nothing before, or since.

Where to now? It was another question Scott wanted to ask, but the words wouldn't form. There was still ground to cover. Ryan was somewhere in here. And Scott wanted to find him.

He looked longingly at the black gun that poked out of the waistband of Noah's trousers.

Noah opened his fingers. The cigarette butt fell to the floor. He crushed it underfoot. His hands went to the straps of a rucksack that wasn't there, patting his shoulders, an almost comical look on his face as he realised its absence.

'Shit,' he swore softly. 'Back that way.'

He moved past Scott, heading back to the chained door that held their classmates captive.

'Wait,' called Scott. 'Do we—'

He never got to finish his sentence. Noise, like that when the headline act appears on the main stage at a concert. A collective roar, feet stamping, bodies colliding. Through the glass of the doors ahead of them, they saw the source of the racket, as the crowd of kids and teachers stormed out of the hall and down the opposite hallway.

'Shit!' said Noah again.

There was still no anger. No excitement like he'd shown earlier, when he herded them from the classroom to the assembly hall. This tone, this expression, was fear.

Nobody looked their way as they streamed out of the hall. It was impossible to distinguish between teachers and students. Nobody helped anybody else. Everybody simply ran.

A few girls at the tail end of the crowd screamed, high-pitched, as though they were going to be left behind, as though they were vulnerable on the fringe. Which they were, Scott saw now.

Noah, blind to the glass and the door that acted as a barrier between him and them, raised the silver gun. From his left side he did a quick draw, doubly armed now, a gunslinger with both hands raised as he pulled the triggers again and again and again.

The glass shattered and rained down upon those fleeing the corridor. The screams multiplied in volume and number. Not just girls, Scott saw, boys too, and the adults, their arms instinctively circling their heads against the unknown direction of the guns.

The anger came to Noah now, finally; it was almost a relief to Scott that he possessed the emotion. He didn't know why he found it a comfort, but he did.

As Noah kicked open the door and marched after the retreating group, Scott felt a vibration in his back pocket.

He pulled the phone out, couldn't remember switching it on. It had been turned off since he entered the school gates that morning. He never had it on in school. He wasn't part of any chat groups or collective message sites like the other kids.

His finger hovered over the red button, fully expecting to see his mother's name on the screen. He hesitated, took one last glance at Noah, almost invisible now so far had he travelled down the hallway, then swiped to accept the call.

'Nan?' he said, tentatively.

Her voice, soothing, like it always was, echoed in the hallway. Scott made to switch it off speaker, but changed his mind when he saw that Noah had vanished entirely from view. He felt his lips twitch. His nan loved him, always had. Sure, she loved Ryan too, but it was as though she sensed the disconnect his own mother had for him and did her best to make up for it.

On the other end of the phone, he heard a gasp, a scuffle, and his mother's voice, 'Give it to me!' Then she was there, sounding breathless, asking if he was okay, acting as if she cared.

He wanted her to put his nan back on the phone, but there was a disconnect in *that* relationship too, one that had been there for as long as he could remember.

'Yeah,' he said, in answer to her question.

Then she was off. Talking about his brother, as usual. *Ryan, Ryan, Ryan.*

Her voice was urgent, echoing around the otherwise deserted hallway. 'Your brother is in the science lab, in a stock cupboard, he's with…'

Scott stopped listening. Noah had reappeared at the end of the hallway. Scott's breath caught in his throat. Standing there in the leather coat, the guns hanging casually out of his pockets, Noah didn't look like a boy any longer.

He looked like a man.

Scott breathed into the mobile. 'Gotta go,' he said. He cut the call and slipped the phone back into his pocket.

'Come on.' Noah walked. Scott followed.

He thought about Emily, the first one to escape, the one he'd led to safety. Had she told anyone yet? Had she proclaimed him as her hero?

'Who was that calling you?' Noah asked suddenly.

Scott, walking a couple of steps behind him, dragged his feet. 'My nan,' he said, 'and my mum.'

Noah glanced over his shoulder and grinned. 'What did they say? What did they ask you?'

Scott shrugged. 'Just if I was okay.'

'She was talking about your brother, right?'

Scott didn't want to answer, wondered if he could get away with saying nothing, but Noah had stopped walking, and stood, arms crossed over his chest, head cocked to one side.

'They always ask about him, right?' he said.

Scott scuffed his shoe on the floor. 'Yeah, sometimes.'

Noah moved, faster than lightning. Scott flinched at the speed of his approach. Noah's arms were on him now, his hand around the back of Scott's neck.

Scott gasped, struggled once, and then stayed dead still as he felt something cold on his collarbone.

Not the guns; from the angle he hung his head, he could see they were both still in Noah's pockets. A blade, then. He remembered the knives that had been in the rucksack.

'Do you wanna change that? Do you wanna do something about it?'

He knew what Noah was asking him. With the cold metal on his throat and Noah's hand on his neck, he felt it. The intensity coming from the boy in front of him spelled it out for him.

Noah wasn't planning on getting out of this.

The knife shifted an inch. Scott raised his eyes to lock onto Noah's gaze.

'I'm in,' he said. 'I'm with you.'

The pressure of the blade lessened, then vanished altogether.

Noah grinned. 'The science lab, right?' He tilted his head, rested his hands on the handles of his guns. 'What're we waiting for?'

33

Sara

Now

She hadn't expected an escape route. She'd thought –
hoped – that like most men, Travis would fall into a deep
sleep afterwards and she would be able to slip from the bed
and retreat to her cabin. She had anticipated a struggle,
either that Travis wouldn't *let* her leave, or that he would
be clingy and cuddly, smothering her with his afterglow
of love. She wasn't sure which one would be worse.

She had been surprised when he hadn't even stayed
with her. Rather, he'd been up and off and out.

She didn't question why, didn't allow for any insecur-
ities to rest upon her. She didn't much care if he'd enjoyed
it or not, though she was pretty sure it was the best thing
to happen to him in a long time. He had that look about
him. One that Mack had once worn, one that showed in
Jojo's eyes whenever he had looked at her.

Not at the end, though, not with Jojo.

It hadn't been about that. It hadn't even been to get
her own satisfaction, like she'd mused on. No, this was all
for Scott. If Travis thought there was something between
her and him, he would be more inclined to help her boy.

Sara shivered as she groped around for her clothes, the Bacardi taste in her mouth threatening to overspill as she recalled the past against her will.

Three days was all it had been since their lives were changed forever. Just seventy-two hours since one boy had come out of the school instead of the three that Jojo and Sara had prayed for. She was barely focused, hardly able to get out of bed. Showering and personal care were a thing of the past. Her mother had gone home, finally, but would no doubt return.

And here was Jojo, on her doorstep when she'd opened the door to his gentle knock.

She couldn't look at him. The man who was the catch of the city, friendly, with a wicked sense of humour. Gentle yet firm, kind, gorgeous.

All gone.

The man in front of her was smaller, somehow. His eyes were red-rimmed, his skin ashen. Three days of stubble at least hid the downward drag of his mouth somewhat.

'I… I want to see him,' he'd said; no greeting, no hug that said he knew what she was going through.

Her heart hammered. Even through the haze of medication, she knew who he was talking about.

Scott.

Why now? All these years later, all those rumours that had abounded, whispered from the lips of Kathy Driver. It had been strange, so typically British. Everyone seemed to know, but nobody talked openly about it. Sara's biggest fear had been that one day these horrible mothers would shout it out to the whole world, breaking the unspoken code. Those who needed not to know would know. Mack, Scott, Ryan.

It was the reason she made no friends. It was the reason she stayed away from the school gates.

Oh, the shame…

The usual panic that had been there for fifteen years pounced before dying.

This time, she thought about it. As much as she could, deep in her well of grief. Mack was gone, he couldn't be hurt by the rumours. Scott no longer had a father. Jojo no longer had a son. She, Sara, had nothing and nobody.

It had been to protect Mack, at first, when he was still alive. She was pretty certain that the extra years he had miraculously lived had been down to Scott. At first, he'd given himself the task of surviving to see the birth of his child. When that happened, he moved the goalposts.

I want to see him take his first steps.

I want to see him say his first words.

I want to see his first day at primary school.

He smashed every target. And while the rumours circulated at the school gates, there seemed to be that unspoken rule.

Mack must not know.

And hats off to those wicked, nasty women. None of them ever told him. Not even Kathy, the worst witch of all.

But Mack had finally given in to the assault on his body. Tragedy had now hit the wider community. Would the Kathys of Farenden say anything if Jojo stepped up?

She'd seen them, on the couple of occasions her mother had coerced her out of the house since the massacre. Their eyes were as glazed as hers were.

Almost as if the rush of thoughts was too much, Sara had sagged against the door, using it to prop herself up.

'I'll think about it,' she managed. 'Just… don't rush me, don't rush us.'

It had seemed enough at the time, the hint of something for him to hold on to. Something that could help *her*, even. Maybe, handled correctly, these fractured people coming together to make a whole would help Scott.

Because so far, he'd said *nothing*. Not to her, not to his grandmother, not even to the police, who had insisted on 'carefully and sensitively' questioning all the survivors before the bodies of the dead were even cold.

He'd mentioned nothing about that day, nor what he had witnessed.

Time… time… time. It was a healer. Or so they all said.

She'd closed the door on Jojo, something passing between them in that last glance: that maybe, one day, things could be something nearer to normal for all of them.

But time had moved fast.

The very next day, Sara had managed to do something so far the police had been unable to.

She had found out the identity of the second shooter.

And twelve hours after bidding goodbye to Jojo, she and Scott had packed up their home and left for good.

Now, in the home of a man who was practically a stranger, things were starting to crack.

Not just starting, she corrected herself mentally. They had been fractured for a year; even more, if she were honest. But now more people were inserting themselves into her and Scott's life.

And that was dangerous.

She cursed as she pulled her shoes on, shoved her hair underneath the baseball cap and let herself out of the cabin.

A light breeze stirred, the leaves in the trees rippled. Knowledge, as clear as day, hit her with a thousand tiny pellets.

She had to speak to Scott. She had to *listen* to Scott.

She shuddered, buttoning up her shirt with fumbling fingers. From her right, near the track that led to her home, she heard a twig breaking.

Travis was coming back.

She ducked her head, moved around the cabin to the far end. She waited until the porch lights went out, followed by the kitchen ones, then doubled back on herself, keeping low, biting her lip as the memory came back to her of the kids streaming out of the school, bent almost in two, as though by making themselves half the size, they could dodge the bullets that would inevitably follow them.

At the curtainless window, she paused; then, reaching to grasp the windowsill, she peered into the room.

Travis's cabin was open plan. She couldn't imagine it, living in a home without rooms to shut yourself up in when the pressure of life and people got too much.

He was standing with his back to her, all lights out now, his silhouette seeming small in the darkness of the room. He was staring at the bed, she knew.

She sighed, lowered herself down to land soundlessly upon the ground, and turned away.

On the road, she breathed a little easier. Her cottage was in view, and she stepped up her pace. Scott's bedroom light was on. She faltered, stopping at the gate.

What did he do up there? There were no books, no DVDs or video games. He had no mobile phone or iPad or any of the other gadgets she saw clutched in the hands of the kids at the Centre.

'Scott…' She breathed his name in the moonlight and remembered her earlier thoughts of talking to him, listening to him.

She passed the white rose bush, plucked a bloom from it as was her habit. For the first time, however, she didn't drop it to the path and crush it underfoot. Instead, she carried it into the house, holding it as though it were a precious thing, the way she'd held Ryan when he was born.

The way she'd never held Scott.

34

Sara

Before

Her first thought was that it was a trick. Or no, not a trick, just a calming technique her mother was using to get her to chill out over not being able to reach Scott herself.

But that made no sense either. She hadn't been hysterical, not like some of the other mothers, not over Scott, not even over Ryan, not really. She had been stressed and worried and fraught, but none of that had shown, either in her actions or her words.

It must be true, then. Mary must have reached Scott.

She lurched forward, losing the robotic stance. 'Give it to me!' she gasped, misjudging the distance and knocking her mother off the kerb into the road.

A tut from Mary, but she gave the phone over willingly.

'Scott?' Sara shouted down the phone. 'Are you all right?'

A long silence, so long that she thought maybe it was a trick after all. Then she heard the breathing from the other end.

'Yeah,' he said.

Yeah. Just like that. As though the school wasn't the site of a massacre. As though it wasn't as bad as a war zone. As though people hadn't been *killed* in there.

'Have you seen your brother?' she asked, for want of anything better to say.

It didn't escape her, the autopilot that had kicked in when she'd spoken to Ryan. Ascertain his location and the fact that he was safe. Stress the importance of keeping hidden. Guilt rose in her now. She had her elder son on the phone and all she could say was his brother's name.

'He's in the science lab, in a stock cupboard with a couple of other boys,' she said. Her intention was to tell him to get to where Ryan was, to hole up together, along with Jaden, because wouldn't it be a win if the three boys came out alive and unharmed?

'Gotta go.' His voice, always small, suddenly seemed even quieter.

Before she could speak, she knew he had hung up.

'Excuse me.' A small voice by her side brought her back to the present.

She let Mary take the phone back and looked to her right. A young girl, a stunningly pretty little thing. The kind of girl who would waltz through life. The thought was sudden, biting in its bitterness.

'I just got out, a little while ago.' The girl spoke breathlessly, her small white hands fluttering around her neck. In her fingers she twisted a slim gold chain, straining the necklace until Sara worried it would break in her grip.

Everything is so fragile, she thought.

'I'm Emily, I was… He had me, held me by my neck.' Her eyes widened as though she was reliving the horror. Sara's heart dipped in her chest as tears spilled from the girl's clear blue eyes.

Another presence, the girl's mother, hustling through the group that Sara now saw surrounded her and Emily. She didn't know the woman, nor this Emily, but she watched the mother, intrigued, as she circled her daughter with her arms and crushed her to her chest. A protective measure, as well as a need to touch the girl, make sure she was real, not an apparition, dreamed up by witnessing the terror of the other parents, their arms aching and empty.

'Come on, home now.' The mother's voice was throaty, her eyes darting left and right and behind her, as if the perpetrator of this crime was going to spring up and snatch Emily away.

Sara understood. If her boys came back, she would spirit them home, lock the doors behind her and close the curtains. They wouldn't be going anywhere again, not on their own. No parks or cinema trips with their friends. No parties unless they were under her roof, the guests carefully researched and authorised by her.

It was an absurd thought, but one that made sense.

They began to move away, Emily openly crying now, her mother herding and rushing her.

Sara blinked after them, and then, just as they were almost at the road, the girl broke free and made her way back.

'I wanted to tell you, I had to say in case...' She swallowed, clearly imagining all sorts of worst-case scenarios, obviously knowing that she was one of the lucky ones. 'Your son saved my life.'

'Oh!' Sara cried. Tears sprang to her previously dry eyes.

Emily's mother was back, pulling at the girl's arm. Sara wanted to bat her away. Instead, she went into a crouch and touched Emily's hand. 'Did he? My son... helped you?'

Emily nodded eagerly. 'We had no way of escaping, then it was just the two of us, and there was this window, like, really high up. He helped me climb up to it, and, like, he pushed me through it.' At this point, she held up her hands. Scratches criss-crossed her palms, grit engrained in them, as if to prove her story. 'He told me to run, and not to look back.'

Sara swayed, her knees weak. A strong hand clamped her shoulder. She didn't need to look up. She'd know that touch anywhere. Jojo was back. But the thought of him and her mother in such close proximity meant nothing now. All she wanted to do was drink in this girl in front of her, the one her son had saved.

'He was so brave,' said Emily.

Was. The past tense hit Sara hard, and what had felt momentarily like euphoria drowned in something dark and nasty. She stood up, helped by Jojo, as the mother won and Emily let herself be pulled away.

'He should have looked after himself,' she said to nobody. Even in these circumstances the words sounded terrible, and she tried to fight the feeling. 'He saved her life,' she said. She needed it validated, heard, and she shook off Jojo's hand and turned to her mother. 'Did you hear her? Ryan saved that girl's life.'

'Jesus H Christ, will you look at that?' Jojo's Irish accent, which thickened at times of high excitement or anger, lent a pitch to his voice. 'Look, do you see now?'

Sara turned to where he pointed. The main body of the school, a hundred metres away; the entrance doors, previously closed, were being pushed open.

'Oh!' she cried. 'Who is it?'

Even as she spoke, she knew the chances of it being her boys, or even Jojo's, were minimal. Three kids out of hundreds. What would the odds be?

'They're stuck!' Jojo surged forward along with the rest of the group that had congregated outside the gates. 'The doors won't open!'

He was right. The double doors, which opened outwards, would only give a few inches. It was enough for the screams and shouts to reach the onlookers' ears.

'They're chained! They can't get out!' The cry came from Kathy, Sara noted.

She looked over at the woman with distaste. The other parents who called and wailed sounded hysterical with fear. To Sara, Kathy simply sounded excited. She felt her fists curl with a barely concealed anger. It wasn't Kathy's child in there; to her, this was simply a high-octane thriller movie that she was watching in real time.

But her fists uncurled, thoughts of Kathy diminished, as the sound of thumping and the subsequent shouts from those trapped within increased in volume.

'Do something,' she whimpered. 'Oh please, someone do something.'

A hand on her arm; her mother's, she saw. 'They're going in,' Mary said, still quiet, still calm.

She was right. The police streamed from nowhere. Not the officers who had been trying to control the cluster of parents at the gate, but men and women with vests and caps and earpieces that looped behind their heads to hidden radios. In their hands they carried guns and canisters.

They didn't speak to each other or anyone else as they moved in. The ones at the front talked with their hands, signals that Sara had only ever seen in American movies. They positioned themselves at points en route to the doors, fanning out, gesturing, raising their weapons.

Other officers came from the rear, slipping down the protective pathway those in front had created. They held tools, Sara saw now. Battering rams and actual tool bags.

Those previously waiting in a crouch reconvened at a signal so discreet, Sara didn't even see it. A semicircle now, poised in synchronicity as a single black-clad man ran in a crouch to the double doors.

The whine of what sounded like a circular saw hushed the crowd immediately.

Only when the chain sagged and snapped and the doors flew open did the armed officers move. The formation changed like a well-rehearsed dance. The semicircle turned into a line, a barricade between the school doors and the gate as the first pupils shoved their way out of their prison.

Not just one kid, a handful... no, a dozen. Even more!

The parents at the gate surged, their children in tantalising reach yet still denied to them as the officers sent them in the opposite direction.

'Where are they taking them?' Kathy's voice again, disappointed, as though she'd wanted to witness the reunions.

Or perhaps she wanted to witness the children who didn't come back, thought Sara. Whatever her motives, she very definitely needed to shut up.

'She's driving me crazy,' said Sara to nobody.

'Yes, not just you.' The voice at her ear was her mother's.

'I-I can't see if any of the children are... mine.' She swallowed, realising belatedly that she had been about to say *Ryan*.

The hand fell from her arm. The sudden absence of support put Sara off balance. She faced front, caught sight of Jojo crushed against the locked gates, pulling himself up by his strong arms. Some of the other parents followed his lead, until the small area by the gates looked like a pitch invasion at a football match.

The police, the non-armed ones who only had batons at their disposal, attempted to calm the situation. They didn't pluck the batons from their belts, however, and for that Sara was grateful. You couldn't punish people for this reaction.

It was purely human nature.

Finally, the men atop the gates were talked down. The formation of armed officers had broken and dispersed.

The children were gone.

An officer on the outside of the gate waved his walkie-talkie in the air.

He was young-looking, thought Sara. Another one who was too young for this job, for this scene. Pale and pasty and seemingly on the verge of throwing up, he seemed momentarily stunned when everyone looked to him, as though he'd imagined he would have to shout for their attention.

'The students who came out are being checked over by the paramedics.' He ran an eye over the crowd. 'Please don't attempt to enter the grounds to find them.'

A voice piped up, a red-headed man who had his arm clamped around a tiny woman next to him. 'Where do we go, then?'

The officer, just for a single moment, looked like a deer caught in headlights. In an instant, he regained his composure. 'Wait,' he instructed.

He turned his back, curled around his police radio now, bursts of static bouncing along the sound waves.

'The community centre!' the officer called. 'But please, we need to do this in an orderly fashion, we need to remain calm...' His words trailed off as the crowd of parents turned and began a fast walk back to where they'd originally come from.

Sara, anchorless without Jojo, without her mother, watched them go.

There was no stampede, which she would have expected. The crying and the random shouts of anger and frustration had died away. All that followed them up the street was silence.

When they had gone, the quiet enveloped Sara as she stood alone at the gates, feeling like she was the last person remaining on earth.

35

Travis
Now

He wasn't sure what to do. Should he check that she'd gone home, or would that be too much?

Nobody liked a needy person, and he didn't want to come off as such. Sara was the one with the need for him. At least that was how it had to be portrayed.

He buckled up his jeans and flopped into the chair in front of the computer.

His gaze wandered to the window, to the black, starless night.

Maybe she was happy. Maybe he'd done his duty for tonight. It couldn't have been easy for her, giving herself up to another man, a man who wasn't her dead husband.

Husband!

Travis sat up straight, recalling the article he'd seen about Ryan's death. He'd wanted to read more, to find out more about this family, but she'd been outside, drinking. He'd been jittery, not wanting her to walk in and find her dead son's name on his computer screen.

She was gone now. She wouldn't be back tonight.

Just in case, he got up and locked the front door, something he rarely did.

Tonight, he would find out all he could about Ryan, the dead husband, the widowed Sara and her one surviving son.

Tomorrow morning, he would make his way along the track with fresh croissants for Sara and Scott. He would be friendly, but he wouldn't be pushy. He would assess the lie of the land when he was there.

Feeling better now he had a plan in place, he switched on his computer and got to work.

It was dire reading. He recalled how at the time, he'd heard snatches and snippets of what was happening. The heartbreaking days that followed as sadness turned to anger. Protests, placards held aloft as Farenden High Street had become a march.

This is not America! proclaimed one of them. As though it was expected in the States, as if because it happened on an almost weekly basis it was fast becoming normal.

But here, it hadn't been for lack of laws. Those gun laws were in place, and for almost twenty years they had worked. Marches and protests would not change anything. This was a terrible tragedy that had occurred because a boy had stolen his father's legally owned firearms and gone off the deep end.

That led Travis on another path, a road that excited and intrigued him in equal measure.

The boy. Noah Miller. What caused a fifteen-year-old kid from a seemingly good home, with both parents around, to kill nineteen people?

Another memory flashed back at him. The first weeks had centred on the victims, the survivors, the funerals and the memorials. Only afterwards, later, would questions arise about Noah Miller.

There had been talk of a second shooter, an accomplice. Kids who had got out mentioned Noah communicating with someone over a radio. He himself had spoken about his friend in another part of the school causing the same kind of carnage.

They hadn't run, the kids said, they hadn't rushed him, because he wasn't alone. He had a partner – he might have had three or four or a dozen in his team – and they could be anywhere.

Nobody knew.

And to this day, still nobody knew.

Travis moved on to the comments left at the bottom of the original piece, falling down rabbit-hole links that led him to other news articles, essays, support groups and chat rooms. Every so often he came back to the comments, hundreds of them, some from strangers, some from left-wing groups, proposing that all guns should be banned. One name jumped out at him, repeatedly commenting, imparting information again and again.

Kathy Driver, aka KDmum.

She had a kid at the school, a daughter, but by some stroke of luck or fate her girl had been off sick that day. Kathy, however, concerned for her community, had gone down to the school the instant she heard, and had stayed almost until the bitter end.

It was Kathy Driver who made the only mention of Sara's name that Travis could find.

> KDmum: I was assaulted while the school was locked down. While all those people were standing at the gates, not knowing if their kids were alive or dead, and one person was still acting like nothing was happening. #BitchInHeat

SuziSue: OMG, KDmum, what happened? Who assaulted you?

KDmum: Sara Fuller. She had a go at me for being there to support my friends, said I should be at home with my Louise. She said I was just there for the gossip! She hit me.

MumOfTash: Like you weren't just there for the drama, KD! ;)

SuziSue: Shut up MumOfTash. KD, do you reckon the rumours about her and Jojo were true?

KDmum: Darling, I KNOW they're true. I caught them at the Palais in Hammersmith. He was holding her face, stroking her like she was a bloody cat. I could never work out what he saw in her. She told him to stay away from her and walked out of the restaurant. I reckon Mack had found out, given her an ultimatum. And Mack was dying, she had no choice but to stay with him.

SuziSue: OMFG!

Working_Mum: Jojo didn't leave her side at Farenden. Even when her mum turned up, he stayed with her. Maybe the affair never actually ended?

KDmum: All those years Mack thought that boy was his own.

SuziSue: You think Scott was Jojo's kid? Poor Mack, he was a really nice guy, didn't deserve her.

Comments for this post have been switched off

He pushed himself away from his desk and moved across to the kitchen. The coffee was still there, hours old and cold now, but he poured it into a mug and swallowed it anyway.

Sara had committed adultery with another man.

One of her children was rumoured to be the son of a man called Jojo.

He sniffed his disappointment and looked out of the window into blackness. It didn't sound like the Sara he knew. His Sara was a classy lady; surely affairs were... beneath her? It was far more likely that this man, this Jojo, had forced her. What was it that KDmum had said? He scrolled back, found the passage.

She told him to stay away from her and walked out of the restaurant.

To Travis, it seemed that Sara, like Kathy Driver, had been the victim of an assault.

And the son who was not Sara's husband's was Scott.

He felt his eyes widen.

It would explain so much. The distance between Scott and Sara. Her wariness of him, her discomfort when in his presence.

Suddenly revived now that he had more to go on, Travis tipped the dregs of the coffee down the sink and rushed back to the computer.

He glanced at the clock on the wall. It was nearing four a.m. Three hours until the bakery up near the Co-op opened. Three hours to find out as much about Sara, Scott and the savage, hideous Jojo as he could.

He had no surname to go on, but the man wasn't hard to locate. He'd had a son, Jaden, and a wife, Amelia. He was from Ireland, which made sense, thought Travis, going by that name. But he had lived in London for a lot of his adult life. He and his wife had divorced before the school shooting.

His presence was heavy on social media, this Jojo. His face smiling, usually a pint of beer in hand. A masculine vibe pulsated from him, a Jack-the-lad. Travis wrinkled his nose with distaste. Sara was far too good for a man like this.

He paused on a Facebook photo Jojo had been tagged in. This time, he held aloft an oversized bottle of champagne. With the other hand he gave the 'up yours' gesture to whoever was taking the picture.

Travis scowled. Jojo was a yob, a thug. A guy who thought he was a geezer. A bully, an attacker of women. A walking erection; the type of man Travis couldn't stand.

Was this why Sara had run? On top of the death of her younger son, she was still being harassed by the thug who had impregnated her against her will?

He clicked back to the comments, the one left by Working_Mum. *Jojo didn't leave her side at Farenden. Even when her mum turned up, he stayed with her.*

By the looks of the comments made by the other mums, they were jealous.

Poor Sara.

His heart ached, thinking of her persecution by such a heathen. And then to be victimised by those… those… *witch-hunters*.

He moved on, clicking on to Jojo's own Facebook page now. He scrolled down, landing on one year ago, all the RIP messages giving him pause for thought.

His hand hovered over a post, tags galore, thousands of likes, hundreds of comments.

RIP Jaden Walsh.

Travis's breath caught in his throat.

The awful man had lost his own son in the tragedy.

Horrible, terrible; not a single one of those kids had deserved to die, not even Jojo Walsh's boy. Just because blood and DNA were involved, it didn't mean the lad would have turned out anything like his father.

Uneasily, Travis twisted in his chair and once again stared outside.

The pit cave. The strange moment when he had thought that Scott could kill him. Scott's words when Travis had chastised him for starting a fire in the cave.

Travis: 'Fumes from fires can be poisonous, deadly even.'

Scott's reply: 'I know.'

If Scott was on the cusp of sociopathy, or something equally dangerous or deadly, where did that leave Sara?

He moved up the page, tired suddenly, weariness covering him like the black sky concealed the forest outside.

He had to keep going. If he stopped now, if he slept, he would miss the bakery opening time. All the fresh stuff would be gone, and he needed to carry on with Project Sara.

She was familiar with being used and discarded, he understood that now. He had to show her that he was nothing like the man who had stolen her joy and left her with the burden of an unplanned child. He would step up. He would love her and show her that there was life after tragedy. But first he had to check on this Jojo, see what he was up to now. If he was as enamoured with Sara as the comments on the newspaper article suggested, it explained why she kept such a low profile. He would not betray her whereabouts; Kielder could forever become her foxhole.

He scrolled up the page, right up to the most recent activity, and frowned.

The last post had been just under a year ago. One week after the Farenden shooting. It hadn't been left by Jojo himself, but by somebody – a relative, if the surname was anything to go by – who had tagged him.

> Be with your son, my darling, and fly high together.
>
> We love you.
>
> We will miss you forever.
>
> Rest in peace, Jojo

Travis's breath caught in his throat.

Jojo Walsh was *dead*.

36

'What happened to the people?' Scott asked as they walked the silent hallways.

'Who?' Noah was distracted, kicking open classroom doors at random, giving a single glance inside before exiting and walking on.

'The… the people who were in the hall.' Scott swallowed. 'How did they get out?'

Noah's face slid into a frown, his thin lips matching his narrow eyes.

He didn't know, couldn't work it out, saw Scott.

Eventually, Noah shrugged. 'Doesn't matter, I got some of them.' He stopped, darted back to Scott and grabbed his arm. 'Look, through there, see?'

They had emerged into a glass-lined corridor that bordered a tiny courtyard. Across the courtyard, in the hallway that ran parallel, was the exit route that the fugitives from the hall had streamed down. The main doors were at the far end. The pathway leading to them was littered with inert human forms. The floor and the edges of the smashed glass wall were sprayed red.

Four or five of them, culled at different points. Random shots by Noah as he chased them while Scott was on the phone to his nan.

'Look, through here. Get a better view.' Noah stepped back, raised his right arm and fired off a round at the glass wall that separated them from the courtyard.

No silencer on the silver gun. It sounded like fireworks. Behind him, beyond a closed door somewhere, Scott was sure he heard a voice. He glanced at Noah, but he was already kicking out at the shattered glass, the racket concealing the sound of what might or might not have been a scream.

He followed Noah, his shoes crunching on the glass-strewn floor. Outside, it was hot, London basking in the summer heat.

'Here, see?' Noah had moved to the other side of the courtyard, was tapping on the glass with the barrel of the silver gun.

With one last look at the blue sky, Scott joined him. Four bodies: two girls, one boy, and an adult he didn't recognise. He knew the boy, though; not to speak to, just to look at, one he had actually looked at mere minutes ago.

Matty Cranshaw.

There had been glass between them then as well.

Now Matty lay on his side, his head resting on his arm. He could well be asleep, if it were not for the fact that his eyes were open and unblinking.

Except for the fact that they were not, actually, open and unblinking. A tear squeezed from the boy's eye. The fingers of his left hand twitched. His gaze moved around, a frown knitting his brow as if he was confused. His eyes settled on Scott. His fingers flickered again, outstretched now, a silent request for help.

It was a horrifying moment, shattered by a loud crack next to Scott's ear.

Scott jumped and skittered sideways. Smoke curled from the end of the silver gun. In the corridor, Matty's fingers no longer moved. His eyes no longer looked to Scott for help.

A whirring started up, whining like a high-powered drill. Scott pulled his gaze away from Matty and looked up. Across the blue sky, a grey shape moved smoothly into view.

'A drone! It's a fucking drone!' Noah whooped, shading his eyes. He bounced over to Scott and shoved him. Scott stumbled, went down on his knees.

'Keep your head down!' screamed Noah.

Scott did as he was told. He brought his knees to his chest and shuffled behind a wooden picnic table in the courtyard.

He heard a click; Noah's lower half came into view as he knelt down, arms raised, the gun – the black one now – sprouting from his hands. He aimed, fired, once, twice, three then four times, all the while shrieking and whooping.

A fizzing sound from above, and then plastic and metal rained down into the courtyard, coming to rest among the shattered glass of the window that Noah had blown out.

Scott watched as Noah tilted his head back and screamed to the sky. 'I got it!' he said when he drew breath. He leaped up and danced through the debris, lifting up his heavy boots, bringing them down hard, crunching the tiny robotic bits into even smaller particles.

Scott smiled but shook his head as Noah invited him to join him.

Eventually the whooping, the cheering ceased. Noah's boots, striding past Scott, moved back to the hallway.

Scott stood up and brushed off his knees.

He looked at the blue sky, streaked through with smoke now. He took a deep breath and followed Noah back into the school.

'We have to move now; they could get in here any second.' Noah was marching with purpose down the hallway towards the science labs.

'What? Who?' asked Scott.

'Them, the police, the army guys.' Noah stopped, backtracked at alarming speed and gripped Scott's arm, turning him around to look back across the courtyard. 'They cut the chains off; my backpack's gone, all the spare chains and locks were in it.'

The backpack. Scott stared into Noah's eyes, wondering if the boy remembered leaving him next to it. He hadn't told him to look after it, though. Hadn't even mentioned it. Absently, he felt the weight of his own bag. Absurdly, it was practically empty, everything that had been in it – the books, those freshly sharpened pencils – still back in the classroom where this had all begun.

'We don't have much time left,' Noah said.

It was nearing the finale. On television cop shows they called it the endgame.

Scott looked at Noah, slightly braver now, having proved time and time again that he was on the boy's team. After all, hadn't he had plenty of chances to escape? Numerous times now he had been left on his own. He could have run at any point, but he hadn't.

He raised his chin. 'What about the others? The other guy, your... friend. You were speaking to him on the radio.'

Noah grinned and pulled his hands out of his pockets, turning them palms up. 'No radio, all bullshit.' His smile was lopsided now, his lips a question mark. 'No friends, either.'

Sadness tugged at Scott. Noah was just like him. Alone, friendless, so much so that he'd invented a partner in crime. There was nobody else running around the school with guns or knives or explosives.

He shuffled his feet and looked down at the floor. 'You got me,' he said. 'I'm your friend.'

The sun moved on from the courtyard, dipping the corridor into something dull and gloomy. When Scott finally looked up again, Noah's eyes glinted.

'Yeah,' he said, his voice a breathy rasp. 'Yeah, I guess you are.'

They didn't seal the deal with a handshake, or even a nod or some other gesture.

Scott's eyes left Noah's face. Carefully, deliberately, he let his gaze travel downwards, to Noah's pocket, a silent request in his eyes as he stared at the second gun.

37

Jojo was back, plucking at her sleeve. 'We need to go to the community centre,' he said.

He was breathless; his eyes, though still dark and stormy, now held a glint of something else.

Excitement. Fear. Hope.

She understood what was happening. The kids who had managed to get out of the school would be checked over by paramedics. Those with just minor injuries and those who were unscathed would be handed over to their parents at the centre.

Those who were seriously injured would go to the hospital.

Those who lay dead and bullet-ridden on the floors of the school would go nowhere.

She gasped. Her hands flew to her mouth as she looked around the now-empty street.

'I want to stay here!' she cried.

Jojo stared into her eyes. 'We have to get to the community centre,' he said.

She nodded, but still her feet remained rooted to the spot. 'But… but what… what if he's not there?'

Jojo let his hand slip from her arm.

'They!' she said, hurriedly. 'What if they're not there?'

This time he took her hand, linked his fingers with hers, just like he had all those times in the distant past.

His hand still fitted, she thought as she gazed down at their fingers. They were still a good match.

'You know you have to do this, don't you?' he asked.

She did, but it didn't make it any easier. She tore her eyes away from his and looked around for her mother. It was rare that she needed Mary; ironically, now that she did, the woman was nowhere to be seen.

'She's escorting Kathy Driver home,' said Jojo, as if he knew who she was searching for.

He did know, she realised, sadness descending like a cloud. She didn't have many people in her life to reach for.

He squeezed her hand. 'Think of the odds,' he urged her. 'All those kids who got out, ours will be among them.'

It was likely, she rationalised. More than likely, really.

Think of the odds.

She shuffled her feet on the spot and found they did work after all. She took a few cautious steps.

'Attagirl.' Jojo pulled on her hand, encouraging her. 'Come on, now. Good girl.'

She let him lead the way.

There were two groups of people, she saw as they neared the community centre where they'd already spent time that morning. There were parents, uncles and aunts and grandparents and friends who couldn't get there quick enough. As they crested the hill and the community centre came into view, those people began to run. Even the old ones, who Sara was sure hadn't broken into so much as a jog in decades pulled on their muscle memory and sprinted for all they were worth.

Then there were the others, those like her. They dragged their feet, slowed their step, stuttering and stumbling. They didn't want to reach the centre, not yet.

She got it now. The longer they were out here on this road, the longer they would have before hearing the news that they shouldn't *ever* have to hear.

But Jojo belonged in the first group, and his hand held hers in a vice-like grip, forcing her along. She had a choice. She could untangle her fingers from his and fall back, let him get to the community centre, get to his Jaden. But his hand refused to let go of hers, and with a heart that beat painfully at treble time, she found herself moving over the threshold of the centre, into the throng of people, back into the panic-stricken world of reality.

She stepped into silence. But even though the room was quiet, the terror was palpable. It throbbed through the space, sparking fear in anyone it touched, until the crowd were locked in a weird, hushed frenzy.

The police were here too now, dozens of them, walking around with clipboards, their radios crackling a static that only served to heighten the tension.

Jojo's phone pinged. He released Sara's hand, plucked it out of his pocket.

'It's Cara, Harry's mum,' he said.

Sara stared blankly. She had no idea who either Cara or Harry was.

He looked up and nodded in the direction of the officers who wound their way through the throng. 'They're going to be calling out names, taking people into another room to… to tell them.'

Tell them what?

Tell them if their children were alive or dead? What about people – people like *her* – who had more than one child at this school? What if she had to go into one room *and* the other? What then? Did she have to come out here and wait in the interim? And which news would be given first? The good, to cushion the blow? Or the other way around?

'Oh God.' Her voice was thick, choking. She clamped a hand to her mouth and felt her cheeks bulge.

'You okay?' Jojo put his arm around her shoulder, his face very close to hers.

Sara pulled away, swallowed repeatedly and looked around the room. Nobody else was vomiting.

Pull yourself together.

'Yes,' she said. 'I'm fine.'

He was about to say something else, but a loud voice rang out over the hushed tones of the people in the hall. A couple of hundred heads turned in unison to see an officer, an older one, standing on a small podium. He had his hands raised, waving them, an unnecessary gesture since everyone's eyes were already on him.

'We're so sorry to find ourselves here, in this position, in our community. I'm sure most of you are aware that a large number of students, teachers, assistants and administration staff have made it out of the main school building. We're processing everyone right now. Those who need medical attention are being taken straight to hospital.' Here, both his gaze and his voice dropped a little. 'This is a large-scale emergency. Multiple hospitals and medical centres are on standby. Please, please wait for us to speak to you. Please do not attempt to make your way to the hospitals or tie up the phone lines. We will advise you, I promise you, and we'll work as efficiently as we humanly can. My officers have lists of names; please go with them when your name is called.'

Ice-cold fingers clawed at the back of Sara's neck. The fine hairs there stood up. It was a lottery, an awful, terrible raffle.

And then the names started to be called out, and Sara found Jojo's hand again and clutched it even tighter than before.

38

Sara
Now

She was waiting for Scott on the landing the next morning, her back against the wall, legs stretched out in front of her.

She hadn't gone to sleep, not since she'd left Travis's cottage. She hadn't drunk anything further, save for pints and pints of water.

At some point, when dawn began to crack a shady light across the sky, she had retrieved the Tramadol, along with all the other pills, and methodically flushed them down the toilet.

The continuous sound of the chain had roused Scott, and he'd called through his door, 'Mum?'

He probably thought she was sick, vomiting from the near-entire bottle of booze at the barbecue.

'I'm fine, go back to sleep,' she'd said.

He appeared to have done just that and hadn't emerged from his room to investigate further.

Now, just after six a.m., she heard the telltale signs – squeaking floorboard, bed springs – that he was up.

She pushed herself to standing, wooziness catching at her, the after-effects of the drink and the exhaustion of the day before, and put her hand on the banister to steady herself.

His door opened, and he wavered as he saw her there, waiting for him. She wondered if he was going to close the door in her face; instead, he looked at her once, warily, before glancing down at his feet.

'I spoke to your nan yesterday,' she said, her words a rush, chucking them out there before she could lose her nerve.

His eyes, heavy with sleep, widened. 'Did you?' he asked.

She faltered, losing her way. Scott took the opportunity to slip past her towards the bathroom.

The door closed behind him, the sound of the tap running.

'I know it's been really... strange,' she said, bleating the words before they could get stuck again like they had so many times before.

The sound of the water ceased; one footstep, two, and then the bathroom door opened.

'I want to... I think it's time...' She took a deep breath. 'I think it's time we talked.'

In one hand he held a towel, which he wrung between his fingers, squeezing, threading, winding it, crushing it.

Killing it.

She closed her eyes, briefly, and when she opened them, the door had been softly closed again. But she had come this far, the furthest she had made it in the last year, and she wasn't going to stop now.

'I found it easier to...' *Pretend* seemed like the wrong word, juvenile and stupid. *Ignore what had happened* was even worse. 'It was really hard to accept the reality,' she settled on. 'But I need to try, I *want* to try...'

'Try what?' His voice, rough yet raw, came through the door.

I want to try to love you.

She clapped her hand to her mouth, as if the words were going to escape.

What *did* she want? To move on? To understand?

She would never be able to move on.

She would never be able to understand.

'I want to hear what happened.' With her hands still at her mouth, she pressed her fingers against her lips.

No, that was most definitely not what she had meant to say! Jesus Christ, the visions she had were bad enough, but to actually hear events straight from the horse's mouth, as it were...

No.

No. NO.

But the door was opening again, her elder son's face appearing in the crack. The towel was around his neck now, his eyes suspicious, narrowed and a piercing green as he stared at her.

Eyes just like his father's.

'It's a lot, I know,' she said. 'We don't need to do this now, it's... it's not the right time. I understand that.'

He laughed, short and sharp, like he'd expected this, as though this were typical of her. The laugh, older than his years, cynical and worn down, grated through her bones.

'You've got some explaining to do,' he replied. He gripped the towel, whipped it down so it was back in his hands again. She flinched at the sudden movement.

It took great effort, but she raised her eyes to meet his. 'Wh-what do you mean?'

For a moment she was afraid that he might reply, and that it would be something she didn't want to hear, didn't want to face, didn't want to admit to. Instead, he dropped his gaze. The look he'd given her, that had spiked terror into her heart, was gone. He was back, the Scott she knew: quiet, demure, troubled.

Somewhere, a tapping sound started up.

Scott looked past her, towards the stairs.

'It'll be for you,' he said, and retreating, he closed the bathroom door quietly behind him.

As she moved down the stairs, she slowed her pace. What had he meant when he'd said, 'It'll be for you'? How did he know who was at the door? Had... had he called someone? Someone official, someone who had figured it all out?

She shook her head as if to swish away the thought.

No. If the police knew what had happened, they wouldn't be politely tapping at the door. They would burst in with battering rams, niceties left at the kerb.

It would be... a relief.

She swayed in the hallway, wondering where that thought had come from. But it wasn't a thought, it was a very real need.

A need to confess.

Because it was the truth that was dragging her down, weighing on her soul.

Maybe she could call someone, one of those anonymous charities, like the Samaritans or something, just to get it off her chest. Maybe a priest was what she needed, she thought as she made her way to the front door.

She pulled it open.

Or maybe, she thought as she eyed up Travis, bakery bag in hand on her doorstep, maybe a therapist. Not just for her son, but for her too.

She opened the door wide. He looked surprised, she thought, as he flashed her a smile and dodged in past her, as though she were going to change her mind and usher him out again.

'Breakfast, literally just freshly baked, still warm,' he was saying as he moved into the kitchen and set the bag down on the table. 'It is the most important meal of the day, after all.'

She tried hard to return his smile. 'I'll put the kettle on,' she said.

As she busied herself getting the mugs out, she tried to remember what it was he'd said that day in the canteen. She had been tempted then, the urge to spill almost over-whelming. Client confidentiality, she'd enquired about. He couldn't say anything to anyone, he'd assured her, unless she made a threat of harm against someone else.

She rubbed at her neck as she put the kettle on.

Nothing to worry about there; the threat had already been. The harm was already done.

'Let me.'

She gasped as his hands landed on her, kneading at the top of her shoulder blades, astonished that he would be so forward. Although she shouldn't be, not really, consid-ering they'd slept together the night before. He wanted to keep it going, sustain the momentum, she realised. And though Scott was just upstairs, and could come down at any moment, she let him carry on.

'I… I think it might help me if I were… honest with you,' she said softly.

His fingers paused, his hands shifted, and he wrapped an arm around her in an awkward hug.

'I'd really like that,' he whispered into her ear.

Don't pull away, don't pull away, she instructed herself. To give weight to her words, and a promise that he would be thrilled with, she leaned into him. His body pressed against the length of her and she felt him hardening. It was too much.

She slipped out of his hold and reached for the kettle. 'I really think it could help me... us,' she said again. 'It's important to be honest, if we're... you know, you and me.'

His face lit up, and he came at her again. She allowed it this time, let him cup her face with his small, effeminate hands.

'You can talk to me any time you want,' he said. He fixed her with an intense stare. 'Any time.'

She matched his look and moved just out of his reach. Her voice, when she spoke, came out harder than she'd expected. 'How about right now?' she asked, roughly.

39

Scott

Before

The science lab was high-tech and state-of-the-art. It was the jewel in Farenden's crown, no expense spared.

Set in the newer wing of the school, it was every student's favourite place to study. The teachers in this subject were recruited immediately upon graduating with their degree and gaining their postgrad qualification. As a consequence, they seemed younger than those in other departments of the school. They were cool, and they understood the kids; and more importantly, the kids understood them.

They didn't play by the rules, the science teachers. They insisted on being called by their first names, they wore denim cut-off shorts and T-shirts, and coloured their hair and showed off their piercings. The older teachers, those who had been at the school for decades, sniffed and whispered, but couldn't deny that the grades coming out of the science department were better than they'd ever been, so they sat back with an air of tolerance.

Like most modern elements, the science lab was streamlined and minimal.

It was also deadly quiet.

'There's nobody here,' said Scott. 'It's empty.'

Noah streaked past him, down between the lines of sterile, clean workstations. His boots left scuff marks on the white-tiled floor.

'Ha!' He pulled open a door that Scott hadn't even seen, set into the rear wall.

Scott's heart lurched.

Noah had found the stock cupboard.

He had found their hiding place.

Inside, three boys huddled, the whites of their eyes showing bright in the gloom.

Scott had never thought there would be a day when his brother looked like this. Vulnerable. Scared. So pale he seemed on the verge of passing out.

Scott's eyes skipped over Ryan and landed on his two mates, Max and Jaden.

They didn't hang around together, these three, not as far as Scott knew anyway. But they were all popular, all outgoing; sporty as well as smart, top grades both on and off the field.

They were everything that Scott and Noah would never be.

'Scott.' It was Max who spoke, and not Ryan.

Scott blinked at the boy, surprised that he knew his name.

'It's a family reunion.' Noah stepped forward.

At the sight of him, Ryan squirmed as if hoping to disappear. Jaden raised his hand to his face and tucked his head to his knees, whimpering as he curled into himself.

'You ain't gotta do nothing, Scott.' In the silence of the lab room, Max's whisper sounded like a scream. 'You ain't gotta do anything you don't want to do.'

Scott did do nothing. His feet were planted, encased in concrete, as he stared in wonder at the three boys, who had diminished in every way. Speech and movement left him.

Ryan and Jaden didn't – couldn't? wouldn't? – look at him.

It was Max, the smallest out of all of them, but apparently the bravest, who spoke again.

'Why have you got that?' he asked, his eyes fixed on the waistband of Scott's jeans.

The other two boys, previously sitting statue-like, finally looked up.

Scott had almost forgotten. Now, his hand flew to the belt of his jeans. He didn't know why; there was no concealing it, he'd never even intended it to be anything other than known. He wondered how he could have forgotten. The weight of it hit him, like a silver metal reminder.

Fluidity returned. He raised his chin. Then Noah was there, his breath hot on the back of Scott's neck.

'You don't need to know. You,' he prodded Max's chest with the handle of the gun, 'don't even need to be here.'

A flash like lightning struck the room. One single cry that trailed off into a thin breath, fading to nothingness.

Max was gone. Face gone. The two words echoed in Scott's head.

Face… gone.

Face gone.

Face. Gone.

So much worse than Mrs Fleecy, or Matty Cranshaw. Their injuries contained to their torsos, the way they had fallen in their deathly slumber concealing the damage, the only visual evidence the pooling or the spray of blood.

That wasn't the case here. Not now.

From someone's throat he heard a telltale clicking noise. His own hands rose to his neck as if to confirm it wasn't him. Someone, either Jaden or Ryan, vomited wildly.

Jaden and Ryan. Footnotes in Scott's brain as he looked down at the gun still in his waistband.

Noah, stepping forward, wisps of smoke curling from the black barrel.

'This is better,' he murmured, stepping around the pooled mess that had once been Max. 'Now it's how it should be, just family, right?'

40

Sara
Before

The process was agonisingly slow.

There were two rooms, Sara saw. To the left of the foyer area was a lending library – not the official main library but one set up for book swaps, children's activities and a thrice-weekly mother and toddler group. The room to the right was the office of whoever the manager or custodian of this place was. Sara had never been in it, but she imagined it to be small, sparse and impersonal.

The office was where they took the parents of the dead. The survivors' families were led to the library.

She hadn't known that, not at first, until the first couple were called and led out of the room.

Every pair of eyes followed them, Sara's included, and watched as they turned right out of view of those standing in the main hall.

A scream came, made all the worse by the fact that it was clearly a man, the husband, the *father*. A thin, reedy shriek joined in.

Sobs erupted, a ripple effect through the people still waiting to hear. It was awful, the sound almost worse than the screams from the manager's office.

Sara reached for Jojo's hand. He grasped it, not looking at her, his mouth tightly closed, the strain showing in his jaw, in the tendons that stood out on his neck.

'Sara.' Another hand, slipping into her free one.

Sara looked down at it, surprised.

'I'll come in with you,' her mother said.

'Okay.' Sara licked her lips, felt the sweat that trickled along her eyebrow. She didn't want to let go of either of the hands holding her, sure that she would fall down without the support. Instead, she swept her shoulder along her eye to wipe away the curious mixture of perspiration and tears.

In the foyer, officers spoke in hushed, urgent whispers, their eyes flickering between those waiting and the library and the office. Noticeboards, large, concertinaed ones, were hastily erected, effectively blocking the view of the foyer from those who stood in the hall.

They could no longer see if those who were called turned left or right, towards life or death.

'Jojo Walsh?' A female officer raised her head, scanned the crowd.

Sara let out a little yelp as Jojo's fingers disengaged from hers.

Her hand, free now, followed a path towards him, her mouth moved with useless words.

Good luck! she wanted to say, absurdly, and so she pulled back her wandering hand, put her fingers to her mouth, and repeated his son's name and those of her own, under her breath, again and again, until Jojo had slipped through the door and behind the screens.

–

'There's something going on! Something's happening!' The shout echoed around the hall.

Sara, cross-legged on the floor now, looked up as the stranger's cry rang out.

'Mum?' she said.

'Wait there,' instructed Mary.

Sara watched as her mother strode purposefully out of view.

As the hush grew to a murmur, she pushed herself to standing and looked around.

A gasp slipped from her lips. Where was everybody? How could there be so few people left? Surely they hadn't all received the alive-or-dead notifications?

She dusted off her hands against her jeans. Just a dozen people milled around, eyes on their phones, faces varying degrees of white and grey.

Sara understood. The parents of the kids known to be dead had been told. Those whose children were safe and well had been taken to them.

The rest of them, herself included, were the unknown dregs.

Mary was coming back, walking with purpose, her face neither white nor grey, still perfectly made-up, rouged cheeks and eyeliner unsmudged by evidence of tears or sweat.

'Where did Jojo go?' Sara asked.

Mary studied her daughter for a moment. 'I should think he's with his son,' she said.

'Did he… Is Jaden…?'

Mary shrugged, her thin shoulders jerking in an up-and-down motion. 'I don't know, but I should imagine Jojo is with him, whatever the outcome.'

Sara heard a groan, wondered where it came from, realising belatedly it was from herself. 'What was that about?' She gestured in the vague direction Mary had come from.

'They're bringing people out of the school.' Mary glanced around at the few remaining parents, who were moving as one towards the doors. 'I think we should go there. We're not going to get any information here, not for a while.'

Sara let herself be led, obediently trailing her mother as once again they followed the herd that trekked back to the school.

They heard them before they'd even crested the hill. Before, when she'd walked this route, there had been silence, the atmosphere thick with fear and tension and worry. Now, the air was thin, but the noise was deafening.

It was over, she realised, and even though she didn't know the outcome, she clutched at Mary's hand.

'It's finished,' she breathed.

But it wasn't. For Sara, it was really only just beginning.

41

He'd thought he'd have to work so hard, chipping away at Sara, being there, proving to her that he was serious in his absolute adoration of her. He would never treat her as abominably as that Jojo had done. He even thought about going so far as to promise her that he wasn't going to leave her by dying like her husband. After all, he took care of himself, with his clean living and Eastern philosophies. No cancer would strike him down.

But *she* had approached *him*. She had begged him for a listening ear. She had let him hold her, touch her. It wasn't ideal. After all, as the masculine one in the relationship, it was up to him to take the lead. And he would, but there was no harm right now in letting her think that her actions were born of her choices.

He didn't mention the information he'd discovered; that he knew all about the scoundrel who had ruined her life. But as she moved listlessly around her kitchen, he wondered, did she even know he was dead? Was she unaware that he could never find her, never hunt her down, never hurt her again? He wouldn't tell her that. She might not be so wary of the world if she knew Jojo was no longer in it. For now, it suited Travis just fine that she preferred to remain hidden.

Jojo's death had been by his own hand; he'd thrown himself off the balcony of the swanky top-floor apartment where he lived, just one week after the massacre that had taken his son's life. Clearly the fact that he'd spawned another son didn't give him enough reason to carry on living.

'Where's Scott?' Travis asked now, as Sara seated herself in a comfortable armchair and looked up at him expectantly.

Slow footsteps answered his question, and he turned to see Scott coming down the stairs.

'Morning,' said Travis. 'How did you sleep? Do you want breakfast? I went to the bakery.' He gestured to the croissants, still in the bag on the table.

Scott's glance flicked between Travis and Sara. 'No, I'm going out. See you later.'

He was gone. Travis looked to Sara, who had reclined in the chair and was leaning back with her eyes closed. It struck him as odd that she wouldn't ask where her son was going, or what time he would be back. Considering what she'd been through, he would have thought she would be an overprotective mother, one of those so-called 'helicopter mums', when in fact she was entirely the opposite.

He narrowed his eyes as he scrutinised her.

She's distanced herself, he thought. Disengaged, cut off her heart and her feelings and her instincts. That way, if it happens again, she thinks she'll be prepared.

It was delusional on her part, but he couldn't blame her. Grief hit people in very different ways.

'I'm ready,' she said without opening her eyes.

Travis felt the pulse in his neck twitching. She was supposed to be timid, insecure, unsure. Right now, she seemed like she was in charge.

It wasn't the way it was supposed to be. Travis was her protector. He was there to guide her. He could let a few things slide, but it was important that she look to him from the start. She needed to know exactly who was in charge here.

'Sara,' he said.

She sighed, as if sensing his reluctance. 'Yes, Travis?'

His name on her lips. Not the gentle, breathy sigh of the night before, but impatient, knowing he was stalling but unaware of why.

'Sara, will you take a walk with me?'

She shrugged, eyes off to one side, suddenly reminding him very much of Scott.

'We'll take a walk.' He smiled, held out his hand. Making decisions. In charge. How it should be.

She ignored his hand, which irritated him again. But he let it go as she stood up all the same, picking up her keys off the side and following him out of the door.

He watched while she locked up, testing the handle, moving across to the kitchen window to make sure it was secure. He was intrigued that she felt the need to make her home so safe, fretting, coming back to the door and trying the handle again. She hadn't done this the other day. He'd been able to walk right into her house.

He blew out his breath as he waited at the end of the path. Optimism settled over him, a comforting wraparound that bolstered him.

He would fix her.

'Rain's coming,' he said as they began to walk.

Sara, at his side, paused and looked up. He glanced up too, saw the cloudless deep blue sky. It certainly didn't look like rain. He smiled, waiting for her questions. When she said nothing, he imparted his wisdom anyway.

'There was a halo around the moon last night, and this morning, the birds were staying close to the ground in flight.'

She stared straight ahead, and he wondered if she'd even heard him. Or, he cringed, did she just think the little bits of information he presented to her were boring and dull. Embarrassment gave way to a small, smouldering fire of anger.

He breathed out to dispel the fury. Try again.

'Frogs croak louder on rainy days too, did you know that? It's to do with mating. Rain puddles create perfect conditions for female frogs to lay their eggs.'

Sara pulled her jacket tighter around her, as if the storm was impending. 'I don't really want to be caught in the rain,' she said.

'Why not?' he asked.

She gave him a strange look, like he was mad. 'Who wants to get caught in the rain?' she asked.

He raised his hand. 'Me.'

And then she laughed.

It was rough, patchy, rusty, but to Travis, it sounded like a church choir. He felt himself puffing up. *He'd* done that. *He'd* made her laugh.

'Being outside in the rain is amazing. The smells, all of nature rising, the feel of it, especially after this heatwave—'

'The wet hair, soggy clothes, damp feet, yes, you're right, I'm wrong!' she said, and laughed again.

Travis felt his breath catch in his throat. Her laugh was so pretty he almost forgave her for interrupting him. 'You should do that more often.'

'What, laugh?' The smile slipped from her face. 'I haven't had too much to laugh about.'

He caught hold of her hand and wrapped it in both of his. 'I'd like to think that's going to change,' he said.

She looked away but didn't remove her hand. Encouraged, Travis linked his fingers with hers and pulled her onwards.

Off the road, heading not towards his cabin but in the other direction. The woods were denser here, less disturbed, and the undergrowth was thick and punishing.

'Watch your step,' he warned. He himself was as sure-footed as a mountain goat, but he realised that for newcomers it could be dangerous. 'The pit caves are treacherous. Some of them you don't realise you're practically on top of until you fall in.'

She pulled away from his grip and shoved her hands in her pockets. 'Is that what happened yesterday? Did you fall in one of those… pit caves? Or… or did something else happen?'

There was suspicion in her tone, and he remembered the night before, Scott insisting he'd been the hero, Sara disbelieving, and then there was Travis somewhere in the middle, unsure of what had happened, only recalling the look on Scott's face, like he could kill Travis, but then rescuing him anyway.

Sometimes there was a familiarity in Scott that was a little too close to home.

'Why do you think someone else was responsible?' he asked her.

'I didn't say that.'

'You didn't,' he agreed, 'but it kind of seems that's what you're trying to say.' He stopped walking and sat down on a fallen tree trunk.

She remained standing, by one of the poplar trees, running her hand up and down the bark before smoothing it over her brow.

'I really think you're wrong about the rain,' she said.

He shrugged and raised his hands, palms up. 'I have been known to be wrong. We're none of us infallible.' And then, because she seemed almost comfortable, he said, 'Talk to me. Tell me about… him.'

She looked at him over her shoulder, a question in her blue eyes.

Braver, bolder now, with the earth under his feet and the protective trees shielding him, he raised his chin. *I'm in charge.* 'Tell me about Jojo.'

The birds were silent suddenly, and the sun dipped behind a cloud that Travis hadn't seen approaching. It was sinister, like it was a result of the words he'd dared to say.

His name.

He knew she was astonished that he knew that name, wondering where he'd heard it, why he was saying it. But it was important; she had to face things, she had to know that Travis was going to help her to do just that.

She kicked at the ground by the poplar. As if only now waking up to his surroundings, he jumped up.

'Careful,' he murmured, and nodded down to the leaf-strewn floor by her feet. To be on the safe side, he circled her shoulders with his arms. She didn't pull away. Encouraged, he held her close to his chest.

'What? Is it a snake?' she whispered.

He laughed, and moved to stand beside her, one arm still holding her close. 'Look.' He scrubbed around with the toe of his boot, moving and pushing at the earth. He heard her gasp when he uncovered the hole.

'A tunnel!' she said.

'A pit cave,' he corrected. 'One of the deepest I've come across.'

'Shouldn't it be closed off, shouldn't there be warnings?' She was down on her knees now, peering into nothingness. Finally, she looked up at him. 'It's dangerous!'

'The rangers came around once, covered over all the entrances with wooden pallets. The villagers objected, started a petition – me included,' he said.

She gaped at him. 'Why would you object to making something safer? Why wouldn't you do all you could to prevent someone from dying?'

It was interesting, he thought, that her thought had immediately been of death, rather than the more likely event of injury from a fall.

The sun had re-emerged from behind the thin cloud, and the birds were at it again, but suddenly it wasn't the same. She was angry, furious, all directed at *him*.

He closed his eyes and saw his error. She wasn't talking about the pit caves any more.

He hooked his hand underneath her arm and pulled her up. 'Come on, forget about the caves. Talk to me, Sara.'

Her breathing quickened noticeably, and she yanked her arm out of his.

'This was a mistake,' she muttered.

He was losing her. 'No, keeping things hidden is a mistake. It eats you up, gnawing away until there's nothing left of the real you. Let me help you.'

She paused, head down, submissive and passive, but he saw the cords on her neck standing proud with tension.

'I will *never* hurt you. I will never behave the way he did towards you.' The words burst out of his mouth before he could stop them.

Her head snapped up and she stared at him, eyes narrowed now with confusion.

'What?'

He'd gone too far to back up now. He pushed on, his theories and beliefs buried underfoot, acting purely on instinct. Feeling his way by her reactions.

'I know he hurt you, and he shouldn't have. I will listen to you, Sara. No judgement.' He held his hands up to her as if to demonstrate his trustworthiness.

She sagged against a tree. The bark scratched at the back of her shirt, ivy curling around her ankles. She was part of the landscape. She belonged here. Her eyes glinted.

Travis breathed out.

A breeze sighed around them, barely rippling the leaves.

For a moment there was silence, and then Sara began to talk.

42

Scott
Before

'What did you mean? You said "just family", what did you mean?'

Scott had flattened himself against a wall; a deliberately chosen place to wait. He could see the door, where men with guns – men who were actually allowed to have guns – would surely appear at any moment. Between him and the door was a pillar, large, square, as thick as a hundred-year-old tree trunk. They wouldn't see him right away. They would see Noah, making no effort to conceal himself; they would see what had once been Max. They would see the two remaining kids, Jaden and Ryan, huddled so close together it was almost like they were trying to merge into one.

'You're his brother.' Noah spun the gun casually around his forefinger, catching it upright and pointing it at Jaden, who flinched involuntarily. 'And he,' he pointed at Ryan, 'he's *your* brother, so you're all, like, linked, right?' He swung the gun, holding it in both hands, and steadied it to aim at Ryan's face. 'Family, right?'

Then he laughed, long and loud, braying out his mirth. 'You didn't know, did you? Ha, like, really? You really, really didn't know?'

Who was he talking to? wondered Scott. Did anyone know? Was this a revelation to all of them apart from Noah?

'Did *you* know?' Noah sprang, landing in a crouch next to Jaden.

'He's not...' Jaden shrugged, apologetically it seemed, 'he's not my brother. I ain't got no brothers.'

Noah laughed again and swung around to address Ryan. He leaned in close to him. From where he stood by the pillar, Scott could hear the sound of his brother's breathing, heavy, fear-filled, desperate.

Noah quietened as he studied Ryan. 'You knew, didn't you?'

Ryan gulped and shot a quick glance at Scott.

'I DIDN'T HEAR YOU!' Noah screamed, high-pitched, spittle flying.

'Yes!' Ryan gasped. He planted his hands on the floor and juddered backwards, even though his back was to the wall, even though there was nowhere to go.

'Who told you?' Noah smiled, the action coming so quickly after the scream he'd just let out, it was dizzying.

Ryan shrugged, inhaling too quickly now, his words short and breathless. 'I just... heard it, gossip, like.' Jerkily, he turned to look at Jaden.

Scott saw it then, as he stared at both Jaden and Ryan. Apart from Sara's colouring, there was no real likeness between Ryan's face and his own. But Jaden... Jaden...

He heard a groan and knew that it came from himself.

The clues were there, always had been: the disconnect between him and his family, the differences between him and his brother, the way his own mother brushed him aside. The breadcrumbs for him to follow had been there all along. Whispers, even, of a woman called Sara. Scott hadn't listened, even though the gossips had shut up when they saw him. It wasn't *his* mother. There were loads of Saras, right? But he had been trusting, too trusting.

No, more than that. He'd been an idiot. He found the gun, previously in his waistband, now in his hand, fingers curled around it as though it wasn't a brand-new experience to hold one.

As though he'd been born to use this thing.

'You knew this?' He aimed his words at Ryan, whose eyes were downcast now, his gaze sweeping left and right across the floor.

Ryan muttered something.

'What?' A fire burned in Scott, replacing the emptiness that had been resting in the pit of his belly for so many years.

Time began to flash. Words and conversation were useless, needless. It was all instinct now. This hadn't even been in Noah's plan. This was just a bonus for him, a lucky strike for him to savour.

Ryan spoke again, and this time he looked up, made eye contact with his brother. He spoke the words quietly, but Scott heard them all the same.

A strange, squared formation: two boys with guns, cocked, safety off, aimed. Two other boys, not related by blood, not even friends during their short lives. But at the very end, their arms found each other, entwined, each pulling the other close, close, closer. An unspoken agreement sent and received: they just didn't want to die alone.

43

Sara
Before

The organisation that the authorities had tried so hard to sustain failed at the end. The armed police were all over the grounds now, and pockets of children and lone teachers and assistants were leaving the school by any means possible.

Windows were smashed, crying teenagers climbing out amidst the jagged shards of glass. Scrapes and cuts didn't matter; dodging bullets did.

The police shouted louder than Sara felt was necessary. Any child who staggered through the gates they caught, manhandled roughly, barking orders, sweeping their hands over bodies, seeking metal, seeking knives, perhaps seeking blood. When they were deemed safe from harm and not a threat, they were shoved to one side.

Parents and strangers alike caught them, held them, smoothing away the police brutality with kindness and relief.

'They're… they're hurting them!' cried Sara.

'They don't know who they are,' said Mary. 'They have to be certain.'

Of course, the second shooter. Did they know who he was yet? Had they discovered his identity? Maybe they'd found his body. Suddenly, without Jojo and his never-ending stream of WhatsApp news, Sara felt alone.

Beside her, Mary stabbed at her phone. 'Who are you calling?' asked Sara, without taking her eyes off the school.

'I'm trying the boys again.' Mary pinched her lips together. A straight line folded the skin between her brows. 'Both switched off. *Shit.*' She tucked her phone into her pocket and stared at the clusters of black-clothed police.

Sara felt tears rising. It was her mother's fault. Mary had sworn. She never, ever did that, no matter how bad things got. Not when Mack had died, not throughout this whole terrible day. Up until now, she had been cool, calm and organised.

That single swear word underlined every single part of the dread that threatened to overwhelm Sara.

The police swarmed through the playground. Their formation was broken, that carefully executed stalking motion of earlier had splintered. The windows with their jagged smashed glass were empty now. All who could escape had done so.

'Where are they?' Sara whispered, her words thin and breathless. She turned to Mary: 'Mum, where *are* they?'

Mary made a strange noise in her throat and took Sara's arm. 'Let's move over here. We don't want to get in the way of the police, do we?'

'What? No. I'm staying…' Sara's words left her as she saw the source of Mary's concern.

Amelia Freda-Whitehall. Jojo's ex-wife.

The other woman was flanked. A medley of yummy mummies stood sentry on her left. On her right, Kathy Driver was back, acting as her bodyguard.

Unobserved, unnoticed for the moment, Sara let her gaze take in every inch of the woman. She was beautiful, classy, double-barrelled, for God's sake. Her hair, although pulled back in a bun, was flawless. Her jeans were tailored, the white shirt effortlessly chic.

Once, when Jojo and his mates had been in the pub, they'd ribbed him that he was punching above his weight. Subsequently, since that overheard remark, Sara had often wondered if that was why he'd gone after her.

Amelia Freda-Whitehall was the kind of woman the Kathy Drivers of the world fawned over.

Sara was the woman they all loved to hate.

Their eyes met, as Sara had always known they would. How they had avoided each other for so long was a miracle in itself. Never had she imagined it would be like this, in the midst of a tragedy.

Nothing apart from the single look passed between them, but it was there all right, the knowledge that whatever had happened, whatever had come before, didn't matter.

Amelia's bodyguards held no such opinion. They glared at Sara, eyes narrowed, nostrils pulsating. Not for the first time, it occurred to her that it was awfully unfair. Sure, she deserved their hatred, but did Jojo not also?

She glanced around again. The last thing she needed was for him to appear by her side again. Vague recollections of earlier came to her: the two of them, hand in hand, comforting one another, the closeness still evident after all this time.

But he was nowhere in sight.

Beside her, Mary breathed out an anguished groan.

Sara looked at her. 'What?' she asked, her voice high and panicky.

Mary stared down at the ground, gripped her daughter's hand and jerked her head to her right.

Sara saw him then, the clipboard man. The one from the community centre who held the dreadful list of the dead in his hand.

Her body began to throb, painful jolts like a flare of arthritis in her limbs, the stabbing of a knife in her stomach and head.

The man continued his approach. She felt the wail spread and grow in her chest.

'Mum...' she began. 'Mum... he's going to—' Abruptly she stopped as Clipboard Man walked determinedly past her.

She sagged, eyes closed, letting Mary hold her up.

A howl, and for a moment she thought it had come from her. She checked herself, hand to her throat. No, it wasn't her, and besides, it was still ongoing.

She turned to seek the source.

'Oh no. No, no, *no*...'

Across the road, the bodyguards surged, holding Amelia's arms as her knees buckled, and she tipped her head back and screamed her pain to the sky.

–

'They were together, Jaden and Ryan. They were hiding together, so if Jaden's gone, what about Ryan? He was with him, they were *together*!' Sara was rambling, some part of her knew that. Her voice was loud, shrill, and onlookers were glancing at her, disgust on their faces that she should dare to worry about her own son instead of consoling the woman who knew for sure that hers was gone.

She covered her mouth, tried to stop talking, but it proved impossible.

'He's gone too, Mum, Ryan was with Jaden, they were hiding, if Jaden's dead—'

'Enough.' Mary's voice was firm but low. With her hands clamped on Sara's shoulders, she forcibly turned her, frogmarching her away from Jaden's mother, nearer to the school, to stand outside the gates that were no longer guarded, and no longer closed.

'I need to know.' Sara pulled out of her grasp and wrapped her arms around herself.

She would wait all night, like she had waited all day. They would bring the bodies out under cover of darkness; it made sense. Nobody needed to see that.

She wasn't sure if she'd shared her thoughts with her mother; if she had said them aloud or if they were just in her head. It didn't matter. Not much mattered now.

She had been wrong. The sun, though dipping in the sky, still cast an almost obscene light as they rolled the stretchers out. Everyone was hushed now, the screams and fury gone; silent tears were all that remained.

Sara's own eyes were wet when she saw them. A small cluster, two police officers, two stretchers wheeled along. Not body bags after all, but instead covered in sheets.

Behind them trailed a single child.

Scott.

A clash of bodies; hers, his, her mother's. The medic who walked beside him unceremoniously shoved aside. She ran her hands over him, seeking wounds, pressing her fingers underneath the rucksack that he still wore on his back and finding nothing. Beside them, two paramedics took over the responsibility of the trolleys that contained the forms of two boys.

A solitary boot was on show. She knew that boot; had purchased it along with its paired mate. Had flinched and grimaced at the cost, but swallowed it anyway.

She said her younger son's name, once, very quietly. Of its own accord her hand reached out to flip the sheet back. A tight grip on her fingers: Mary, shaking her head, preventing her. The paramedics and police officers crowded in, forming a human barrier between her and the stretchers.

'You don't need to do that.' The gravelly voice of an older officer rumbled around her head.

She looked into his eyes and saw they were wet and red-rimmed.

His face told her everything she needed to know.

44

Sara
Now

It was the first time she had spoken of how that day ended. She hadn't even thought about it before now. Oh, sure, her brain had tried; sometimes it screamed at her to recall it, to relive it, and some part of her knew it was essential to allow the grief in in order to eventually move through it.

'There are stages of grief, I think,' she said now to Travis. 'How many are there?'

She looked up at him for the first time since she had started to talk. What she saw made her blanch. His face was ashen and slack. His eyes seemed damp. Just like the police officer back at the school. A streak of anger rushed through her, hot in her veins.

He was a therapist. He was supposed to be stoic and attentive, not sad and crying. This was *her* grief, her story, her life among all the death.

'Why are you crying?' she demanded.

He coughed and scrubbed at his face. 'Hay fever,' he croaked, his voice hoarse.

She didn't believe him, and for a moment she wondered about his abilities. 'This is all in confidence, right?' she blurted. 'I mean, you said so, you have to take an oath as part of your job, don't you?'

She saw the impact her words had, and the subsequent change in him. He didn't want to lose her, not now he was so close to gaining her confidence.

He pushed himself off the tree he leaned against and came to sit beside her. He didn't look at her, and for that, she was grateful. She didn't want to see her own pain mirrored in somebody else's eyes.

'There are many stages of grief. Shock, pain, anger, denial.' She felt a slight pressure on her fingers, which were as numb as her heart. Looking down, she saw he had her hands in his. 'There is more to this, isn't there?' he asked gently. The pressure tightened. Her knuckles whitened. 'Jojo?' he probed.

She pulled her hand free, the wedding ring that she still wore catching painfully. At last, some feeling.

In spite of the muggy heat, she shivered. How did he even know about Jojo? And why was he so fixated on her former lover? The way he spoke about him was almost familiar, as if he'd known him. He couldn't have. He must have read something online. She shuddered to think of the websites where the school-gate mothers had posted. It was why she'd come offline; why she'd taken the batteries out of the Scott's phones and stashed them in the back of a cupboard.

'You don't need to speak about him,' she said. '*We* don't need to.' She corrected herself, trying to steer the conversation away.

None of this was about Jojo. She didn't even want to go there. That was something else she couldn't – wouldn't – think about, let alone discuss.

'What *do* you want to talk about?' he asked.

Confused, she edged away from him on the fallen tree trunk. She had talked already. She had relayed to him one of the very worst things that had ever happened to her. What more was there to say?

Lots more, a little voice whined in her head. *The truth, for a start.*

She shushed herself. Beside her, she felt Travis eyeing her.

'I think that's enough, for today anyway.' She pushed herself up, her body heavy and lethargic. In the clearing, the heat punched at her and she pulled at the front of her shirt.

Travis was right. Rain was coming. There was an oppressiveness in the air, like the whole of the forest was weighed down with something she couldn't even see.

Perhaps that was what had her feeling so strange. Didn't they say things got really weird before a storm?

'I'll walk you back.' Travis stood up too.

She nodded in his direction and pretended not to see the disappointment on his face.

They walked in silence, her following him, stepping where he did, barely listening to his murmurs of warning when they strayed too close to the dangerous entrances of the old caves.

'Did Scott have many friends back in London?' he asked casually.

She shrugged, even though he couldn't see the motion, and felt the familiar downward drag on her face as she thought about her elder son. 'I don't know. I guess.'

Beats of silence. In the stiff way he held himself, she could tell that he was forming a question, contemplating the best way to phrase it.

'Was he friends with Noah Miller?' he asked.

She stumbled, her ankle twisting over to one side. In an instant, he was there, one hand on her elbow, the other around her waist. 'Yikes,' he said, 'that's got to sting.'

She looked down, saw the blackberry bramble trailing her path, the barbed-wire-style wound it had inflicted on her ankle, the beads of blood that dotted the skin.

He was wrong. It didn't sting. She felt nothing on her flesh. All the pain was internal, hammers and knives in her body, beating on the inside for release.

'Don't say that name,' she said quietly, brushing his hands away and limping onward.

He obliged, falling mercifully silent, and not for the first time Sara wondered what on earth she had been thinking. If she was going to talk about this, any of this, perhaps all of this, she shouldn't have chosen Travis. There were so many problems that were bound to surface.

She'd slept with him, for Christ's sake; not only that, but she worked with him. Scott seemed keen on the art classes, and on top of that they were practically neighbours.

She'd known she was close to spilling it all; it was far too much for one person to carry. God knows, she'd have been far better off travelling to the city and finding someone there to open up to. Someone she would pay. Someone she wouldn't have to see each and every bloody day.

Bad idea. All of this had been a bad idea.

And worse than that, she hadn't even told him the half of it.

Back on the road, out of the shadows of the woods, she tipped back her head and breathed. The air here was still hot, stifling, burning down her windpipe. Travis paused, hovering beside her, talking in hushed tones about dehydration, alcohol consumed the night before, and offering her *a nice cup of tea*.

Just stop. She wanted to say the words, spit them at him even, but she knew her turmoil wasn't really aimed at him. He was being kind, but his attention was cloying, controlling and claustrophobic.

'Why don't you come for dinner?' he asked. 'I don't want to blow my own trumpet, but I'm a pretty good cook.' Uninvited, his hand moved to graze her ribs. 'You could do with feeding up.'

That irritation again, but she pushed it down, swallowed it, and simply moved out of his reach.

'Scott can come too, both of you.' She heard a twang in his voice, something almost like desperation. How badly he wanted to save her.

His face lit up as though he'd been suddenly struck with a wonderful idea. 'We can all talk, if you like. A group thing, but just the three of us.'

This was new. She'd thought it would send her running, but his offer buzzed around her like a fly.

Could that work?

Would Scott finally talk?

Could she bear to listen?

She needed to; she knew that much. This limbo had lasted almost a year. Twelve long months of pushing the memories and the half-knowledge away. It wasn't healthy. It was killing her. It was killing them both.

In spite of the turmoil that swamped her, she made a decision, ignoring the part of her brain that told her opening up to him was a mistake. 'All confidential?' She looked him in the eye.

His upper lip twitched. Just once, slightly; a giveaway to his anticipation.

It's so important for him to save me, she thought. Why does he need this – us, me – so badly?

'No police?' she asked, determined to clarify the bottom line here.

That question seemed to alarm him. His small pink tongue darted out to touch upon his dry lips. She felt a shiver. No, he wasn't alarmed. He was *excited*.

He recovered quickly. Friendly now, he moved to her again and took hold of her arms. 'Anything you tell me is between you and me. Both of you can trust me.'

Finally, she saw what she needed to, even if it wasn't really there and was simply in her head. Sincerity. The need to spill it all now was overwhelming. 'Tonight, then. And thank you.'

45

Sara
Before

Night and day had no meaning, no distinction. There was no sleep, no set times for meals.

Mary was there sometimes, and then Sara was alone. Faces peered at her – a doctor, her mother – but her elder son stayed away.

She called to him on occasion, knowing he was some-where in the house, but since that moment when she had seen him stumbling out of the school, he had not approached her.

One day, or night, she fumbled with her mobile and rang her mother.

'Where is Scott?' she asked, thought she'd asked, but no words emerged. She coughed, great hacking whoops, and tried again. 'Where's Scott?'

'He's here with me,' Mary said calmly. 'We're down-stairs. Do you need anything?'

They were downstairs. Sara didn't give a fig where her mother was; she'd just needed to know that Scott was somewhere... safe.

She hung up the phone and laid her head down on whatever bed she was lying on.

Many hours later, or days, she smelled the familiar scent of her younger son. It filled her senses, and she was crying before she'd even opened her eyes.

His bed. She was in Ryan's bed.

Later, there was a minister, or a vicar – some member of the clergy – downstairs. Sara sat and half listened, plucking at the hem of the clean shirt she wore, wondering how Mary had bathed and dressed her when she had absolutely no recollection of it.

Once the man in the dog collar had left, she asked some questions.

'How many?'

'Twenty,' said Mary. 'Nineteen students, one teacher.'

'Jojo's son?'

'Gone.'

'The kid that did it all.' Sara's lip curled in self-disgust that she was even asking about him. 'Noah?' she spat.

'Dead.'

She nodded. 'Good.'

Mary hesitated. 'They say there was maybe another one, a second shooter, but they don't know who it was.'

There were plenty more questions on the cusp of Sara's mind, but none that she needed the answers to right now. Just that short conversation had been too much, too exhausting. It wasn't the end, either. There was a funeral, and some sort of horrible fucking decision that all the parents would attend the funerals of all the children, or so Mary told her in her no-nonsense way.

'A mark of respect and support. You're all in this together.'

Nineteen funerals. Sara leaned over the arm of the chair and dry-heaved. She could hardly stand to attend her own son's service, let alone eighteen others.

'No way,' she said.

Mary nodded. 'Think about it,' she said.

Mary took it upon herself to take Scott out frequently. One time, when Sara was home alone, Jojo knocked on the door.

He looked bloody awful, she thought. He looked like a shadow or a ghost. He wanted to see Scott, now that he didn't have a son of his own. Sara wasn't offended; she understood that if she'd told him fifteen years ago, he would have accepted Scott as his own, regardless of Mack, regardless of his own wife.

Regardless of what other people thought.

Later, in the days after Ryan's funeral, which Sara didn't remember, she had awoken. She was slightly more alert, more aware of conversations going on around her. She was really bad still; the days were like wading through mud. Yet though her thoughts were fragmented, jagged yet blunted, one thing struck her.

How would Scott feel about them opening up their life for someone who had been up until now a stranger? Would he accept Jojo as his father?

She went in search of him, stumbling outside Ryan's bedroom door. Unconsciously, her hand reached to open it. How easy it would be to sink back onto his bed and let sleep and darkness take her.

She clenched her fingers, altered her trajectory and carried on to Scott's room.

It was empty. She stood in the doorway, listening through the constant whine of sadness that settled and multiplied in her head.

The house was quiet. Mary had taken him out again.

As she stepped into his neat room, vaguely she wondered where her mother went with him. She wondered if they talked, or if he remained resolutely quiet with his grandmother as well.

She was about to back out of the room when the bag caught her eye.

Scott's rucksack, kicked under the bed, the sunshine streaming through the window casting a dappled glow on its corner.

She didn't know why she approached it. Tidying was hardly on her mind. Maybe because she knew that it had been in the school that day; maybe Ryan had even touched it as the boys walked to school together. Ryan's own bag was missing, lost in the carnage of personal items and belongings in the school, which was still cordoned off.

Sara fell to her knees and dragged it out from under the bed.

It was stained, dirty, a splash of crusted brown paint splattered along the front.

She scratched at it absently, some part of her brain dimly aware that this was most unlike Scott, that out of her sons he was the neat one. Ryan was too busy – *had* been too busy, she corrected herself painfully – to take care of his things. Friends calling, sports to play, girls to chase. She smiled, lost in thoughts of her boy.

The bag lay heavy on her thighs, and the smell of it pulled her back to the present.

She sniffed. It didn't just smell bad; it was horrific. Not like an unwashed gym kit, but something darker, something she'd never smelled before.

It wasn't paint, she realised; the bag had come from the school, and inside that school were rivers, lakes, *a sea* of blood.

But confusion still pricked at her. Scott had been unscathed. He had walked out of there without so much as a scratch or a bruise.

Unzipping the bag, aware that her breathing was loud in the otherwise silent house, she upended it.

A single notebook and a couple of pencils dropped to the floor, a block of Post-it notes that would have told her this was Scott's bag even without seeing his name on the notebook.

One more item, caught in the bottom. She put her hand in, closed her fingers around metal and yanked it out. It clattered onto the floor to lie beside the discarded book.

Colours burst behind her eyes. The floor rushed up at her, the room moving crazily around her. Had she not been kneeling down, she would have fallen. As it was, she planted both hands on the ground, locked her elbows and squeezed her eyes tightly closed.

Bile stung the back of her throat. She freed her right hand and clapped it over her mouth.

The room settled around her.

The buzzing in her ears stopped.

The house was once again silent.

She remained like that, frozen, staring and staring, unable to pull her eyes away from the gun on the floor.

Like a puzzle, the pieces suddenly fitted. Not only was Scott the elusive second shooter the police had so far been unable to identify, he had also sent his own brother to his grave.

-

He came home, dropped off by Mary. Her mother ushered him inside, and Sara watched from the darkened living room as he sloped off up the stairs.

'You need anything? Dinner, drink?' Mary took one step inside. 'A chat, darling?'

Sara shook her head and retreated into the shadows of the sofa. 'Nothing, thanks.' Her voice was hoarse as she flicked a hand to dismiss her mother.

When the door closed behind Mary, Sara charged up the stairs and flung open the door to Scott's room. He sat on the bed, the room dark around him. At his mother's sudden movement, he flinched, ducked his head and rolled off the other side of the bed to stand at the far end of the room.

Sara kept coming, arms out, hands gripping his shoulders. 'What did you do?' she hissed, fingers digging into his arms so hard she could feel the bones and gristle of his slight frame.

From the pocket of the oversized cardigan she wore, she pulled out the gun, not caring enough to be careful, not caring if it went off and a bullet hit him, or even her.

'It wasn't mine!' he said, scared, a small voice that she hadn't heard from him since he was a toddler. 'It doesn't belong to me.'

She gripped the gun tightly. Her fingers pulsed, something terrible urging her to strike him with it, again and again.

'He was so good!' She gasped the words as images of Ryan flickered through her mind. 'He saved a girl, he put someone else first over his own life, and then you... you... you took it!'

For the first time, Scott looked invested. 'What girl?'

Sara, thrown, blinked at him. From outside her own body, she saw herself, her fingertips white from the pressure she'd put on Scott's upper arms.

Suddenly she was exhausted.

'What girl?' Scott asked again.

Sara searched around in her memory. Flashes of memory came back, the trembling lips, the tear-filled eyes. *Your son saved my life.*

'Emily,' she said dully. She fell back to sit on Scott's bed. He remained where he was, staring at her, an intensity in his eyes that made her heart jolt. 'What?' she asked.

'Nothing.' He folded his arms. 'I didn't hurt him. I didn't hurt Ryan.'

The cold metal of the gun that she'd forgotten she held told her otherwise. She supposed she needed answers, reasons – why, why, why? The question bounced around in her head, rattling like the pills in her otherwise empty stomach. But the words wouldn't come.

'What did you do?' She asked it again, a whisper this time.

Scott raised his chin and opened his mouth.

Suddenly she couldn't bear to hear his answer. She turned away from him and walked to the door. On the landing, she stood with her back to him. 'We need to leave,' she said, one thought, one decision, finally managing to push through the fog. 'Pack what you want. I'll be back soon.'

46

Travis
Now

Travis set the scene with precision. In his bones he knew that this was going to be the most important night of their lives. This tragedy that had taken one of Sara's sons but for some reason spared the other had burrowed inside and infected them both like a poison.

Tonight, Travis would start Sara on the road to recovery. He would show her that under his careful guidance, she would thrive.

On the stove, a large pot of chilli simmered gently. It could stay there all night without fear of spoiling. He imagined that she wouldn't arrive here with much of an appetite, but there had to be a casual ambience in his home for both of them to feel they could open up.

On the table was a large bowl of fragrant rice. Salad beside it, already wilting in the heat, he saw with disappointment.

For beverages he had thought long and hard. Sara liked a drink, and alcohol was probably necessary for her to talk tonight, so he had put out a bottle of vodka. It looked hard and a bit crass, so he softened it with a jug of fresh cranberry juice. Just for one night, he told himself. Eventually she would need to be weaned off the booze. He would help her with that. Sometimes, though, it was vital that she had some – if he sensed she was closing up, slipping back into old ways. But it was he who would decide when, and how much.

He surveyed the table, eyeing up the Coke for Scott and iced water for himself.

Tonight, he would not drink.

Tonight wasn't about himself.

Tonight was the start of the future.

The table was set, and the place looked homely and welcoming. He fussed with the lighting, turning it down low. In the lounge area there were three armchairs set around a low coffee table. He would sit by the fireplace, in the darkest part of the room. He would be concealed, and the spotlight would be on Sara and, to a lesser degree, her son. Hopefully they would forget about him, and they would talk, and Travis would discover the roots of their disconnect.

If they struggled, he would use all his skills to steer them back onto the right path.

He had heard the worst of it now. The moment she had realised her second son was dead.

He imagined it, as he had back then when she was telling him. The sheet that covered him, the older police officer who had clearly been crying.

And yet she had never spoken of it until now.

He felt himself puffing a little with pride, happy that she had trusted him with her grief. It buoyed him, gave him strength to listen further.

Tonight, perhaps Scott would talk.

It occurred to him then that Scott had been there in the locked-down school, watching classmates and friends as their lives left them, one of them his own brother.

Suddenly the way the boy was made sense. That look on his face, the near sociopathy that Travis was sure he'd glimpsed. The confusion, the despair, the sadness, the terror; all of these might have collided, creating something akin to excitement.

Travis could identify with that.

With one last look at the room, he moved to straighten the cutlery he'd laid out on the table. Then he moved outside to the porch to wait for his guests.

-

They came through the trees, silent and pale, like two little ghosts. They seemed to take care to walk with a gap between them, eyes looking up, down, all around; anywhere apart from at each other.

He put on a smile and held up his hands. 'Welcome again, so glad you both came!'

He beckoned them inside and watched as they entered his home and moved in different directions. Scott wandered over to the table, staring down at the food that Travis had prepared. Sara stood by the door, one hand on the frame, and looked around.

They really were fractured, he thought, and not for the first time, he reflected upon how therapists' offices were usually rather small. In a single room, there was nowhere to run.

Here, there was too much room, and if Travis wasn't careful, this would turn into a social occasion, reminiscent of last night. Sara would drink, Scott would escape into the forest at the first opportunity. He needed to manage this and exert some much-needed control.

'Sara, sit down. Do you want food yet, or shall we chat?' Casual, yet with an underlying instruction. Travis preened with his foresight.

Reluctantly, Sara edged fully into the cabin. Travis slipped behind her and closed the door firmly.

'I-I guess we'll eat?' Sara shrugged and looked to Scott, still staring down at the table.

Without looking at his mother, he nodded, pulled out one of the chairs and sat down.

'Great.' Travis clapped his hands together and, without touching her, steered Sara to the table. With him at her back, she paused, looking at the five other chairs.

'Here.' Travis pulled out a chair on the same side of the table as Scott, leaving a space in between them, mindful that sitting opposite each other, eye to eye, face to face, might be too overwhelming.

He was nothing if not thorough.

'What is this?' Scott spoke up, his voice unusually sharp, his tone suspicious.

Travis drew in a breath and glanced at Sara. She looked a thousand miles away, her gaze fixed on the window. Outside, the trees moved in the early dusk.

He cleared his throat. 'I know what happened to you, Scott, to your brother. And before, losing your dad. It's a lot to cope with.' He paused and lowered his eyes. 'It's a tragedy, and it's clearly disconnected the two of you. We thought maybe we could have a chat, talk about how you're feeling, if there's anything we can do to help each other.'

Scott stared at him, his eyes dark, his expression impossible to fathom.

'No, I meant what is this?' He lifted a hand and jabbed at the wooden spoon resting in the pan of chilli.

'Oh.' Travis felt himself burning. How did this boy always seem to make him feel small, belittled? To cover his annoyance, he forced a jovial laugh. 'Well, that's chilli. Are you hungry?'

'No.' There was a scraping sound as Scott pushed his chair back.

Panic rose in Travis. Sara remained where she was, looking outside, as though she hadn't heard any of the conversation.

He was losing Scott. It looked like Sara was already lost to him. He fought against the anxiety.

'Sit, just for a while,' he said. 'Please,' he added, 'I'd like to listen, to try and help.'

Just talk, he begged, though he didn't say the words aloud. *Just start a dialogue. Anything, even if it's a torrent of fury, of hurt, of anger or pain.*

Just. Say. Something.

Scott's face was granite, like a stone carving. Travis held his breath. The boy was on the edge; he could see it in his expression, in his hands, the fingers clenched into tight little fists, in his spine, straight as a spear, and in the dark, scrutinising gaze that moved away from Travis to settle upon Sara.

She flinched, as though she'd been burned.

'I didn't lose my father, did I?' Scott's voice belied his posture. His tone was low, calm. Too calm, thought Travis. Eerily calm.

Sara looked at him. 'What?' she asked.

It was time to step back. Travis cursed himself. The dialogue he had so desperately wanted had begun, but it was all wrong. They were supposed to have been sitting in comfort, in the armchairs he had so strategically placed. Travis himself was supposed to be in the semi-darkness, there but not there, and yet he was here, caught midway between the kitchen and the dining area, a spotlight on him, highlighted instead of hidden.

He tried to move soundlessly, slipping to the darker end of the table, where it met the kitchen counters. He was reminded of that deer again: mustn't startle them, mustn't pull them out of the essential discussion that was *happening right now*.

Holding his breath, he sidled into the kitchen and moved to the window. There he remained, arms folded across his chest.

Carry on, he silently begged mother and child.

Scott raised his chin and pointed a finger towards him.

'*He* said I lost my dad. But I didn't, did I?' He faltered, just for a moment, before apparently deciding to push on. 'He wasn't my dad. You lied. All my life, you lied, and everyone knew about it but me.'

Under the low lighting at the table, Travis watched Sara's face carefully. Her cheeks were pale, as bone white as her fingers, which clenched the table edge in a death grip. Then, as the seconds ticked on, a tide of colour rose from her chest, spreading to her neck. She put a hand to her throat.

'Who… who told you that?' Her voice was a gasp, as though her breath wouldn't come, and the words hitched out of her in a painful effort.

Scott leaned his forearms on the table and shifted his chair so that he faced her directly. A full-on assault.

'Noah Miller told me.' The name rang out in the otherwise silent room, and from the effect it had on Sara, it could have been accompanied by knives and bullets.

She let go of the table and fell back in her chair. 'No!' she cried, pitifully, her hands to her face now, fingers dragging at her cheeks.

Travis felt his breath quicken.

'Yes.' Scott was back to sullen now, his face creased in a scowl.

Sara let her hands fall to her lap. A change overcame her, as though she'd remembered something, a weapon of sorts, and despite himself, Travis closed his eyes.

'That's… that's why you did it?'

Travis heard the scrape of a chair. His eyes flew open. Not Scott's, as he'd anticipated, but Sara's. Half standing now, bent double as though in pain, her eyes wide and flashing with fury.

Scott pulled back, leaning away from the sudden change in her. 'Wh-what?' he asked, his chest heaving. 'Why I did what?'

Travis saw her hands come up, and for a dreadful moment he thought she was going to strike her son. Unable to stop it, unwilling to step in, he held his breath.

Sara's fingers twitched before curling into fists. She brought them down onto the table, pounding the wood time and time again.

The tabletop darkened. The fleshy sides of Sara's hands glowed red in the low lighting.

'Sara!' Travis said her name, horror in his voice that she didn't even seem to be aware that she was bleeding.

The beating of the table slowed and faltered. Throughout, her eyes never left her son's face.

'That's why you did it. That's why you killed your brother.'

47

Sara
Now

A whole year had passed and she had never been able to say the words. Now they were out there, falling from her lips to land on the table and nestle among the blood that splattered the worn wood underneath her hands.

She gazed at it, distracted for a moment by the stain. She wondered if it was really there, and if so, whose blood it was. She put a fingertip in it, swirled it around, seeking proof that it wasn't just a vision.

For Sara saw blood everywhere these days; a stark reminder of all that had been spilled that day last year. Blood leaving her son's body, blood caused by her other son.

'You know, it wasn't Ryan who saved Emily's life.' Scott spoke up for the first time. His voice had a tremor to it, and was quiet, forlorn almost. 'I did that. I got her out of the building.'

Sara removed her hand from the stained table and looked at her fingers. They were red and wet. Maybe it wasn't blood. Perhaps it was wine that had been spilled. She licked at it, tasted iron and winced.

To her left, someone cleared their throat. The sound made her jump. At his end of the table, Travis leaned forward.

'Scott is explaining the events leading up to... uh, the...' He trailed off miserably, before trying again. 'It might be good to listen to him.'

She inhaled deeply and forced herself to look at her son.

'What were you saying?'

'It wasn't Ryan who saved Emily. I never even saw him until the end. He was hiding, through all of it. I saved Emily, and others too. I could have left the school with her, but I didn't. I went back for *him*.'

'To... to hurt him.' *To kill him*, she wanted to say, but she'd already said it once, and she didn't think she could say it again. It was like a knife inside her ribs the first time.

'No!' Scott swiped at his eyes, and she watched with fascination.

He hadn't cried. Even afterwards, at the funerals, the memorials, the burials, he had been dry-eyed, emotionless.

'Go on.' She felt it moving closer, something that had previously detached from her, something vital that a year ago had cut its own cord and floated away.

Where only grief had been, now there was a kind of strange curiosity to hear his story.

'It was Emily's fault. She mentioned Ryan. I didn't even know she knew him, which was stupid of me, because everyone knew him.' An odd, whisper-thin gasp escaped from Scott. 'Everyone loved him. So... so I knew I had to go back.'

'You went to find him?' Sara was partially aware that her hands had crept back to the table, sweeping back and forth through the rapidly drying bloodstain. 'You looked for him, went back to find him, to hurt—'

'NO!'

She blanched at his shout, the volume and intensity striking through the numbness.

'I went back for him because I knew you loved him best. And if you knew there was something I could have done but didn't, and he got… hurt…' Scott paused, swallowed and looked across the room at the far wall, 'then I knew you'd love me even less than you already did.'

Beside her, Sara heard a sigh.

Travis. She had almost forgotten about him.

'You went back inside, towards danger?' He spoke up, irritating her. She shot him a glance, but for once he wasn't looking at her. He was looking at Scott.

'Yeah.' Scott seemed relieved to have someone else asking questions. Questions that were not accusatory in their nature.

Sara frowned at Travis, wondering what he made of this. At the thought of what was coming, the confession – for surely Scott would spill, eventually – she reminded herself that he couldn't do anything with the information he heard.

He had an oath to follow.

Safe in the knowledge of no more consequences, she shifted in her chair to face her son.

'You had a gun,' she said, blackly, feeling the fury twist and shiver in her. 'I found it in your bag.'

She darted a glance at Travis, perversely pleased to see the shock on his face. *See*, she wanted to say to him. *It's not me being unkind or unloving. He had a gun!*

'He gave it to me,' Scott said, his expression solemn. 'At the end, Noah trusted me. He gave me a gun.'

It was like a punch. Even though she'd known it all along, the fact that he admitted there had been collusion, and trust, left her feeling winded.

Her fingers spider-walked across the table towards the cluster of bottles. The urge to read the labels and find the one with the highest alcohol content was strong. Once again, her hands twitched.

'You said you saved others.' Travis's voice rang out. Sara's hands skittered, peeled back to lie once more in her lap. 'Who were they, and how did you save them?'

For the second time, Scott seemed relieved that a question had been asked. He sat forward, and this time his face seemed eager, alert and open.

Something that felt a lot like guilt rattled through her. She saw it then, that she should have done this before now. She should have taken Scott somewhere, to someone, anyone, so he could have spoken about this.

How much further damage had she caused her already wounded boy?

'They were in a hall, loads of them, teachers and kids; he put them all in the main assembly hall.' Scott was talking now, and Sara forced herself to listen. 'He chained up all the doors so they couldn't get out. The glass in the door had a bullet hole in it. It looked like... you know, like, when a stone hits a car windscreen.' He held the heels of his hands together and splayed his fingers wide. 'It was all cracked; it wouldn't take much to punch the glass out.'

'You did that?' At some point Travis had crept closer, was leaning on the table now, his chin in his hands, fascination painted on his face.

Scott shook his head. 'No. I left Noah's bolt cutters propped up against the glass. Matty saw me. I couldn't say anything, couldn't smash the glass myself or Noah would have…' He looked down, swallowed. 'I hoped he'd got my message. I hoped he would break the glass that was already cracked, get the tool, cut the chains off, escape.'

Sara's breath hitched as she remembered. The sudden flood of people that had emerged from the school. The great escape.

Scott had done that?

No. No, he hadn't done that.

'None of them said that,' she said.

Scott looked at her. 'What?'

'That Emily, she didn't say you'd saved her. This… this Matty, he would have said if you'd helped. Why didn't they say that?'

Scott drew in a breath and levelled his gaze at her. Suddenly, for the briefest moment, he looked like the adult. 'What did Emily say?' he asked her. 'What did she say to you?'

Reluctantly, Sara took herself back to that moment. Even though she tried desperately hard to block everything about that day, it wasn't difficult to recall.

'She said… she said…' The recollection came in a flash. As soon as it had, she realised her mistake. She remembered it verbatim. The beauty of the girl, those blue eyes and the tears that fell from them. Even crying, she had been gorgeous.

I wanted to tell you, I had to say in case…

Your son saved my life.

We had no way of escaping.

A window that Sara's son had helped the girl through. Palms that were criss-crossed with scratches, the gravel still pressed into them.

He told me to run, and not to look back.

Not once had Emily said Ryan's name.

'It was you.' The three words were a sob. Her fingers danced on the table again. The sole of her shoe tapped out a rhythm on the hardwood floor.

Scott nodded, and despite the new-found knowledge, Sara wanted – *needed* – more.

'The other kid,' she demanded. 'Matt?'

'Matty,' said Scott.

'Matty Cranshaw.' Travis spoke up again, startling them both.

'How do you—' Scott started.

'I remember his name. From the news site.' Travis nodded apologetically towards where his computer sat. 'He… he died, didn't he?'

Scott nodded solemnly.

Impatiently, Sara reached across the table, her hands within inches of her son. The need to know now was fierce, and it was terrible that she wanted to skirt over the names of the victims, the poor dead children whose lives had barely started. But her need was here, alive, and the urgency to finally understand pulsed in her.

'What happened?' she urged. 'What happened at the end?'

48

Scott
Before

The words that Ryan had spoken to him: 'It doesn't matter to me. You're my brother. I love you.'

The words were shocking in themselves. The brothers didn't speak like that; teenage boys rarely did. Those words, in those last frantic, frenetic moments, sparked a heat in Scott that was love returned.

It was the truth, Scott realised. But more than that, he had known it anyway. Ryan was a pain, he induced an envy in Scott like no other, but *none of that was the kid's fault*. These were the mistakes of their mother, of Jaden's father, maybe even of Mack Fuller, because God knows Sara wasn't a wicked woman. There had been discord there for her to go to another man. And it didn't matter.

It didn't matter.

What did matter was three of the four remaining getting out alive.

And that had always been Scott's endgame, from the moment he pushed Emily out of the window, saving her life.

Her life wasn't the important one here, no matter how popular she was nor how pretty.

She had said his brother's name, and in that moment, Scott had realised that he could do this. That he *must* do this. Not just for his mother, but because it was what Ryan would have done for him.

He had been frozen at first, but then it had clicked in his mind. Noah had seen something in Scott, something he thought they shared. A kinship, a binding, a partnership. *A second shooter.*

And Scott had known that the only way to get his brother out of this was to go along with it. The plan was formed.

Now there was someone else. He didn't matter as much as Ryan, but Jaden had done nothing wrong. Ryan had done nothing wrong. It was up to Scott to save them from the sins of their parents. He didn't know how Noah knew this information about his family. His random thought corrected itself: *everyone* seemed to know this rumour. Everyone apart from him. Because he hadn't listened. Dismissive, he hadn't wanted to know.

But it didn't matter. All that mattered was living, and saving.

Now, it would end.

Scott lifted the gun, wrapped his right hand around the handle, held his wrist steady with his other hand.

Noah sensed the double cross. Maybe he'd known it was coming all along. Maybe he didn't think they shared a kinship, that there were no ties to bind them; maybe he had never needed a second shooter. Maybe he just wanted drama and excitement and an ending to end all endings.

Crack!

Crack – crack!

Three bullets, discharging at an incredible velocity.

Three bullets, finding their targets.

Smoke and gunfire, Scott's vision gone as a thick fog covered him. And then, belatedly, an alarm sounded, shrieking through the school.

Code purple! Code purple!

It had been mentioned on induction day; code purple meant the students and teachers should evacuate to the nearest meeting point. Code red was the highest level: *Disregard any fire alarms. Intruder alert/hostile situation – lockdown required.*

Even now, even when it was so very nearly over, they didn't hit the correct alarm.

The alarm shrilled on and on. The smoke thinned, dimmed and finally cleared.

Scott collapsed back against the pillar. He wished that the fog would come back.

He closed his eyes so he didn't have to look at the scene in front of him.

49

Travis
Now

Scott's story of how that day ended was pitifully short.

How simple it had been for those boys. All they cared about was surviving. Scott, quiet, unassuming, forgotten-about Scott, had taken it upon himself to save his brother's life.

It was admirable and beautiful and heartbreaking and bittersweet.

It was also very, very troubling.

Scott had killed someone. Another boy, someone of his own age. What had that done to him?

Uncomfortably, Travis thought back to the pit cave. That look in Scott's eyes. The fire he had started. The answer he had given when Travis had warned him that smoke fumes could kill.

I know, he had said.

And Sara had seen it. From the start, she had assumed her other son's guilt. It was there, it was there inside him. It had to be, to pull that trigger and then carry on as normal for an entire year.

Travis's heart thumped painfully in his chest.

Travis identified with Scott. The loner, the one cast aside. The one who didn't matter, not to family or society.

The familiarity was uncomfortable. And familiarity bred contempt.

Unconsciously, Travis withdrew from the table. He moved carefully, slowly, stealthily to the darkened kitchen area. He didn't say a word, but he observed them carefully.

For the first time since Scott had finished telling his story, Travis looked at Sara.

Her face was wet, he saw, but she made no move to wipe the tears away. They continued to fall from her eyes, a river on her cheeks.

And still nobody said a word.

A crack at the window, like a thousand little hands tapping on the glass, startled all three of them.

'Oh!' said Sara. 'What... who is...?'

Travis's heart had barely slowed from Scott's retelling of the last day at Farenden. With the noise at the window, he put his hand to his chest.

What now? Intruders? Here, in Kielder?

The sound moved around the cottage, surrounding them with what now sounded like multiple bullets.

Travis backed up, the kitchen worktop pressing painfully into his spine. Not here, not in his forest, not in his life of calm and order and peace. Frightened now, he looked at Scott.

What have you brought here? he thought. What have you brought to my door?

Scott moved with no hesitation, stalking to the door, for the first time seeming to Travis like so much more than an innocent kid.

'Scott!' he managed, as the boy reached for the door handle. 'Wait, you don't—'

304

Paying no heed, Scott pulled the door open. Pellets rained down upon him, flying into the room, slap-slap-slapping on the wooden floor.

'Hellfire!' Travis wasn't sure if he said the word, or thought it, but his motion echoed it as he threw himself to the floor.

A scrape of a chair, footsteps, exclamations, and then… laughter.

What?

Slowly, Travis reached out his hand and pulled himself into a half-crouch. From his hiding place in the kitchen, he watched as Sara and Scott drifted out of the door. They were silent now, no more laughter.

He shivered suddenly. Had they really been laughing?

The onslaught lessened but didn't stop. Outside, darkness covered the forest, cloaking it in black, but not enough to disguise the…

The rain.

It was raining. Bucketing down, as his dad would have said. Inside the door, fragmented white balls littered the floorboards.

Hail. Hail and pounding, frightening rain.

Just rain.

Not bullets.

Ashamed and embarrassed, Travis straightened up and picked his way to the door, stepping over the rapidly melting hailstones.

They were out there in the downpour. Still standing apart, but somehow together for the first time, he noted.

They were not talking, and the laughter he had heard before while he had cowered beneath the countertop had stopped. They didn't look at each other, but the discord, the disconnect, had diminished somewhat.

She wouldn't need Travis any more. If she fixed things with her son, all her attention would be on Scott. There would be nothing left for Travis. He felt his breathing quicken with alarm. His hands curled into fists by his sides.

The rain, which had lessened for just a minute, re-formed in the thunderclouds above the branches and let rip again. Now, Sara did speak to Scott, though over the rain Travis couldn't hear what she said. She pointed back towards the cabin; Scott nodded, hunched over as though it would protect him from the storm, and they hurried back to the porch.

'All right?' asked Travis as he took a step back, clearing the doorway for them to duck inside.

'It's really cold.' Scott shivered. 'Like, it was blazing hot today, but now...' He trailed off and stared outside until Travis closed the door.

'Maybe we'll eat that chilli now,' suggested Travis coolly. Before they could reply, he ushered them over to the table.

'We won't stay too much longer,' said Sara as she took a seat. 'I think we have things to talk about.' She gave a sideways look at Scott beside her.

Travis watched as her fingers did the little dance on the tabletop again. There was hesitation in her movement, but this time they skittered all the way over to Scott's hand. They rested on his fingers, intertwined briefly. One squeeze before she let his hand go and picked up her fork.

He was losing her, Travis realised. Amends had been made as far as she was concerned. It was evident in the way she shovelled the chilli first onto her plate, and then into her mouth. Travis thought of the other times he'd seen her eating. She picked at things, no appetite, food just fuel to keep on living, though for what, she hadn't known.

Didn't she realise that it wasn't as simple as this? Didn't she know that there were still months, years of therapy ahead? Not just for her, but for Scott, too? That the feelings she had carried for Scott for so long, even before Farenden had happened, wouldn't just go away overnight with a ten-minute explanation and a hot dinner? Didn't she realise that what Scott had done had probably opened up a whole other persona in the boy? A fresh new personality that Travis had already been partially privy to? A personality troublingly like his own?

He was the one who picked at his food now, staring gloomily into the bowl.

An hour later, there was a break in the rain. Sara peered out of the door.

'I think we should go now, it's not raining too hard,' she said.

Obediently, Scott moved to stand beside her at the door. Balancing on one foot, he pulled a trainer on, then the other.

'Thanks for dinner,' he said, his voice a monotone.

Travis nodded and scratched his head as he watched the boy. Scott hadn't taken his eyes off his mother.

'You could stay here,' he said, clutching at anything so that Scott and Sara wouldn't be alone together. 'Sometimes storms like this can knock the electricity out; your place could possibly be in—'

The lights in his own cottage flickered, dimmed, once, twice, before going out altogether.

'Shit,' he swore, and then, because he was a gentleman, he apologised. 'Sorry.'

From the darkness came laughter, hers again, and Travis let the sound run over him. It was like music, or the ocean on a summer's day. A blue, cloudless sky. It was beautiful. It was tragic that he was excluded from it.

'We'll just leave you to it, okay?'

In the pitch-black, he couldn't see her, but already he felt her moving away from him.

'Wait!' He bustled around, thankful that the layout of his home was imprinted in him. He opened drawers, gathered candles and matches, ones he kept for just this situation, because Travis was nothing if not prepared.

Slowly, the room came back into view, and he looked at Sara's face, lovely in the candlelight, and felt a sad smile on his own lips.

'Scott, you go on ahead,' she said suddenly. 'I'm going to help Travis clear the table. I'll be right behind you, okay?'

Scott shrugged, his usual non-committal reply to most things he was asked, thought Travis snippily, but he was thankful that the boy left, leaving Sara alone with him.

'You don't need to help,' he said. 'Sit down, have a drink, talk to me while I clear the things away.' He looked at the bowl of chilli, still half full. 'I can put some in a carton for you to take home, heat it up tomorrow, maybe.'

Her hand on his arm stopped his speech and his thoughts. The dimly lit room blurred around her, the only clear thing her face, her features, so close to him.

'I didn't get to talk tonight, and that's okay, because I really, really needed not to talk. I needed to listen, and I needed to hear, you understand?'

He stared, aghast at her tone. She seemed in control, with a mission, lighter somehow, and *it wasn't the way it was supposed to be.*

'But you need to hear me, you need to listen to me now, because I think Scott and I could be on our way to some sort of...' she broke off, her eyes far away as she searched for the right word, finally settling on 'recovery'.

He didn't like that, didn't care for how easily she had taken the explanation Scott had given her, taken what she needed from it and discarded the rest, but something told him that now wasn't the time to say that so he simply nodded. 'Go on,' he said.

'I found that gun,' she said, 'in Scott's bag. And... well, you know what I thought, what I felt. But there were other things after that that made me the person you first met.'

Without warning, her eyes blazed for a moment before filling with tears. 'I need to be heard, too.' Her hand came up, found its way to his arm.

He flinched, involuntarily, as though her touch burned him.

He didn't know why, but his heart began to race again, high up in his chest, heat spreading out to his limbs. Dread enveloped him, but he met her eyes and nodded.

It wasn't over. She still needed him.

'I'm listening,' he said.

Sara began to talk.

50

Sara
Before

There was no thought process, just an instinct that took her to Jojo's apartment. She knew where it was, a smart new luxury high-rise block that sat the other side of the school. She had never been there before, didn't even know which flat he lived in, but his name was on the bell. Top floor. The penthouse, she supposed, looking skyward.

She dithered, the gun burning a hole in her pocket, and she cursed herself for bringing it, for touching it, for finding it in the first place.

How different things would have been if she'd remained oblivious. If she'd never found it, she would have eventually carried on, the same way she had after Mack. Minus half of her family, but still with one, and with no knowledge of this terrible, horrible secret.

Jojo knew secrets. Jojo was kind, forgiving, but most importantly, he understood her. He had a vested interest in Scott. He would tell her what to do.

She pressed the bell and held her breath.

–

He drew her in, exclaiming over the sight of her, drenched, hair dripping, shivering. She hadn't even realised it was raining, and she told him so.

His face changed as he put a towel around her.

'You need help, Sara.'

Her breath caught in her throat. Yes, yes, she did, it was why she had come here. Something akin to comfort tickled at her.

She had known Jojo would understand.

He didn't offer her a drink. Instead, he moved slowly over to the coffee table that sat in the centre of the open-plan living area and picked up his tobacco. She watched as he rolled, his fingers steady; unlike hers, which trembled uncontrollably. He held up a cigarette. She reached for it, sucked at it greedily.

'I think it would be a good idea if Scott came here to stay with me.' He slid open the patio door and ducked his head outside. 'The rain's stopping,' he said.

Through the heavy tobacco haze, Sara squinted at him. 'What?' she asked. 'What did you say?'

He leaned against the hip-height wall of the balcony and struck a match. It illuminated his face. Once, the most beautiful face she'd seen. She knew every contour of it, every line, scar and bone.

'Scott needs to be with someone... who can help him.'

'H-h-help *him*?' Sara flung the towel off her shoulders and crossed the room towards him, cigarette dangling, forgotten.

Jojo's lips pinched to form a straight line. His eyes, which once upon a time were only laughing, smiling, cheeky, burned into her. 'You're not coping. You don't even talk to him.' He took a deep drag and leaned forward, the cigarette pointed at her as if to make a point. 'He lost his brother, he was there, he needs to talk to someone. He needs someone to listen to him. You don't even get out of bed.'

Sara was speechless. His words stung like pebbles against her skin. How did he even know this? Who had he been talking to – her mother?

As suddenly as the hurt had come, she was struck by fear. Was it possible he had talked to Scott himself? Had he followed her boy and told him her deepest, darkest secret?

Another fear sprang at her. If he took Scott from her, she would have nothing.

Nobody.

Her entire family gone.

'No!' she said. 'You're not taking him away from me!'

She came at him, the barely smoked cigarette flying as her hands came up and batted at him. Some part of her mind, previously numbed by the massacre, the pills, the shock, the devastation, was suddenly alive. Now she was living, burning, feral with a need to protect. It didn't escape her that for the first time since she had become a mother, she actually felt like one.

Later, back home, she sat in the lounge in the dark. The aftermath of the rain lingered, cloying in her nostrils, her clothes drying to release a pungent, damp scent that clung to her. Another scent, this time of alcohol. Not her, for once. When she had pummelled at Jojo, she had smelled it then. He had seemed in control, in charge. In truth, he was flailing and failing as much as she was.

She smelled the other aromas of Jojo, once so dear and familiar, and in a more recent memory she watched his crumpled form turn away from the blows that landed on his chest. She heard his gasp as she thumped at him with the heels of her hands, and she saw his face as he slipped quietly over the edge of the low balcony, eyes wide with shock as he went, down, down, down.

Now she remembered the awful sound his body had made, the rain scattering around him to wash away the pieces of his insides that were now on the pavement. Her knees buckled beneath her.

Then, she had heard and seen nothing but her own desperation. Now, she remembered everything.

51

Sara
Now

It had been more cathartic than she could ever have imagined. More than she had hoped for. But she hadn't told Travis the truth. For a while, she had been like an audience to herself, listening to the story she was telling him, shame and relief mixing like oil and water as she distorted the true ending of her meeting with Jojo even as she relived it in her mind.

She knew then that she'd never tell anyone. This shame would be her own to hold, always.

'He... he jumped to his death. After, later,' she added hurriedly.

In all fairness, Travis hadn't said very much at all. For that she was grateful. And suddenly she was desperate to leave his cabin and be with her boy.

The rain had started up again. Heavy, possibly even more violent that it had been before. She made her excuses, draped her coat over her head like a makeshift shelter, expecting Travis to ask her to stay, not looking forward to having to turn him down.

Better not to even give him the chance to implore her to remain with him, she thought as she left the cabin and entered the downpour. He had opened a door that had been closed, locked, bolted and boarded up. His job was done.

She wanted to be with Scott. For the first time – not just since Farenden, but for most of his life – she wanted to *be with him*. She wanted to hear about that last day again – if he was up for it, that was, she reminded herself. She mustn't push him. It was painful.

But it was also therapy.

They had so much time to make up for.

No, not 'they'. She did. *She* had to make it up to *him*.

As she emerged from the forest, she gasped as she stepped into a flowing river. The track that was laughingly sometimes called a road had flooded. It was bad, she realised as she moved back onto the bank and stepped carefully towards her home, clutching onto tree branches so she wouldn't get swept away.

Anxiety, never far from the surface, but all the more poignant and pronounced in the short time she'd felt something other than the emotion, grabbed at her.

Had Scott got back to their cabin okay?

She stopped and looked at the torrent that rushed down the track.

Their home was on the upper part of the road, just below the crest at the top of the hill. There was no danger that the water would reach it. If anything, she noted as she cast a look around in the rain-sodden night, it would flow down into the forest. Travis's place was more at risk than hers.

She dismissed the thought of him. He was an adult; he was experienced in the world of the outdoors and extreme weathers. Scott wasn't. Scott was at home, waiting for his mother.

Suddenly the need to see him was as fierce as the anxiety had been a moment earlier.

She stepped off the bank, into the flowing tide, gasping as it came up to just below her knees.

Wading through it, she welcomed the battle, feeling stronger than she had for months – for years.

She was relieved to see the glow of the porch light in the cabin. The electricity wasn't out here, then. One final push, and she staggered up the bank on the left side of the track. In the distance, in the next village over, church bells rang out, muffled against the rain, but there all the same.

Sara caught her breath. Yesterday had come and gone; today was a new day.

It was also the one-year anniversary of the Farenden massacre.

In front of her, the door opened. Scott stood just inside, his eyes darting left, right, assessing the damage of the storm before settling on her.

'It's bad out there,' he said. He raised his voice over the sound of the downpour.

Beside the white rose bush, she stopped to catch her breath. 'Yeah, really bad,' she agreed.

A beat or two that moved from silence into something nearing awkwardness.

Scott broke it by stepping forward and stretching out an arm.

She looked at it for a moment, before reaching out and taking his hand.

'Thanks, son,' she said, as he hauled her up the path and into the house.

–

'Why didn't you tell me sooner?' she asked.

They were sitting by the fire, both in dry clothes, a towel around Sara's wet hair.

Scott shrugged. Sara felt annoyance flitting around her.

'No,' she said. 'That stops now.'

His face in the firelight was wounded, hurt, and she took a breath.

'It's okay for normal teenage things, like if I ask you to clean your room or whatever. But this, it's really grown-up stuff, and I need you to be open and honest with me, okay?'

His lips twitched in something close to a smile. 'Since when you do ever need to tell me to clean my room?'

He wanted to move on, she saw, and that was incredible, and wonderful, but there was so much more to say. They hadn't even scratched the surface back in the session with Travis, not really.

She didn't smile at him in return. 'This is important, Scott. Please?'

He moved a little, his face half in shadow, and when he spoke again, his voice was soft and low, and scared.

'I... I shot someone, I took his life, and I... I didn't want to have to...' He shrugged, caught his mother's eye and apologised. 'Sorry, it's difficult for me to... Anyway, I just didn't want to have to pay for what I did. You know, prison, and all that.'

Sara felt her lips settle into a thin line. They had thought exactly the same thing, but for different reasons. She had made them up and leave because she thought he had killed Ryan, and if it were to become known, she would have lost two sons.

'You thought I'd hurt Ryan.' Scott's voice broke into her thoughts. She chanced a look at him, saw something in his eyes that made her glance away. 'Do you really think I could do that?'

Yes, she wanted to say, but she knew she never could. And now that it was clearer, and she knew what had actually happened, it seemed ridiculous. Scott had always been a good son. Minimal trouble, quiet, unassuming. A pain stabbed at Sara's heart. She wanted to throw herself at his feet and tell him how sorry she was, how terribly she'd behaved, how wrong she'd been.

And how much she loved him.

'I wasn't myself,' she said instead. 'I... Jesus, I really wasn't myself. I'm... I'm so sorry, Scott.'

'It didn't work, anyway. I wasn't quick enough.' His lips quivered. He looked very young in that moment. 'I don't understand how he could have got both of them faster than I got him.'

Got. It didn't escape her that he didn't use the proper terms. Shot. Killed.

He pressed on. 'You thought he was alive still. All this time, up until really recently, like, you put out dinner plates for him.'

As he spoke, a faded memory came to her. Scott, raising his voice, shouting at her. Horrible, awful words. *He's dead, Ryan's dead.* When was that? She had sobbed, turned from him and bolted. Her feet had been bare, and when she stopped running, she was shivering. Winter, then. Months and months ago.

As far as she could remember, they had not spoken of it again. Whenever she referenced Ryan, after that day, Scott had never again tried to remind her that he was dead. He had gone along with it. At times, she'd even heard him talking out loud to his dead brother, mimicking her and her behaviour, her denial. How fearful he must have been, watching his own mother play pretend all this time, as though she were a child or a dementia patient.

And he'd pretended back. For her.

Her heart splintered as the fragmented reminders of what she'd put him through became clear.

All the time she had known Ryan was gone, but it was so much easier to simply not address it. She said as much to Scott now, and watched his face carefully as he listened to her.

'Losing your dad, then... then Ryan,' she took a deep breath, 'it made me feel... it was too much, Scott, do you understand?'

He nodded, but he was no longer looking at her. Instead his gaze settled on the window, the rain that pounded the glass relentlessly.

She had lost him again, she realised. He had inverted, and somehow he seemed smaller. It was the mention of Mack, she realised, as she remembered what he had said back at Travis's place.

He wasn't my dad. You lied. All my life, you lied, and everyone knew about it but me.

They needed to talk about Jojo. But where to start? At the beginning, when she'd cheated on her faithful husband with a man-about-town? In the middle, when she'd discovered at practically the same moment that Mack was dying and she was pregnant? Or at the end, when she'd killed the father of her firstborn son? Sending him toppling to his death, just days after the demise of his own son?

She couldn't explain it to him, couldn't even begin. She couldn't even unpick it herself, and it had been fifteen years.

She had adored Jojo. Not at first, of course; it had been a fling, a reaction to her husband's cold shoulder. She'd thought Mack had fallen out of love with her. Rejected, she had turned to another man. Later, and even now, she had loved Jojo deeply, but back then, from the moment she had found out she was pregnant, shame had overshadowed the love. Every time she'd looked at Scott, she'd seen Jojo and what she'd done.

Ryan, her husband's child, had been a fresh start on a clean slate. Mack's extended life had been nothing short of a miracle. The arrival of Ryan was how it should have been all along. There was no shame in Ryan.

There should never have been any shame in Scott.

The mistakes were hers, for cheating, and Mack's for concealing his diagnosis.

She covered her eyes. Her failings were so clear now it was blinding. Her love for Scott, sudden and all-consuming, as if he were a newborn, crippled her. Fifteen years after the event, her maternal instinct had arrived.

'Mum?' Scott was up close to her, his eyes dark with concern. The vision of him wavered, grew blurry through her tears, and she gasped as she reached her hands out for the boy she could no longer see.

She cried. Floods, rivers, as heavy as the rain outside. A year and more's worth of tears that had been caged since they had all gone: Mack, Jojo, Ryan, and all the others who hadn't made it. Her mother, who had proven herself during those dark days, yet Sara had pushed her away too.

Noah Miller had lit the fuse of a bomb that had been built a long time before.

For a long while, Sara wept. Scott didn't move. He didn't put his arms around her, but he let her clutch onto him. Outside, the rain hammered the windows.

Normally, birdsong and sunlight woke Sara. That morning, there was neither.

At some point in the early hours before dawn, the thunder had moved in. Jagged lightning pierced the darkness of the lounge, where she sat twined around her son. In the white glow, she held her breath as she watched Scott's face. In his sleep, he was free from troubles. The frown that he wore throughout the day vanished. Even when the thunder was directly overhead, he didn't flinch.

Sara cried some more as she studied his sleeping form.

Where did she – *they* – go from here?

She wanted a relationship with her son, but now that the lines of communication had opened, how far should she go with the truth?

She needed to tread carefully so she didn't screw it up again.

A crack sounded; not the dull thud of thunder, but the noise of something splitting. A tree, she thought, and she visualised a trunk, one of those thick hundred-year-old trees in the forest, caught by a lightning bolt, the withered and weathered bark spiking off in all directions.

Her body was stiff and unyielding as she disentangled herself from Scott and moved over to the window to peer outside.

The rain was lessoning, she was sure. It was still coming down, but no longer in sideways sheets. Now it was just heavy, fat drops. Towards the west, the sky was pale. The new day was slow in coming, but it was there on the horizon. She craned her neck, looking upwards.

A brand-new sky for a brand-new day. Suddenly she didn't want to miss the birth of the dawn.

She breathed deeply as she walked back to a still-sleeping Scott.

'I'll be back, sweetie, okay?'

He murmured in reply, his eyes opening to small slits. Behind half-closed lids, his eyes studied her, his pupils large and black and covering his irises entirely.

She concealed a shiver and pulled her cardigan tighter around her. 'Back soon,' she whispered.

52

Travis
Now

Travis hadn't slept at all.

It wasn't due to the storm, even though it had been the worst he had ever encountered in his time here.

No, it was the story Scott had shared. It was the story Sara had told him after Scott left. It had ended too suddenly, and she had withdrawn into herself, glancing at the locked door, seeking escape. She had chosen not to trust him after all, and that disappointed him. There was still so much work to do with Sara.

He had let her go. He had wanted to mull over her son's tale of that fateful day, and the way Sara had changed when she'd finally learned the truth.

Scott was a hero in her eyes now.

This news wasn't good for Travis.

Before he could think of a new direction to take, the rain had returned tenfold, thundering against the windows.

'I need to make a run for it,' she had said, her face anxious as they both turned to watch the downpour.

'Be careful,' he managed to say, without conviction, as she draped her jacket over her head and darted out into the night that was thick with rain.

It was late, past midnight, and – a first for him – he didn't finish clearing up. He cast a glance at the table, strewn with glasses, chilli congealing now in the bowl. Belatedly, he remembered he'd offered Sara some to take home and heat up later. He felt a chill as he pictured her at the door, about to face the rain with that jacket a makeshift shelter. She'd looked back into the room. Had she been looking longingly at the food that he had promised and then forgotten to give her?

He blinked the memory away and went into his bedroom. The bed that she'd been in just the day before. He hadn't washed the sheets. Even from here in the doorway he fancied that the scent of her lingered. It spurred him on. He needed her. He just needed her to need him too.

Outside, thunder boomed, followed almost instantly by a crackle of lightning. Emotion was rising as he made his way back to the door and unlocked it. He opened it onto fire and brimstone, and after a moment's pause, he slipped outside. Every weather phenomenon had been called to the forest. He welcomed the sense of self-flagellation as the wind took his breath away and the rain punched at his bare arms.

Crab-walking across the porch, he set himself down in the easy chair and let the storm rage around him.

It was a stupid idea to be out in this; even though the porch roof sheltered him a little from the rain, he wasn't totally safe. This was confirmed moments later, when a jagged bolt flashed, turning the night momentarily into day. It hit in the forest, not too far from the cabin. A splintering thump, a puff of smoke, and then the long-drawn-out sigh of a tree coming down.

He breathed heavily, the sound audible even over the racket out there. This was what he needed, he realised, to be in a place of anger, pain and hurt. Because right now, that suited his emotions just fine. The rain would wash away his confusion. In time, he would know how to move forward.

—

He wasn't sure if he slept, but when he woke, his legs curled beneath him, cramped and tingling, and his neck aching from the odd angle it had sat in for hours, he moaned.

He was freezing, and soaked through.

He muttered to himself, levering himself up by his arms – the only part of his body that didn't ache – and then paused.

Maybe he did sleep. Maybe he was still sleeping.

He swallowed. This had to be a dream.

But no, the vision approaching him was real enough. Sara.

His arms, supporting his weight on the chair, collapsed. He crumpled back into the seat and moved his hands to his legs, patting at them to get some feeling back.

'Sara,' he croaked, 'morning.'

She gave him a wave, and his heart knocked against his chest. She was so carefree, so... so casual! Almost as though the confession from her son – of murder, no less – had lifted the weight she had carried for the past year.

'Travis, hi.' She ducked under the porch and smoothed back her wet hair. Behind her and all around, the rain still came down. 'Have you been here all night?'

'I needed to watch the storm.' It occurred to him that it was a ridiculous choice of words. Who *needed* to watch a storm? He cleared his throat, mad at himself that he hadn't yet formulated a plan of action to keep her close. He looked past her into the woods, as though the forest would bring him clarity. 'What can I do for you, Sara?'

'What's wrong?' She ignored his question, directing one of her own at him instead.

The black clouds opened to reveal a slice of blue sky. Slowly an idea began to form.

'Where's Scott?' he asked.

She gestured behind her. 'At home.' She smiled, open, happy, real.

All wrong for Travis.

He sighed. 'Look, I've been troubled. I haven't slept, and I feel...' He stopped and assessed his words. He allowed his partial thought to bloom and grow. 'We need to speak to the police,' he said. 'We need to tell them exactly what Scott told us last night.'

As soon as he said the words, he felt a flush of enlightenment wash over him. The police would come; they would take Scott away. He had killed, and even though there had been extenuating circumstances, the bottom line hadn't changed. He would need to be questioned at length, there would be a prison sentence, surely, for the concealment as well as the crime.

Sara would be left alone. They wouldn't take her too; she'd been oblivious until last night. She would need support and guidance, love and care and direction.

She would need Travis.

His nose twitched at the words he had spoken without mulling them over. It would have been better to make an anonymous call to the authorities, and he cursed himself internally.

Salvage this, he told himself. *This is important.*

'Wh-what do you mean?' Sara came towards him, her feet loud in the sudden stillness.

The rain had stopped. The sky, previously black as night, was yellowing. He breathed deeply, a half-smile on his face. It was a sign. He was doing the right thing.

When the door at the top. Sara told him that she didn't feel well, sudden chills —

I hear you told Travis, his eyes slowly blinking open, winced while I described it, waited a few moments our line. Traves on her. He was telling the doctors.

53

Sara
Now

Blindsided, she stared at Travis.

What? *What?*

She looked at him, at his surroundings. He had clearly spent all night out here, in the midst of the storm. Had the lightning struck him? Had he been hit on the head by flying debris, whipped up by the strange, howling summer wind that had chased the storm through the forest? Had a bang to the head driven him insane?

Everything that she had begun to feel after their session last night melted away. The new start, the feeling of hope fled. Suddenly the woman of the past year was back. She felt it in her stance, in her face, that familiar dragging feeling, pulling her downwards. She could almost see her own anxiety permeating the air around them.

'It's okay,' he said, pushing on, a little bit of the old Travis, optimistic and positive, emerging. 'Once it's done, when you tell them everything he told us, things will get better.'

Still she couldn't believe what she was hearing.

'What do you mean?' She was imploring now, panicked, her arms wrapped around herself protectively. 'I'm not going to go to them. It's… it's done and over.

Now I need to be there for *my son*.' Her last two words were a snarl, a tone she knew was unlike anything he would ever imagine coming from her.

'I have a responsibility. A duty of care. This will help both Scott and you. The other parents have a right to know what happened. You need to acknowledge it to be able to move on. Sara, you must—'

'You have a duty to me! An oath of confidentiality. You can't go to the police, you told me that yourself!' She was aware of her chest heaving, her breathing hard and fast. She watched him, wringing her hands now, panic growing as he dropped his gaze from her face.

'I don't.' He cleared his throat and averted his eyes, looking across to the trees, a frown knitting his brow, as though this conversation wasn't going the way he'd planned. 'I'm not a qualified therapist, Sara. I'm an art teacher, with a very real, very serious dedication to various therapies. But I took no oath. I have to do what I feel is right.' He moved then, coming up to her fast, fixing his eyes on her. 'I have a duty of care to *you*, my love.'

Last year, she had fled. Out of fight or flight, she had chosen the latter. She'd thought she was finally done with running. Started to believe that the days of hiding were over.

She was wrong.

Slowly, not taking her eyes off Travis, she backed down the porch steps. On the floor of his forest garden, the sodden ground seeped through her shoes.

She ran, feet sinking as they pounded the earth. Not in any particular direction, not back home. The awful familiarity of it struck her. In some part of her mind – perhaps the same part that had known all along that Ryan was gone – she knew she ought to slow down, to pause, reflect, plan.

The urge to flee was overwhelming, though, and she found she couldn't stop.

Branches snagged, arms reaching out to clutch at her. Inside her fragile mind, the shapes of the trees morphed into people from her past. Those women, the ones who had judged and scorned, along with faces from before: Mack and her mother, Jojo and Ryan.

A scream sounded, piercing enough that a flock of jays crashed from their resting place, swooping high and far. A magpie, she thought, or a crow, but the noise continued, and she realised it was coming from her. Clamping both hands over her mouth, she carried on running. The slushy pounding of her feet changed, movement was moment-arily halted, an invisible fence at her ankles. The sudden rush of water swirled, changed direction. Footsteps were suddenly easier, and then unstoppable. Then the ground beneath her feet shifted, from earth to river, causing her to stagger as she was swept along in the flow. The forest tilted, the world at an angle, until the gnarled tree roots met her eyeline and the sky whirled and then vanished. Painfully, the floor dragged at her, then there was water, foul-smelling and ink-black, filling her mouth and nostrils. She tasted warm grit, rotted vegetation. One single moment where she snatched at air, before darkness enveloped her.

Then, for a long time, there was nothing at all.

–

A caress to her face, and half awake, Sara felt her lips curl into a smile.

Ryan was just over a year old and a master of escape. Each morning he negotiated the high bars of his cot and the closed door of his room to journey to Sara and Mack's bed. He would clamber up, crawl up in between their sleeping forms and wake his mother with feather-light strokes to her cheek.

She would awake with a full-to-bursting feeling of joy, her gaze flitting between her younger son and her husband, healthy and well for the time being.

Responsibilities had interrupted. Mack had been worried about Ryan's early-morning wanderings. Too much danger; he could fall from the cot, he could misjudge the landing and topple down the stairs, he could get his hands trapped if the bedroom door slammed on him.

Sara wanted to protest. Thought about fitting stair gates, child-friendly door closings, a spare mattress beneath the cot for a soft landing.

'That's just because you want him to keep visiting you in the wee hours,' Mack had chastised gently as he got his tool bag out.

Sara was confused. Yes, she did want to wake up to Ryan's feathery touch each morning. Was that bad? Was it wrong? Was she supposed to stop his morning gifts of affection?

Mack did all the necessary DIY, and eventually the memories of those visits, and the touches, and the pure joy upon awakening faded.

Now they were back, and the same smile stretched and grew on her lips as she reached out her arms.

She touched a wall, cool under her fingertips, rough and unyielding and... wet.

She opened her eyes to darkness and had absolutely no idea where she was.

A psych ward or a prison cell, those were her first thoughts, and momentarily she was confused as to why those two options would come to mind. Then the recall came, glaring and terrifying. She had killed a man she had thought she loved. And her son was dead. She was getting her remaining son back, she loved him, because he'd done *nothing wrong*, and now, a man wanted to have him removed from her life again.

She moaned, but stopped immediately as the sound echoed around her, multiplying her pain and throwing it back in her face.

She thought about calling for help, but for the life of her couldn't remember who was still around to be able to assist her. Mentally, she ticked them off: her mother, not here; Mack, dead; Jojo, dead; Ryan, dead. Scott was at home, oblivious. Travis had turned traitor.

Dear God.

In the darkness, Sara blinked. The rising panic gathered in her chest, threatening like vomit. With everything she had, she pushed it down.

Think.

Look.

Feel.

It was possible she could do the latter. It seemed to require the least effort, and so she reached out her arms and swept her hands around. Underneath her fingers, the walls were slick, damp and cold to the touch.

Think.

It came to her in fragments, memories of conversation rather than experience.

Watch your step.

The pit caves are treacherous.

Her own reply. *Shouldn't there be warnings?*

She was inside a pit cave. Just like Travis had been yesterday. Something had altered him in there, even though he had all the knowledge about them. All the history, all the facts, and yet he had been frightened upon his exit.

That fear had lingered inside him, clinging to his clothes and skin just like the downpour of rain had.

The thought of him left a bitter taste in her mouth. The man she had let into her life had lied to her. He had pretended to help, but he had lied. And now he was going to finish off her and Scott by going to the police.

A scream of fury burst out of her, thin and weak, so weak it only served to infuriate her further. She opened her mouth wide and shouted, a series of nonsensical words, just emotion. She banged her hands against the mud-smeared walls of the cave and kicked her heels against the floor.

'Sara!' A shout, close by, her own name, which came again and again. 'SARA, SARA?'

Her heart and voice stilled. Beside her, her hands curled into muddy fists.

Another shout, closer now, along with an accompanying splash of water. She remembered that sound, she remembered the feeling of an obstruction before the river caused by the storm had gripped her in its current. She had gone down, reached out for something, anything, to stop her journey. It hadn't come to an end, though, not until the unforgiving river had deposited her in the cave she sat in now.

Thoughts churned around inside her mind. She needed to warn him, make him pull up and get back onto the forest path before it was too late. If he came hurtling down here too, nobody else would come along to rescue them.

A second thought came hot on the heels of the first, overtaking it before the original had fully formed, and she sagged with something that was almost relief.

Nobody else would rescue them.

She cupped her hands around her mouth. 'Travis! I'm over here!'

A long second of silence. He could have moved on past, she realised. He would have seen the newly formed river. He lived here, Jesus, he breathed this land. He wouldn't be as stupid as she had been.

And as soon as she'd had *that* thought, there came a thump, a cry – of pain? – and a large shape careened past her.

Another memory, and to her surprise it was Scott this time. A water park, on their one holiday to Florida. Coloured plastic tubes criss-crossed for what seemed like miles. Scott, seven years old and fearless, flying down them, finding some sort of body-bending bone manipulation that only children seemed to possess, emerging to execute a perfect swan dive. Ryan, the daring one usually, had sat on the edge of the pool, for once quiet, watching as his brother drew cheers from the onlookers.

'That's a nice memory.' She spoke out loud, interrupting the groan that came from below her.

Below her.

The memory dissipated, *puff*, gone.

'Hello?' she said, tentatively, fearfully.

Another groan. Down there, something shifted, and the splash of water could be heard.

For the first time, Sara tried to take note of her surroundings. Suddenly, perhaps because she was no longer alone, she felt alert.

Above her, probably within reach, she could feel air on the back of her neck.

Turn around, she urged herself silently. Stand up, turn around and walk out of here.

Time stretched on. The moans of pain from below grew weaker, quieter, then stopped altogether.

Eventually, all Sara could hear was the sound of her own breathing.

54

Now

Travis

She needed rescuing, again. He set off after her, confident that in his forest he would find her, soothe her, make her understand that what he planned to do was for the best. She needed a protector, and it was him.

Outside what he thought of as his garden, the forest engulfed him. Knowing he could not pause, he nonetheless slowed his step slightly as he looked at the damage caused by the storm. Bark hung in strips from the maple that bordered his small patch of land. A ribbon of it rose and swung in a sudden gust of strong wind, and rain that had caught in droplets on branches soaked him.

He glanced up through the canopy of trees and could just about make out slivers of sky. Not bright blue, not even the ghostly white of storm aftermath, and not the pale lemon yellow of moments ago, but black, a fiery sun all but concealed somewhere up there.

His breath caught in his throat. He knew that sky as well as he knew the Kielder floor. The storm wasn't yet over. It was merely taking a break, just minutes of breathing time, gathering energy, waiting above the trees until it was ready to unleash havoc once more.

He put his head down and moved quickly onwards.

He stepped out onto the track that led up to Sara's house. Only it was no longer the road so familiar to him. It was a newly formed stream, fast-flowing, and cold enough that it took his breath away.

He crab-walked sideways, aiming for the other side of the track, confident that though the forest floor would be sodden, it would only be unpleasant rather than dangerous.

He heaved himself up the verge, staggering off the road, feet squelching as soon as they hit the mulch. He looked down at his boots and felt a grim satisfaction. Barefoot was fine, but sometimes shelter and protection were called for. He was just glad he knew when to bow down to nature.

He called her name, then listened to it bounce back through the trees. It was the only sound. Even the birds had vanished. No thumping from rabbits or hares announcing their presence. Above him, the sky darkened further. The wind stilled for a moment.

That was when he heard it. Her voice. He shivered, looked back just once at the road-river before forging on.

As he pushed further into the undergrowth, the trees shifted. He exclaimed aloud as he watched a Sitka spruce uproot itself, the purplish crinkled cones scattering as a stray branch drew a trajectory in front of him. The path was swallowed by rushing water, far fiercer than it had been on the road. It took his feet from under him, shifting the landscape upside down.

Belatedly, he realised it wasn't the imposing tree falling. It was him.

Something struck him in various places on his body as he streaked through the mud concealed by the flood. Pain flared all over, then localised itself. Agonising wounds to his leg, his back, his skull. Winded, all he could do was moan as the velocity took him.

Nothing for a while, mercifully passed out, and then he was woken rudely. A dark place, cold, water to his waist, and pain that stabbed and tortured, accompanied by anguished groans.

Despite the rainwater that flooded around him, he picked up the scent that he knew so well: chalk and concrete, along with a metallic tang that might or might not have been his own blood.

Water flowed down the walls at an alarming rate. He thought of the black cloud overhead, of what would come out of it when it cracked open, and what it would mean for him down here.

He wasn't alone. He knew this instantly, the way a mouse knows a hawk is in the vicinity before it has even made the dive. Even the youngest mouse knows the hawk is a threat.

Her voice, when it came, held a note of fear.

'Hello?' Tremulous, wary.

She shouldn't be fearful, because he knew she wasn't in danger, even if she wasn't aware of that herself.

This pit cave, the deep one he had pointed out to her yesterday, had a lip just two feet from the entrance. A shelf that ran part way around it. She had been stupendously lucky to land on it. If she stood up, if she dared, she could pull herself out.

Vaguely, he wondered if she knew this yet.

Probably not. Not many people knew that. Just Travis, because he was the king here. This was his forest. He cared for it, tended to it and respected it.

And yet, in a cruel twist of irony, it had eaten him alive.

He began to laugh, because Travis was nothing if not an optimist, and laughter was always better than tears.

His mirth must have scared her even more. He sounded like a madman, even to himself. He heard the shift as she moved, feeling her way along the structure on which she had landed. He sensed rather than saw movement. The swish of clothes slapping against wet skin. The dim light was eclipsed for a moment before the cave shone a little brighter than before.

The silence told him that he was now alone.

Clarity, awful and terrible. Yesterday he had been scared when Scott had left him in a pit cave. He needn't have worried; Scott threw himself into danger to rescue others. Sara was a different story. She was a lioness, protecting her cub. Her baby, whom Travis had threatened. She would not return to save him.

The water that crept a little higher on his thighs with each passing minute told him that time was running out.

55

Sara
Now

When she had fled Farenden, Sara had acted on instinct. She didn't think about it, about what *he'd* done, about what *she'd* done. Hole up, find a secure place where nobody knew them, where they could survive quietly. She had thought they both had a terrible secret to hide. She'd been wrong, she knew that now. The only crime was hers and hers alone; a crime she had now repeated, only this time it had been a conscious decision.

She had thought it was clear that she was beyond redemption. Now, however, she let her thoughts linger on the possibility of actually living. Not just surviving, not just getting through each day, but waking up without a cloud of doom hanging over her. Spending time with her son, with Scott. Knowing him. Appreciating him.

Loving him.

She forged on through the forest, circling away from the cave, not daring to approach it again. She avoided the road, which was now not so much a river as a lake. The track couldn't even be seen any more. Kielder would be cut off for days, maybe a week or more. But that was okay too.

The water level had risen to the lower branches of some of the trees. She passed pit caves that ordinarily would have remained unseen and anonymous. Now, their small openings bubbled like gutter drains. Her courage grew, and she began to move with purpose. She hoped she would find the right one, believed she would, because *this was how it was supposed to be.*

The blind faith that she'd carried with her that day a year ago had found her again, after the initial desertion. Now that she was carrying it like a talisman for bad things, she was sure it would work. Bad things found Sara with a magnetic force.

She found the entrance to the pit cave with ease, as she had known she would. The water had risen, and like the others, foul-smelling sludge flowed out of it. Scattered nearby were large chunks of rock. Paying no heed to the splash that she made as she fell to her knees, she picked up a few of them.

She recalled a leaflet in the tiny tourist board office near the Co-op, informing visitors that the famed Girdle Stone, a huge mass located on the border between Northumberland and the Jed Forest, had collapsed. There was a typical doomsday legend, a tale steeped in folklore, that if anyone should find any of the shards, they should avert their eyes and leave them alone. It was the sort of fable that Jojo, with his Irish roots, would have fancied, and she had imagined him beside her, in another time and place and town, with no ex-wives and no widow status, no complicated half- or stepchildren, no angry women-of-the-community and definitely no massacre in their history.

Now, she disobeyed the superstitious fable and gathered up as many pieces as she could fit in her pockets.

They were weighty, so much so that she heard a seam rip somewhere.

Holding her clothes close to her body, she turned back to the entrance of the cave. This close, she could see that even though the sludge still churned out of it, the lip that had saved her wasn't yet covered. Beneath it, maybe halfway up the walls, the water lurked, black as night. Lower still, somewhere down there, lay the body of a liar.

She was numb now, whether through cold or terror she didn't know. It didn't matter. She clutched the rocks close to her, keeping them firmly in her hold.

She thought: nobody will do this to me again.

Pause for thought, allowing that earlier notion to creep back in. She could dig out her mobile phone, charge it and call her mother. Her son was waiting obediently back at home. Somehow, a breakthrough had occurred. Was it possible that relationships could be mended, bonds tightened, new ones formed?

She wondered if she deserved a future. The answering realisation sang loud like the magpies.

Perhaps she didn't, but Scott deserved a mother, a real one, a *good one*. And her own mother deserved a daughter.

She drew in a sharp breath, which emerged as a cry.

The stones and rocks clicked and chipped against each other as they spilled to lie once again on the ground.

Sara stepped over them as she made her way back to the cabin, and back to Scott.

Acknowledgements

As always, I'm so grateful to have so much support. Firstly, I send so much love and so many thanks to my parents, Janet and Keith Hewitt, and to all of my family.

And to Marley, my unconditional friend and constant writing companion.

My wonderful agent, Laetitia Rutherford of Watson, Little, for constant support and championing my books. My editor, Louise Cullen, and also Siân Heap, thank you for your support, warmth and enthusiasm. Copyeditor Jane Selley, who did a wonderful job as always, picking up those things that need detail or attention, big and small.

Thank you to Kelly Taylor, for your invaluable help on school procedures.

The crime fiction community. The writers, bloggers, publishers, and book clubs, everything you do is appreciated.

Finally, a huge thanks to you, the reader, and as always, as long as you keep on enjoying my books, I'll keep on writing them.